Dark is the Sky

Jessica Chambers

For the one who inspired the character of Scott Cameron.
Without you, this novel would never have been written.

Acknowledgments

I have to say a huge thank you to Adal, whose knowledge of investment banking and company fraud proved invaluable, and to Nadia for pushing me, never letting me get away with half measures.

I'm also indebted to my critique partners at The Next Big Writer: Molly, Diana, Rory, Tina, Caroline, David, Louise, Joy, Cathryn, Nathan, Clarissa, Sharon, and anyone else I may have unwittingly forgotten.

Thank you so much for helping me make this novel the best it could be, and most of all for your unwavering support and encouragement.

Prologue

The cemetery was deserted. Oblivious to the December chill seeping through her jacket, the woman sat at the graveside and watched the sky darken over London. The dome of St. Paul's and the slender finger of Big Ben stood starkly against the dull canvas, both as familiar to her and as meaningless as the wallpaper in her office. For twelve years she had lived and worked like a shadow in this city, existing without being part of it, separated from everything around her by a wall of grief. She went through each day in a state of limbo, unable to let go of the past, refusing to move forward.

Well, not anymore.

Reaching out a hand, the woman traced the inscription etched into the gravestone. Frigid air nipped her fingers, but she scarcely felt it over the pain, the soul-rending sense of loss. She pressed a palm to her heart, as though doing so would somehow make the agony more bearable. It had been so long since she'd last been here, since she had let herself feel. The tears overflowed before she could stop them, scalding against her numb cheeks. She dashed them away with the back of her hand. *Pull yourself together, for pity's sake. This is no time for falling apart. You have a job to do.* Squaring her shoulders, she tilted her face up to the steel-gray sky.

"I'm so sorry," she said softly. "I know it's taken me a long time, but I'm ready now. I'm going to find out the truth."

Part 1
Friday

One

Olivia fought a rising hysteria. Why had she let Vi talk her into this? She took a huge slug of gin and tonic, trying to organize her thoughts. Since her sister had suggested this dratted get together in the first place, surely the least she could do was be here to lend a capable hand. But, no. She was far too busy for anything so mundane as slaving over a hot stove, and too wrapped up in being the revered barrister to spare a thought for anyone else. Olivia sighed. That was unfair, she knew. Vi always worked so hard, perhaps too hard, and it must have cost her a great deal of courage even to contemplate this reunion.

Raking a hand through her hair, lank from the steam fogging the farmhouse kitchen, she surveyed the chaos. On the table dominating the room, carrier bags spilled their contents over its scrubbed-pine surface. Dirty saucepans and crockery littered the worktops, waiting to be loaded into the dishwasher, which hadn't yet been emptied. She still needed to liquidize the leftover Christmas turkey for soup, chop the Everest of vegetables to go with the roast lamb, and throw together a trifle and apple crumble for pudding. Olivia's head throbbed with the enormity of her mental checklist. Even once she'd prepared dinner, there were beds to change and bathrooms to clean, not to mention the considerable task of making herself presentable. In her current state, she would send her guests screaming from the house in terror. God, she'd never be ready in time!

Olivia gulped another mouthful of gin. Normally she would have looked forward to spending a weekend catering for her family. She loved entertaining, and when Violet first suggested the gathering some months earlier, she had jumped at the idea. But that was before everything changed, before her world crumbled and left her standing alone in the ruins.

"I can't do this," Olivia had told her sister in a desperate phone call the previous week. "I'm going to have to cancel."

"Why?" Violet sounded concerned. "This isn't like you. What's happened?"

Unable to confide the truth even to her sister for fear that her brittle self-control would shatter into a thousand pieces, Olivia could only mumble something vague about getting cold feet.

"For heaven's sake, Liv," Violet said. "You're being ridiculous. It's twelve years now since … since it happened. Do you want this big, black cloud to hang over us forever? We need to move on. *I* need to move on."

Her sister's pain was evident even through her impatience. How could Olivia refuse her? No matter that her own heart was in shreds, she had to be strong for Vi. Now she faced the elephantine task of spending an entire weekend with her family, of putting on the vivacious front they expected of her and wishing them a happy new year while keeping up the pretence that all was well. She wasn't sure she was up to the challenge.

Swallowing the last of her drink, Olivia glanced out of the kitchen window. Snow fluttered past like confetti, draping the grounds in a fluffy eiderdown, and the laden sky promised more to come. Perhaps her family would decide the driving conditions were too treacherous and stay at home. She could hope.

"Mum!" Lottie's voice drifted through the house. "I need you."

"Sweetheart, I'm a bit tied up at the moment. Can you come downstairs?"

"But I've just got out of the shower."

Olivia rolled her eyes. Reducing the heat on the simmering turkey carcass, she sculpted her features into the cheerful mask that had been so natural only weeks before, and hurried along the narrow passage to the hall. Lottie, her seventeen-year-old daughter, stood on the landing at the head of the stairs. Her golden-brown hair, so like Olivia's, hung in a dripping curtain down her back and a pink towel clung to the long, slender body she'd inherited from her Aunt Vi. Olivia was always telling her how lucky she was to be so slim, but Lottie complained that she looked like a boy and hankered after her mother's curves.

"You're keen," Olivia said. "No one's due for a few hours yet." *And thank heavens for that, or her family would think they'd wandered into war-torn Kabul.*

"I wanted to get in there before you and Dad hogged all the hot water." Lottie looked away, twirling a strand of wet hair around her finger. "Mum, can I borrow your black top for tonight?"

"Black top." Olivia searched her muddled brain. "Which black top, sweetheart?"

"You know, the tight one with the silver, glittery bits."

"Gosh, I'd forgotten I had it. Yes, of course you can. In fact, you may as well have it. There's not much chance of me squeezing into it again without going on a crash diet."

"Wow, thanks." Beaming, Lottie blew her a kiss and dashed away along the landing.

Olivia smiled. It wasn't like her daughter to take so much trouble over her appearance. She spent most of her time in cords and baggy jumpers, either galloping around the Denninshire countryside on her beloved horse or curled up by the fire with a book. Still, it was so long since Lottie last saw her cousins and Olivia suspected she'd always been a little in awe of Emma's beauty. It was natural Lottie should want to look her best. Not that she need worry. With her sweet, oval face, soft mouth and hazel eyes, she was far lovelier than the overconfident Emma; at least, Olivia thought so.

Halfway along the passage to the kitchen, she froze as the shrill ringing of the telephone pierced the silence. Almost at once, the sound was cut off; Joel must have picked up. Olivia's stomach lurched. Please, not again. Heavy with dread, but unable to resist torturing herself, she crept to the half-open study door to listen. Joel sat at the desk with his back to her, body hunched around the receiver as though to conceal it from view.

"What do you take me for?" he was saying in a low voice. "Of course I haven't … No, she doesn't suspect a thing, I promise."

An invisible fist squeezed Olivia's heart; she couldn't breathe. How much more of this could she take? Bile burned the back of her throat and Olivia swallowed it down. Don't let me be sick, she thought. Shock and nausea drained the strength from her legs and she put out a hand to steady herself against the doorframe.

Joel glanced around and saw her. The color leached from his face, leaving it chalk-white beneath the fringe of black hair. He met her gaze, features tight, dark eyes pleading for understanding. Olivia looked back at him until the tears stung her eyelids. She wanted to scream from the rage and anguish tearing at her insides. *Don't fall apart, Liv. Not now.* Turning from his guilty expression, she stumbled away.

***

Lottie unearthed the prized black top amongst the jumble in her mother's wardrobe and took it back to her room, where she laid it on the bed beside her best jeans. The outfit would look great with the cowboy boots her parents gave her for Christmas. She hugged herself and waltzed around her room, letting the towel fall to the carpet. In just a few short hours, she would see Adam again. The thought spurred her heart into a canter and her skin tingled with anticipation.

Due to the rift between her dad and Uncle Tim, Lottie saw little of her cousins while growing up. What they fell out over, she didn't know. She sensed it had something to do with Cameron's, the family investment bank of which her dad was once a director. Years before, too far back for her to remember, he had left the business to start up on his own, producing vegetables for local restaurants, but his reasons remained a mystery.

"It all happened too long ago to concern you," was his only reply whenever Lottie asked him about it.

Even her mum, normally so open, claimed not to know what caused the bad feeling between the brothers, although Lottie didn't wholly believe her. Dad must have confided in her, if no one else.

Whatever the basis for the estrangement, Lottie hadn't seen her cousins since Granddad Cameron's funeral eight years ago. This was why, when their paths crossed by chance two months earlier, she and Adam failed to recognize one another. They met on a geography field trip to Exmoor with their respective schools, and by the time they made the connection, it was too late.

Retrieving her towel, Lottie sat on the edge of the bed to dry her hair. Would things have been different if she and Adam had known of their kinship from the outset? She didn't think so. Surely nothing could have prevented the immediate attraction that sparked between them as they caught one another's eye during dinner on the first night, or stopped them forging a bond that strengthened with every moment they spent together. They'd been inseparable for the entire week, talking endlessly as they studied the moor and surrounding area by day and escaped to quiet corners of the hostel in the evenings. In fact, Lottie didn't think she'd ever talked so much. Always shy, especially with boys, she was both amazed and delighted how easy she felt with Adam.

She touched her lips, remembering the warm softness of his mouth on hers, the thrilling weight of him as they'd lain together on the narrow bunk bed in her dormitory while the other students watched a firework display outside. Her pulse sped up. Just think, a whole weekend to spend with Adam, showing him around the rambling grounds she adored, stealing kisses in the many secluded spots, and all the while keeping their relationship secret from their family. Not that they were doing anything wrong. It wasn't illegal to fall in love with your cousin, even if your dads were twins; she'd made a point of looking it up on the Internet. Yet, Lottie suspected their parents wouldn't be happy if they discovered what was going on. Not happy at all.

***

Joel opened his mouth to say something, he didn't know what, but Olivia had already gone. Hands shaking, he returned the phone to his ear. "Look, I have to go. We'll talk later."

He dropped the receiver back on its cradle, cutting the female voice off mid-entreaty, and put a palm to his aching forehead. Damn and blast it. How could he have been so careless? With a sigh, Joel hauled himself out of the chair and left his study to trudge along the passage. The kitchen door was shut, but he ignored the hint, slipping into the room and closing the door behind him. At least he could shield Lottie from whatever might be said between them.

Olivia acted as though she hadn't heard him come in. Joel watched her empty carrier bags, slamming bottles and jars into cupboards with unnecessary force; it was a miracle they didn't smash to pieces. Her lips were compressed in a tight line, a sure indication she was fighting tears. As if he needed anything to make him feel worse.

"It's not what you think." The words sounded lame even to his own ears, not least because he'd repeated them so often over the past two weeks.

Clearly deeming the remark unworthy of response, Olivia carried a heap of carrots over to the worktop and began skinning them. She wielded the knife with such ferocity Joel guessed she was imagining doing the same to a certain part of his anatomy. He winced.

"Liv," he tried again, "You've got it all wrong."

"Have I?" She looked up at him, eyes flashing like jade in her flushed face. "So who were you speaking to just now?"

Joel dropped his gaze. "No one important. Just … just someone about work."

"Silly me, I should have realized. So what did the restaurant order that's so top secret you can't tell me about it?" She flung his own words back at him. "'She doesn't suspect a thing, I promise.' What're you up to, Joel? Slipping cannabis in the veg boxes? Give me a break."

"I know it sounds unlikely —"

"An out and out bloody lie, you mean."

"All right," Joel said, "so it wasn't a client, but that doesn't automatically mean I'm guilty of what you think."

"And what *do* I think?" Olivia's sneer clashed with her soft features. "Or are you so eaten up with guilt you can't even bring yourself to put it into words?"

"No. I'm just not willing to give your accusation any credence by naming it."

"Don't you patronize me! I suppose you're going to tell me next I've imagined the whole thing: the way you put the phone down whenever I come into the room, your mood swings, the endless dropped phone calls."

"Like I said, those were probably just wrong numbers."

"Funny how it only happens when I answer the phone." Olivia thrust the knife towards him, and for an instant Joel feared she would run him through the heart. "No, the only thing wrong with those phone calls was that the woman on the other end got me instead of you. What I don't understand is how you expected to keep something like this from me. I thought you knew me better than that."

"Yeah?" Joel's temper rose. "Well, that makes two of us. I never believed you'd be so quick to jump to conclusions. Why can't you just trust me?"

"Trust you? After the way you've been sneaking about lately? That's hardly the behavior of an innocent man, Joel." Still holding the knife, Olivia crossed her arms over her chest and drew a shuddering breath. "Okay, if you're really not having an affair, what is it?"

He flinched from the plea in her expression, the faint glimmer of hope. "I can't tell you."

There was a long silence.

"No," Olivia said, voice catching, "I didn't think so."

He raised his head to see her eyes brimming with tears.

"Liv." He started forward, wanting to put his arms around her, to tell her everything was all right. But it wasn't all right, and they both knew it.

"Don't touch me," she hissed. Shoving him aside, she threw open the kitchen door and stormed out.

Joel fought the urge to charge after her; what would be the point? He was the last person Liv wanted around right now, and who could blame her? Hell, what a God-awful mess. As if his marriage heading for the rocks wasn't bad enough, he now had to contend with a whole weekend playing gracious host to his family. Compared with that, the prospect of his enraged wife knifing him in the chest was almost appealing.

***

Olivia resisted the temptation to slam her bedroom door; she didn't want Lottie to know anything was wrong. Once alone, she flung herself on the bed and sobbed into the pillow. How could Joel do this? Did eighteen years of marriage mean so little to him that he could risk it all for the sake of a cheap thrill? As well as the good times they'd shared, they had been through so much together, helping one another come to terms with the horror of that long-ago summer and struggling to get by financially when Joel left the family business. Yet he had tossed it aside as though it held no more value than the weeds he extracted from his vegetable patch.

If someone had asked her a few weeks before to name her most painful experience, Olivia would not have hesitated to say childbirth. However, labor paled to a mere twinge in her memory beside the anguish of first overhearing Joel on the phone to his—she could scarcely bring herself even to think the word—mistress. Excruciating though giving birth had been, the memory faded the instant she held Lottie in her arms and gazed in wonder at the perfect life they'd created. She doubted the pain of Joel's betrayal would diminish for as long as she lived.

Gripped by a sadistic desire to torment herself, just as she would prod a bruise as a child to test how much it hurt, Olivia recalled her first encounter with Joel. She met him during the second of her wild student years. True to form, that Saturday night found her in a London nightclub, wearing out her ridiculously high heels on the dance floor and pouncing on every good-looking young man unfortunate enough to catch her eye. She spotted the Cameron brothers several hours into her alcoholic marathon and discovered afterwards that they'd been out for dinner first to celebrate Scott's eighteenth birthday. Struck by the possibilities posed by four such handsome specimens, she reeled over to their table.

"So, which of you sexy beasts can I tempt to a dance?" she slurred, or so the brothers claimed. Olivia had been too paralytic to remember, and to this day suspected they were having her on.

"Not sure that's such a good idea," Joel said, reaching out to steady her as she swayed. "Perhaps you should sit down."

"Sit down? I've hardly started." To endorse her words, Olivia seized his hands to drag him to his feet, and fell flat on her back in a drunken stupor.

The next thing she knew, she awoke in a strange bed to find a handsome young man watching her with serious dark eyes. Joel later explained how he'd left his brothers at the club and ordered a taxi to take her back to his flat. Olivia supposed she should have been alarmed, all alone at the mercy of a stranger, but it was impossible to doubt his kindness. He cooked her an enormous fry-up, which she ate with enthusiasm at the kitchen table. Afterwards, they sat on his balcony in the autumn sunshine, getting to know one another over endless mugs of coffee. When Olivia arrived home later that afternoon, she had a glow on her cheeks and an invitation to dinner the following evening.

Their relationship blossomed despite the differences in their personalities, or perhaps because of them. Joel proved a steadying influence on Olivia, while she taught him to laugh at himself. In addition, they shared the bond of losing their mothers at a young age and being brought up by career-obsessed fathers. Less than twelve months after passing out at his feet, Olivia discovered herself pregnant and Joel proposed. With absolutely no regret on her part, and earning her father's unerring disapproval, she abandoned her English Lit degree at the start of her third year. Lottie was born the following June and Olivia had never looked back. Until now.

She clenched her fists against the rending pain in her gut. Frequently over the years she had sent up prayers of thanks for her good fortune in finding a man like Joel, pitying the couples she knew who were not so blessed. She'd believed her marriage was solid, that it really was till death do us part. What a fool she had been, and how smug.

Shoving the memories aside, Olivia wiped her eyes on the sleeve of her jumper and sat up. Pull yourself together, she scolded. Your world might be in pieces, but there's no sense crying about it when you have a million things to do. Taking deep breaths to calm her sobs, she went to stand by the bedroom window and rested her hot face against the glass. The snow swirling past her in thickening flakes gave the illusion of peering into a snow globe. It transformed the grounds into a picture from a Christmas card, hiding the tired grass under a white carpet and dressing the bare trees in glittering cloaks. Joel's greenhouse and the stables where Lottie had so often re-enacted the nativity as a child looked like enormous iced Christmas cakes.

The beauty of the scene cut through Olivia like the wind howling down the chimney. She couldn't tear her eyes away. The idea of leaving this place, of selling up and splitting the proceeds, was almost as devastating as losing Joel. Not that it didn't harbor its fair share of ghosts. In those terrible days following the tragedy, they'd seriously considered moving away to escape the constant reminders. However, to the incredulity of their families, Olivia and Joel's love for the old farmhouse remained intact. This was their forever home, the place where they envisioned spending the rest of their lives. They couldn't bear to leave it. Gradually, the happy memories overshadowed the bad and, though they never forgot what happened, they somehow learned to live with it.

Locking her emotions away in the secret compartment of her heart, Olivia turned from the window and glanced at her watch. Heavens, she needed to get on! Her guests would arrive in just over two hours, expecting to be fed, entertained and made welcome. More importantly, they needed the chance to put the past behind them at last, Violet most of all. For this one weekend, she must set her own troubles aside and channel all her efforts into ensuring the visit went smoothly. Only once it was over would she allow herself to confront her uncertain future.

Two

Miraculously, by the time the doorbell chimed to announce the first guests, everything was ready. Olivia had even managed to bathe and wash her hair. Tucking her gypsy blouse into a floor-sweeping skirt of crimson velvet, she took a last look at herself in the dressing-table mirror. A pair of green eyes gazed back at her, their strain visible even beneath the make-up she'd piled on to disguise any trace of tears. My hair could do with a trim, she thought. I look like a hippy. Still, too late to worry about that now. She practiced her smile in the glass. Perfect. No one would ever know how much it cost.

Olivia clomped along the landing in her ankle boots, a little unsteady from too many gin and tonics. Please, let it be Violet. Apart from itching to give her an earful for leaving her in the lurch, she had never been in greater need of sisterly support. She reached the top of the stairs just as Lottie opened the front door. Olivia's prayer ended in a groan. Carla stood on the step, her slender figure framed against the night sky, golden hair gleaming in the light from the hall. Emma hovered at her shoulder with Tim and Adam bringing up the rear, their hands full of luggage. Where was Joel? Surely he wasn't going to leave her to deal with his sister-in-law alone.

"Darling," Carla exclaimed, swooping on Lottie. "And how's my favorite niece?"

"I thought we agreed I'm your only niece." Lottie returned the hug as naturally as though she saw her aunt every week.

"You'd be my favorite no matter what. Here, I have something for you." Carla thrust a bulging carrier bag into Lottie's arms. "I was clearing out my wardrobe the other day and thought these might do for you."

"Wow! Thanks, Aunt Carla."

"Don't mention it, darling. They were destined for the charity shop, anyway, but I thought you could make better use of them."

Oh, because poor Lottie is so deprived and her parents so destitute she doesn't have any clothes of her own? Was Carla being deliberately malicious, or just insensitive? Olivia chastised herself. It wasn't like her to be so uncharitable. She scarcely recognized the embittered woman who'd recently taken possession of her body, and didn't much care for her. Determined not to spoil Lottie's obvious delight, Olivia rearranged her features into a welcoming expression and tottered down the stairs.

"Hello, everyone," she gushed. "Do come in out of the cold. It's so lovely to see you all."

"We almost didn't make it," Carla grumbled. "These country lanes are a death-trap in this weather." She touched her cool lips to Olivia's cheek. "How are you? You're looking peaky."

"Oh, can't complain," Olivia said. In truth, beside Carla's tall elegance and expensively cut hair, she felt both frumpy and over made-up.

"Don't listen to her, Liv." Tim set down the cases to embrace her. "You look lovely as ever."

Olivia tried not to cling to him, overcome with the impulse to bury her face in his shoulder and weep. Must be the stress getting to her, intensified by the amount of alcohol she'd drunk. And Tim so resembled Joel with his strong bone structure, athletic build and the black hair falling over his forehead. All that distinguished the twins was the faint scar on Joel's left cheek, and only those who knew them well could tell them apart. Tears burned Olivia's eyes. So many wasted years, when they had all missed out on the love of this gentle man: Joel as a brother, Lottie as his niece, and she as a friend.

Don't think about that now. Getting her emotions under control, she turned to her niece and nephew, both as blond and beautiful as their mother.

"Did you have a wonderful Christmas?" she asked, hugging Emma tight.

"Awesome," Emma said. At nineteen, she exuded the same confidence in her own loveliness as Carla. "Mum and Dad bought me a Porsche."

"Wow," Lottie breathed, eyes wide.

Olivia blinked. Cameron's must be thriving, indeed. "But didn't you have a Ferrari?"

"Smashed that up weeks ago. I was driving home from a club one night when this lamppost just appeared in front of me, and crash! Dad wasn't keen on buying me another car after that, said I couldn't be trusted behind the wheel, but I talked him round."

"Well, as long as you weren't hurt." Olivia marveled at her niece's casual attitude to her possessions, an attitude born of having wealthy parents who never refused her anything. Of course, that could so easily have been Lottie, had things turned out differently. Not for the first time, Olivia was thankful Joel's grief had driven him to give it all up.

"What have you got there?" she asked, smiling at her nephew. "The kitchen sink and all the china?"

Adam grinned, and for all that he had inherited his mother's good looks and self-assurance, his smile was Tim's. "Mum said we should be prepared for every eventuality."

"Very wise. We could wake up to a heat wave tomorrow."

"No," Carla retorted, "but if this weather keeps up, there's a chance we'll be snowed in."

Please, God, no! Olivia suppressed a shudder. Playing hostess to her family for the weekend was going to require all her will power—a second longer and she would end up in the loony bin. If only she could wave a magic wand and banish them all in a puff of smoke.

"Wow! Versace," Lottie said, rummaging in the carrier bag. "How cool are these?"

Olivia threw off her mean-spiritedness and examined the jeans. "They'll look fab on you, sweetheart. Why don't you take that lot upstairs and show your cousins where they're sleeping?"

Emma opened her mouth to say something, but Carla silenced her with a look. Olivia cast her daughter an anxious glance. Had she noticed anything? Lottie, however, was already halfway up the stairs, beckoning for her cousins to follow.

Once they'd gone, Olivia turned gratefully to Carla. "Thanks for that. You know Lottie doesn't remember anything about last time."

Carla shrugged. "She's lucky. I'm sure we'd all give a good deal to forget. You know, Liv, this place hasn't changed a bit from my memory of it."

Olivia bristled, aware of Carla's critical eye taking in everything through the drawing-room door: threadbare carpet, faded curtains and furniture that had seen better days. She and Joel scraped a comfortable living, she as a moderately successful novelist, he growing vegetables to sell to local restaurants. Yet much of their income went on the running of the house and paying for Lottie's school trips and textbooks, not to mention the upkeep of her money-guzzling horse. This left little for new carpets, and many of Olivia's own clothes came from charity shops.

Until that moment, however, Olivia hadn't noticed quite how shabby everything looked. This was a home, not a show house, and she loved it too much to mind foam leaking from the sofa or the coffee stains on the rug. Soon, though, she would have to consider how the house might look to a prospective buyer. Her heart ached at the thought of leaving this place, of strangers tramping through the home into which she'd poured so much of her soul. She didn't think she could bear it.

"Do make yourselves comfortable," Olivia said with forced brightness, leading them into the drawing room. "Just dump your cases in the corner for now and we'll take them up later."

As though sensing her unhappiness, Tim touched her shoulder. "It's lovely to be back here, Liv. Thanks so much for inviting us."

"You're welcome." Once again, Olivia battled tears. "I wish I knew where that husband of mine's got to. He should be here to greet you."

"He's here," Joel said, appearing in the doorway. Olivia had the distinct impression he'd waited till the last possible moment to show himself. He shook hands with his brother and pecked his sister-in-law on the cheek, neither gesture displaying any warmth.

Olivia looked away, struck by the contrast of past and present. No one witnessing the scene would guess Tim and Joel had once been close, as close as only twins can be. Something happened twelve years ago that opened an unbridgeable gulf between them, and, though she had implored him countless times to confide in her, Joel refused to speak of it. Now he never would and it no longer mattered. Soon this family with their festering resentments would be none of her concern. The tears threatened to spill over. She couldn't break down, not in front of everyone.

"I'm so sorry to abandon you all," she managed, "but I must check on the lamb. Joel, if you could organize drinks." Steeling her heart against her husband's silent appeal, Olivia fled.

***

Lottie avoided Adam's eye as she led him and Emma up the stairs; she was bound to blush and give herself away. Best not to risk looking at him until they were alone.

"Wow," Emma said, taking in Lottie's room. "This is exactly how I remember it."

Distracted, Lottie stared at her. "What're you talking about? You've never been here."

Emma's eyes widened. "So Mum was right. You really don't remember." She moved farther into the room, examining everything. "I remember the bookcase, and that chest of drawers. They must be ancient. I'm sure the walls used to be pink, though, not yellow."

"Mum decorated a few years ago." Lottie tried to make sense of her cousin's excited chatter. "So, when were you here before?"

"Yonks," Adam said right behind her; Lottie started. "You were only about five, so it's no wonder you can't remember."

Lottie melted at the sound of his voice; soft and deep, it resonated an assurance beyond his seventeen years. She ached to look at him, but didn't dare under Emma's perceptive gaze.

"You're the same age as Lottie," Emma said, "and you have some memory of the last time we were here." She turned to Lottie. "I slept in your room, on that exact same camp bed, and Adam slept on a mattress on the floor because he was too chicken to sleep on his own. We stayed up late scaring each other with ghost stories, and played for hours in the—" She broke off at a look from Adam. "In the garden," she finished, but Lottie suspected that wasn't what she'd been about to say.

"I don't remember any of it," she said, staring at the carpet. The thought of herself and Adam once sharing a room, albeit as small children, sent heat rushing to her face. "I don't get it."

16

Emma opened her mouth, but, at another warning look from her brother, she merely shrugged. "You were only five, like Adam said. Not everyone has vivid memories of when they were little."

Lottie nodded. There was something going on here she didn't understand. For the moment, however, desire to be alone with Adam overshadowed curiosity.

"Will you be all right while I show Adam where he's sleeping?" Lottie asked Emma, fingers crossed behind her back. *Please don't insist on coming with us.*

"I'll be fine." Emma took one of the cases from Adam and laid it on the camp bed. "I need to change for dinner, anyway."

Lottie looked at her cousin, already gorgeous in black jeans and a cashmere jumper that hugged her curves, then down at her own clothes. She'd thought the slinky, black top so sexy a moment ago; now it seemed dowdy and noticeably second hand.

"Shall we go then?" Adam said.

Nodding, Lottie showed him from the room and along to the stairs at the end of the passage. Nerves and anticipation fluttered like a caged moth in her stomach. She tried to think of something witty or interesting to say, but tension whipped her thoughts into chaos and they ascended to the attic in silence.

"This one's yours," Lottie said, leading him into the room on the right of the tiny landing.

Adam closed the door behind them, and they were alone. Lottie's heart rate picked up. After almost two months of her longing for him, of secret phone calls and passionate emails, he was here. Suddenly shy, Lottie edged away to stand by the window while Adam inspected the room.

As the silence stretched between them, she stole an anxious glance at him from beneath her lashes. His tall frame filled the space, his head almost touching the sloping ceiling. She found herself seeing the room through his eyes: tiny, with scarcely enough space for a bed and chest of drawers, bare floorboards covered by a frayed rug, paint peeling from the frame of the one Velux window. What a contrast to the grand penthouse where he lived. Though she hadn't been there since the day of Granddad Cameron's funeral, the image of the elegant rooms with their marble fireplaces, large windows and ankle-deep carpets remained fresh in her mind. Adam, in his designer clothes, was horribly out of place in this shabby room, and, for the first time in her life, Lottie burned with shame for the only home she had ever known.

"It isn't much," she said, desperate to break the silence. "Not like you're used to."

Adam snorted. "What, you mean a show house where you can't sit on the sofa without feeling you're messing up the cushions, and anyone who leaves so much as a fingerprint on the coffee tables is doomed? Nothing's more than a couple of years old. Except us, that is."

Lottie laughed, though she felt more like crying. Silence formed a chasm between them once more and she shifted from one foot to the other, her entire body prickling with embarrassment. Over and over she had imagined their reunion, how he would hold out his arms and she would run into them as though they'd never been apart. The image of his face, the blue eyes bright with intelligence and amusement, had haunted her day and night as she counted down the hours till they could be together again. She never envisioned this awkward torment, that the connection they'd shared on the field trip would have snapped, leaving them with nothing to say to each other. Before she could stop them, tears of disappointment sprang to her eyes.

Adam was beside her in an instant. "Lottie?"

"It's okay." She brushed a hand across her eyes. "I understand."

"Glad you do, because I'm lost here."

"Well, you must have loads of girls after you. I was stupid to think you'd wait around."

"You're stupid for thinking I wouldn't, more like," Adam said. He slipped his arms around her waist and pulled her to him. "And there was me worrying you might have someone else."

"Seriously?" Lottie looked up at him, searching his face.

"What do you think?" Adam drew her closer and kissed her. The instant his mouth touched hers, the feel of his lips both familiar and exciting, Lottie's doubts evaporated. He was here, holding her. Nothing else mattered.

***

"So," Tim said, filling the painful silence, "how's business with the vegetables?"

From his stiff-backed position on the sofa, Joel stared coldly at his twin and sister-in-law seated on either side of the drawing-room fire. "Evidently not as prosperous as yours. Olivia and I had to forego buying Lottie a Porsche this year."

Carla let out a tinkling laugh. The sound stabbed through Joel's aching head and he cringed.

Tim's expression flickered at his curtness, but he smiled. "And I'm sure Lottie is much better off for not being spoilt like mine have been. You're doing all right, though, aren't you?"

"I'm earning a living, if that's what you mean. A *good, honest* living."

If Tim noticed the slight behind the words, he didn't show it. "I'm glad."

"You are?"

"Course I am. You can't think I'd want you to fail."

Joel said nothing, knowing the skepticism was plain to read in his eyes, and Tim bowed his head. Silence smothered the room, broken only by the crackle of the fire. Joel's resentment burned as fiercely as the logs in the grate. How could Liv do this to him? She knew how he felt about Tim and Carla, even if he had never been able to confide in her the reason behind his hostility. Yet, she'd forced him into entertaining them for a whole bloody weekend, when all he wanted to do was fight to save his marriage. If this was her way of paying him back, she couldn't have dreamt up a more effective punishment.

"Think I'll go and get ready for dinner," Carla said, and set her empty wine glass on the mantelpiece. "Okay if I have a shower, Joel?"

He didn't look at her. "You know where the bathroom is."

"Joel, your hospitality overwhelms me. With manners like that, you should open this place as a hotel."

Once Carla had gone, the men sat in mute awkwardness, staring into their whiskey and sodas.

"What's wrong?" Tim said at length. "Besides your problem with me, I mean."

Joel raised his eyebrows. "What makes you think there's anything else?"

"Come off it. We may not be close anymore, but you're still my twin. I can see when something's bothering you, and I wish you'd tell me what it is."

Joel looked away, chest tight. He and Tim were once inseparable, all the closer for being best mates as well as identical twins. They shared everything, celebrating one another's triumphs and picking each other up when they fell. What a relief it would be to cry on his brother's shoulder, admit the mess he'd made of his marriage, and let Tim calm his fears as he used to. But that was out of the question. Joel's fingers clenched around his tumbler. Tim had forfeited the trust between them and there was no getting it back.

"It's nothing," Joel said, voice hard. If Tim thought he would forget his betrayal, let alone forgive him, he had better think again.

***

"Aunt Liv," Emma burst into the kitchen in a state of panic, "it's so awful!"

"What is?" In the midst of checking the roast potatoes, Olivia slammed the oven door shut and turned. Visions of accidents and wounds pouring blood streaked across her mind.

Emma brandished her mobile phone. "I've been trying and trying, but I can't get a signal."

"Is that all?" Olivia said, laughing. "I thought the end of the world had come."

"This is the end of the world. I promised I'd ring my boyfriend to let him know I got here safely. If he doesn't hear from me, he'll think I've been in a car crash or … or gone off him. Can I possibly use your phone? I promise I won't be ages and run up a massive bill."

"Of course you can, darling. Use the extension in my bedroom so you can be private."

"Aunt Liv, you're a lifesaver." Emma gave her a swift hug and dashed from the room, just as the doorbell rang. Olivia's heart leapt. That had to be Violet.

"I'll get it," Emma called, and the next moment her voice echoed from the hall. "Hi, Uncle Rafe. Wow, love your coat, Aunt Phoebs. Is it real fur?"

Olivia left the sanctuary of the kitchen, concern tempering her irritation. Where on earth was Vi? Could she have had an accident on the icy roads? But her sister was such a fastidious driver. Subduing her anxiety, she emerged into the hall where upon Emma, having completed her duty, dashed upstairs.

"Liv, my dear," Rafe boomed, pinching her bottom, "how splendid to see you."

"And you." Olivia stifled a wince. At forty-two, Rafe was the eldest of the Cameron brothers. Shorter and stockier than the twins, his ruddy complexion and spreading waistline spoke of too many long lunches and glasses of good wine. He was still an attractive man, though, and what he lacked in height, he made up for in confidence.

"Hello, Phoebe." Olivia turned to Rafe's wife. "Emma's right, that is a beautiful coat. Let me take it for you."

"Thank you." Phoebe gave her a shy smile, which seemed to cost considerable effort. "So kind of you to invite us."

Olivia accepted the heavy fur, trying to conceal her shock. Phoebe looked dreadful, painfully thin, her arms little more than twigs that might snap at the slightest pressure. Her eyes, huge and dark in a prematurely lined face, darted around the hall as though expecting danger to leap out at her from the shadows. Olivia remembered the pretty brunette, her cheeks flushed with anticipation, who'd arrived on her doorstep twelve years before. Could this really be the same woman?

"Amazing," Rafe thundered, interrupting her thoughts. "Nothing's changed since we were last here."

Phoebe shot him a frightened glance, but Rafe didn't notice, or else didn't care.

"I have to hand it to you, Liv," he went on. "I'm not sure I could have done it."

"Done what?" Olivia took the parka he thrust into her arms; they sagged under the weight of both coats.

Rafe looked surprised. "Why, gone on living here. I know I couldn't have done it after what happened, but you and Joel are clearly made of sterner stuff. I would've seen ghosts everywhere."

"Rafe, don't," Phoebe begged, shuddering.

"We love it here," Olivia said, "and it isn't as if we'd have anything to fear from these particular ghosts, is it?"

She regretted the words the moment they left her mouth. Phoebe's white face grew even paler and she looked about to faint.

"Ignore me." Olivia attempted to repair the damage. "There are no ghosts here, only memories, and so many of those are good ones. Would you excuse me while I hang your coats up and check on dinner? We're just waiting for Violet now, so it should be about half an hour. If you go through to the drawing room, Joel will get you both a drink."

"Just what the doctor ordered," Rafe said. He shoved the bulky suitcase into Phoebe's hand. "Be a love and take this upstairs. I need to have a word with Joel. He's so elusive these days, anyone would think he's avoiding us."

Chuckling, he disappeared into the drawing room where he could be heard greeting his brothers in voluble fashion. Olivia stared after him, aghast. His wife was plainly under considerable strain, and yet Rafe had dismissed her as casually as though she were a servant.

Hoping to spare the other woman's embarrassment, she pretended to have noticed nothing untoward. "I expect you'd like to get settled in. I've given you the same room as last time. Do you need any help?"

"Thank you, but I can manage." Phoebe cast Olivia an apologetic glance and clutched the suitcase like a talisman. Then she hurried away up the stairs, rather, Olivia thought, as though fleeing some grisly discovery.

Three

Olivia stared out of the kitchen window at the snowflakes drifting like scraps of lace in the blackness. Vi really should have arrived by now. To stave off the anxiety dragging at her stomach, she took a gulp of her replenished gin and tonic. The same image continually buffeted her mind: Violet's car tossed into a ditch, her body crumpled and twisted in the wreckage. Olivia shook her head to clear it. Perhaps her sister had simply decided she couldn't face coming, that she'd been expecting too much of herself. No one could blame her after everything that had happened. Still, Olivia shrank from the possibility. Without Violet, she didn't have a hope of getting through the weekend.

The instant the doorbell pealed through the house, Olivia threw off her oven gloves and hurtled along the passage to the hall, where she almost collided with Joel. Clearly desperate to escape the drawing room, he reached the front door a fraction before she did. They clashed in a silent war of wills over the door handle, Olivia meeting his pleading look with one of mingled entreaty and accusation. She won. Joel flung his hands up in reproachful surrender, and slunk back to rejoin his brothers.

When Olivia opened the front door, her sister strode in, wearing a tailored black trouser suit and carrying a leather briefcase along with her holdall. As always, Olivia had the sense of looking at a taller, more angular version of herself. Violet was softer once, a long time ago. Grief and bitterness had sculpted her face into hard lines that made her appear older than forty, and her green eyes held little trace of the animated young woman she'd been twelve years before.

Shaking the snow from her shoulder-length hair, Violet pecked Olivia's cheek. "Sorry I'm late."

With her sister finally there, the strain of the past couple of weeks crashed over Olivia. Relief mixed with frustration and despair rushed up inside her, lodging in her throat.

"Just dump your stuff down there," she blurted, then sought refuge in the kitchen where she busied herself banging saucepans onto the hob.

Violet joined her a moment later. "Is everything all right?"

"It's fine," Olivia said jerkily. "I was worried, that's all. Thought you must have been in an accident. What kept you?"

"I have a really important case coming up. You know how it is. I can't drop everything for a family gathering."

"A family gathering you organized, no less."

"Liv, what's got into you?" Violet sounded annoyed. "I admit I expected more of a welcome after driving for two hours through a blizzard. I'm sorry you were worried, but it couldn't be helped."

Olivia opened her mouth, a snarl on her lips, and burst into tears.

"For heavens sake." Violet sighed, though her tone softened. She came to put an arm around Olivia in an awkward gesture. "You'd better tell me what's happened."

"It's Joel." Olivia sobbed into Violet's expensive jacket. "He's having an affair."

"What? Are you sure? I mean, has he admitted it?"

"Not in so many words, but I know him well enough to realize when something's going on. Now I'm stuck entertaining his family for a whole weekend and I don't think I can do it."

"Yes, you can. We'll help each other through it. Christ, I'll kill Joel for this."

"Not if I get to him first." Olivia smiled through her tears. In her practical, no-nonsense way, Vi had always managed to make her feel better as no one else could.

Neither sister remembered their mother, who died of breast cancer when Olivia was a baby and Violet only two years old. Nor could they recall a time when their father was anything but a remote figure in their small household. What limited enthusiasm Hugh Brown possessed he chose to expend on rising through the ranks of the insurance company of which he'd been an employee all his working life. Brought up chiefly by Hilda, a German nanny with a permanently sour expression and nothing in the way of a sense of humor, the sisters accustomed themselves to relying on one another for comfort or advice. Now their father resided in a specialist care home for patients with Alzheimer's, unaware even that he had two adult daughters. Beyond eliciting the occasional duty visit, he played as insignificant a role in their lives as he'd ever done.

"Sorry for being a cow," Olivia said, sniffing. "I really am so glad you're here."

"I expect you are," Violet said. "It's a disaster area in here."

Brushing a hand across her eyes, Olivia surveyed the pots, pans, dishes and chopping boards cluttering every surface. "It's what you might call organized chaos."

"Chaotic chaos, more like. Come on, let's get this evening over with and then we'll talk."

***

"Wish I knew what I'd done to make Joel hate me," Tim said as he buttoned his clean shirt.

"Darling, don't fret about that now," Carla begged. They had discussed this so often over the years; it never did any good. She stood before the full-length mirror to hook on her earrings, turning her head to see the effect. The sapphires matched the color of her dress and brought out the deep blue of her eyes.

"But I need to understand what went wrong," Tim said. "We were so close. He was my best friend in the world, and, just like that, he cut me dead."

He looked so troubled, Carla went and put her arms around him. "You mustn't let it get to you. The only thing you've ever done to upset Joel is marry me. If anyone should be asking what they've done to offend him, I should. He's never liked me. None of your family has."

"That's not true," Tim said.

"Oh, I think it is." Carla smiled, loving him for his loyalty and need to protect her. "But I'm too thick-skinned to bother about what anyone thinks."

"Even Rafe?"

"What about Rafe?" Carla's voice came out sharper than she intended.

Tim chuckled. "Don't look at me like that. It's hardly a secret you and Rafe loathe one another. Still, if you two could refrain from sniping at each other for one evening—"

"Snipe? I'd like to do more than that. What does he think he's playing at, making Phoebs come back here? You saw the state she was in. She's a nervous wreck."

"Don't you think you're being unfair? We all know Rafe can be a bit, well—"

"Selfish?" Carla supplied. "Incapable of thinking about anyone but himself?"

"No," Tim reproved gently, "but he does sometimes have trouble seeing things from another's perspective. I should know. I've worked with him long enough. It might look as though he's being callous, but he's sure to have Phoebe's best interests at heart."

Oh, but of course, Carla thought, because Rafe has never been anything but considerate where his wife's concerned.

Out loud, she said, "I'm sure you're right. Anyway, I promise to be on my best behavior. In fact, I won't even speak to Rafe if it can be avoided."

Tim rewarded her with his sweet smile. "I'm sure Olivia would appreciate it. Poor love seemed a bit fraught."

"Aren't we all?" Carla pushed a strand of hair behind her ear and glanced again at her reflection. "So, how do I look?"

Tim traced her lips with the tip of one finger. "You look stunning, as you very well know. You'll knock 'em dead."

They froze, his words hanging in the air between them.

"God, darling, I'm sorry," Tim breathed, pulling her close. "I didn't

25

mean … I don't know what I was thinking."

"It's okay. Doesn't matter."

"Yes, it does. What a stupid, tactless thing to say. It's hard enough for you being back here without me opening my big mouth."

"It's fine, really." At any other time, the notion of her husband having a big mouth would have been funny. "It's just as hard for you as it is for me. Scott was your brother, after all. Besides, I think the whole purpose of this reunion is to help us put the past behind us, and, however hard it might be, we have to try."

***

"Joel didn't seem particularly pleased to see us," Rafe drawled, adjusting his cufflinks. "Wonder what's eating him."

Phoebe kept her face blank and said nothing. Rafe didn't expect an answer, in any case. Why should he, when she had nothing of value to say? Instead, Phoebe examined herself in the mirror, face pale and lined with fatigue, premature gray streaking her once glossy curls. *Gosh, you look a fright. Is it any wonder Rafe despises you?* Tears stung her eyes; she blinked them away. Returning to this room after twelve years reminded her poignantly of the girl she had been, so eager and hopeful for love. Now the glass reflected only sadness and disappointment.

"Give me a hand, would you?" Rafe interrupted her thoughts, sounding irritated at having to ask.

Phoebe turned at once and hurried to help him with his tie. Really, what had she expected, marrying a man like Rafe Cameron? He was so handsome, so confident and successful; a dull mouse like herself hadn't a hope of holding him. Hah, she'd been unable even to bear him a child to carry on the business and family name. As ever, her insides contorted in the agony of loss for the children she'd so longed for but never had.

"Please let us adopt," she had begged over and over during those awful months after the doctors discovered the cysts on her ovaries. "There are so many unwanted babies out there, crying out for a good home and people to love them."

Rafe's answer never varied. "Over my dead body. There's no way another man's bastard will ever inherit Cameron's."

And in the end, just as she always did, Phoebe backed down, though the ache wrenched at her heart even all these years later.

"What's got into you?" Rafe demanded as she fumbled with his tie.

"Sorry." Phoebe took a firmer grip, but was trembling so badly the silk slipped through her fingers.

"For Christ's sake, I'll do it myself." Rafe slapped her hands away and went to stand in front of the mirror. "I wish you'd pull yourself together. You're no good to me like this."

"Sorry." Phoebe bit her lip; she hated him being displeased with her. Even as she looked at him, so dashing in his gray suit, her heart flipped over. Despite everything they'd been through, all the disappointment and heartbreak, she loved him as deeply as when she'd first set eyes on him. She would have done anything for him then and that hadn't changed.

"Well, I'm going down," Rafe said, straightening his tie with evident satisfaction. "Coming?"

"In a minute." She wasn't ready to face them all. Not yet.

Once Rafe had gone, she went to stand by the window. Immediately, just as she'd known they would be, her eyes were drawn to that spot beyond the hawthorn hedge. There was nothing to see save for a dustsheet of snow, but still the memories flooded her mind: the limp figure sprawled on the grass, the eyes sightless and staring.

Phoebe started at a light touch on her arm. She hadn't heard anyone come in. Without needing to look, she knew it would be Carla, her best friend of childhood and, in spite of everything, her best friend still.

"You'd best come down," Carla said. "Olivia's ready to dish up."

Phoebe nodded. Still, like a child terrified by a horror movie but unable to stop watching, she couldn't tear her gaze from the snow-covered grounds.

"Come away now," Carla persisted. "There's nothing to see. It's all in the past."

"Yes," Phoebe said, but knew it was a lie. For her, it would never be in the past.

***

"I've missed you," Adam said against Lottie's neck.

They lay on the narrow bed, limbs entwined, breathing ragged. Lottie's head whirled from the hard leanness of Adam's body molded to hers, the heat of him burning through their clothing.

"Not as much as I've missed you," she told him. "Do you think your family suspects anything? Does Emma?"

Adam's breath brushed her skin in a chuckle. "This is my sister we're talking about. She's too wrapped up in herself to give a toss about anyone else. What about your parents?"

"Dad certainly can't have a clue or he'd never have let any of you through the front door."

"Yeah, he'd love the excuse to ban us from the house. What about your mum?"

Lottie tried to think straight; Adam's lips on her collarbone made it almost impossible. "She hasn't been with it lately, probably having trouble with her novel, or I'm sure she would've guessed something was up. I've been going around in a dream ever since the field trip."

"Nothing new there." Adam raised his head to smile at her. "That's the first thing I noticed, you sitting at dinner with this smile, like you were in another world. I knew right away you were different."

Lottie opened her mouth to protest but he silenced her with a kiss. She closed her eyes, losing herself in a world of desire and sensation where no one could follow.

"Lottie!" Aunt Carla shouted up the attic stairs, sounding alarmingly close, and they sprung apart. "Adam, Emma, downstairs now, please. Dinner's ready."

"Better go." Lottie scrambled into a sitting position and ran a hand through her disheveled hair. "I'm sure they'll all take one look at me and know what we've been up to."

"That would be an interesting topic for the dinner table," Adam said. Throwing off his crumpled T-shirt, he dug a fresh one from his suitcase and slid it on.

Lottie stared, unable to take her eyes from the taut muscles of his stomach and chest. He caught her looking and she blushed. Grinning, Adam pulled her up to kiss her, and then they stole from their haven and down the stairs.

As they neared her parents' bedroom, Lottie made out Emma's voice through the half open door and poked her head around it. Her cousin was sprawled on the double bed, the phone cradled to her ear.

"Sounds amazing. Wish I was there, rather than stuck out here in the middle of nowhere with my boring family." Emma caught sight of Lottie in the doorway and had the decency to look sheepish. Covering the receiver with her hand, she mouthed, "Won't be a minute."

"You need to come now," Lottie hissed. "Dinner's ready."

"Okay, okay." Emma re-settled the phone against her ear with a pout. "Sorry, babe, I have to go … Yeah, I'll try. Think of me while you're partying all night … I know, I wish I was there, too … Speak to you tomorrow … Love you, too … No, love you more … Okay, bye." She replaced the receiver and clambered off the bed, looking put out. "I can't believe I'm missing the party of the century, and for what? A whole weekend with my family, who don't even like each other. Without me there, Jerry will probably get totally pissed and have it off with some tart."

"He wouldn't if he could see you now," Lottie said.

"You like it then?" Emma pirouetted to show off her outfit: a cherry-red dress made of some clingy material, which barely covered her thighs in their black tights and made no attempt to contain her full breasts.

"You look amazing," Lottie assured her.

"No," Adam said, "she looks like some cheap lap-dancer."

"What would you know about lap-dancers?" Emma stopped twirling to smirk at him. "And for your information, this dress was nowhere near cheap. Besides, seeing as I can't be at the party, I might as well have some fun."

Lottie didn't trust the mischievous glint in her cousin's eye. "What sort of fun?"

"You'll see." Emma grinned, and, slipping her arm through Lottie's, led her along the landing.

***

"So, how's life at Cameron's?" Olivia asked to fill another awkward silence.

Joel glared at her from his opposing position at the foot of the table, provoking an automatic twinge of guilt. She quelled it. Too bad if he didn't like her choice of topic. He'd made no attempt to help her keep the conversation going and had rebuffed all Tim's efforts to draw him out, greeting them with disdain.

"Business is great." Rafe's eyes gleamed at the mention of his pride and joy. "Positively booming, in fact. A very different story from the last time we were here, that's for sure."

Joel's spoon slipped, splashing turkey soup onto the tablecloth. Olivia resisted the reflex to shoot him a sympathetic grimace. So many of their competitors in the financial world had fallen during that recession of the early '90s, but their family lost far more than any amount of money could replace.

"I'm glad," she told Rafe neutrally. "More soup, anyone?"

"Not for me." Carla, who had barely touched hers, patted her flat stomach. "It's absolutely delicious, Liv, but so rich. If I eat any more I won't be able to manage another thing."

"Well, I'll certainly have some," Tim said. "Carla's right, it is delicious."

In the flurry of bowls being passed up the table and replenished, Olivia tried to think of a subject that would move the conversation away from the company. Rafe, however, had other ideas.

"Yes," he went on as though there had been no interruption, "I couldn't be more positive about the future, although I do sometimes wonder who I'm doing it all for. It's not as if I have a son to pass the business on to, after all."

The remark was spoken lightly, but Olivia's cheeks burned on Phoebe's behalf. How could Rafe throw that in her face, and in front of her family? Phoebe had wanted a child every bit as much as he, probably more so, and was utterly devastated upon discovering she was barren. Remembering how she had always doted on Lottie, Emma, and Adam, Olivia's heart squeezed in pity.

Phoebe appeared not to have heard him. Sitting stiff as a corpse in her chair, she pushed her soup around her bowl, eyes continually darting up and down the table as though expecting one of them to pull a gun on her.

"Don't worry, Uncle Rafe," Emma said, fluttering her eyelashes. "At least you'll have me to take over the business for you."

"I'm glad to hear it." Rafe's eyes strayed to the copious amount of cleavage spilling from his niece's dress; Olivia shuddered. "I don't doubt that you have considerable assets to bring to the company."

Emma beamed. "I hope so. It's about time Cameron's had some female blood."

"Ah, but you've just hit on the problem. Once you marry, you'll no longer be a Cameron. I haven't devoted the best part of my life building up the company's reputation only for the next generation to put their own name to it. I need someone to carry on the family line."

"You're so old-fashioned, Uncle Rafe. Not all women change their names these days, and I have absolutely no intention of changing mine. Either my future husband takes my name, or I don't marry him."

Rafe nodded his approval. "I'm glad to see at least one member of my family shares my own commitment, which is more than can be said for your brother. I don't suppose you've finally seen sense, Adam?"

"'Fraid not," Adam said, leaning back in his chair with a grin. "Finance just doesn't do it for me. I want to be a lawyer like Vi."

"Good for you." Violet regarded him with interest. "Give me a call when you've qualified and I'll do what I can to help you."

Carla pursed her lips in evident annoyance. Any normal mother, Olivia mused, would be proud that her son harbored such an ambition. But then, Carla had always set such store by the family business. Turning to shoot Adam a commiserating look, she was in time to catch her sister's smug expression. Doubtless she'd made the offer with the sole purpose of getting Carla's back up. Not for the first time, Olivia wondered why Violet had been so determined to reunite the family when she'd spent the last twelve years avoiding them. Surely she could have made peace with the past just as successfully by coming alone?

"A lawyer, eh?" Rafe's snort interrupted her thoughts. "I can see Tim hasn't brought you up properly. No son of mine would be so ungrateful as to pass up a position in such a reputable firm, a firm, no less, that his father had worked his balls off to make a success. What about you, Lottie? Are we to have the pleasure of welcoming you to Cameron's in a few years?"

"You wouldn't want me," Lottie said. "I'm rubbish at maths. I'm going to be a vet."

"Clearly your father's done an equally poor job of instilling any sense of pride in you," Rafe scoffed. "Still, I can't say I'm surprised. I wouldn't expect anything more from the man who abandoned his family when they needed him most. Some might call it cowardly."

"And some," Olivia retorted without thinking, "might call it extremely brave, leaving a secure position in the family business to set up on his own."

There was a stunned pause. Aware of Joel attempting to catch her eye, Olivia got up to collect the empty soup bowls before escaping to the kitchen. Why on earth had she jumped to his defense? She supposed the habits of eighteen years were hard to break.

Joel stomped in a moment later, slamming the soup tureen onto the worktop. "This is a bloody nightmare! Who needs family, anyway?"

"Tell me about it," Olivia said.

Their eyes met and, for a split second, everything was as it should be, the two of them united against the world. Then reality barged in, shattering the illusion.

"Here." Olivia forced a bottle of red on him, her voice sharp to disguise the break in it. "Give everyone a top up and tell them dinner won't be a minute."

***

Halfway through the roast lamb, Olivia finally allowed herself to relax. Aided by plenty of food and a good deal more wine, the strain defrosted. Relieved from the chore of keeping up a constant stream of pleasantries, she leaned back in her chair and let snatches of conversation eddy around her.

"Wish I'd driven my Porsche down," Emma was saying to Lottie on Olivia's right. "Then we could have gone into town or something. Do you have a car?"

"Not yet. I'm still taking lessons. I have a horse, though. I'll introduce you to Gypsy tomorrow."

"Thanks, but I think I'll stick to cars. Less smelly."

On Olivia's other side, Adam and Violet were discussing the legal profession.

"How come you want to be a lawyer? Been watching too much *LA Law*?"

"I never even thought of it before I started taking Law A-level. My tutor's so cool, getting us re-enacting the crimes. Really brings them to life."

"He's certainly doing his job right if he's inspired you so much. Just bear in mind that the reality is somewhat different, harrowing even." Violet broke off, looking thoughtful. Olivia wondered which of her cases she was remembering.

Beyond them, Rafe had turned his back on his pale, silent wife to talk to Joel. "This business of yours, what vegetables do you grow, exactly?"

"All sorts." Joel's face had lost its stoniness, although he still refused to look at either Tim or Carla. "But mainly more unusual ones—celeriac, tomatillos, Jerusalem artichokes—to sell locally to organic restaurants."

"And is it lucrative? What's your annual turnover?"

"Who're you? My accountant? Trust you to bring it down to profit margins. What happened to job satisfaction?"

"So, Liv," Tim leaned past his daughter to call down the table, "how's the new book coming on?"

"Fine." Olivia quailed inwardly, reminded of the impending deadline she would be unable to meet.

Tim smiled. "I know we haven't seen much of each other over the years, but I always look for your latest novel."

"You do?" Olivia blinked away the ever-ready tears. "You've no idea how much that means to me, although I wouldn't have thought they'd be your thing."

"You'd be amazed," Carla said. "Tim's quite the romantic."

"Hey, don't go letting the world in on my secret." Tim put his arm around her, winking at Olivia. "Incredible that it was twelve years ago we were celebrating your first book being accepted."

Olivia groaned. "Don't remind me. You're making me feel old."

"We were all a lot younger the last time we were together like this," Carla mused. "In fact, it's been far too long. I'm glad you organized this reunion, Liv. It's just like old times, isn't it?"

"No," Violet said, "it isn't."

Perhaps alerted by her tone, everyone stopped talking and turned towards her. Olivia noticed Lottie exchanging curious glances with her cousins, and she flashed her sister a warning look.

Violet raised her eyebrows. "What're you all looking at me like that for? Of course it isn't like old times. How can it be?" She paused, as though summoning courage. "Things can never be the same again. Not without Scott."

Four

Phoebe dropped her knife and fork to her plate; the resultant clang echoed in the silence like a gunshot. Olivia's heart stuttered with the same shock evident on almost every face. Only Violet appeared unperturbed, observing their reactions with detached interest.

"Well," Olivia said, getting up, "if everyone's had enough, I'll just clear this lot away and we'll have pudding."

The matter-of-fact clatter as she collected plates dispersed the awkwardness, and the others began helping to stack the empty dishes. Only Phoebe still appeared paralyzed, knuckles straining to break the skin as she gripped the edge of the table.

Arms full of crockery, Olivia threw her sister a significant look. "Do you think you could give me a hand?"

Violet nodded. Expression torn between wariness and defiance, she gathered up the heaped dishes and followed along to the kitchen. Olivia nudged the door shut with her hip and crossed to dump her load on the draining board.

"Was that really necessary?" she reproached. "This is hard enough for everyone as it is, without you dragging it all up again."

"Dragging it up?" Violet slammed her own pile onto the worktop, eyes glittering. "Is that all Scott is to you? An unpleasant memory to be swept under the carpet?"

"No, of course not." Olivia extended her palms in apology, but her sister surged on.

"Have you any idea how these past twelve years have been for me? No, of course you haven't. You think you understand, but you don't. You haven't got a clue what I've been through. The longing, the guilt, the never knowing whether it might have been my—" Violet broke off and turned away, but not before Olivia glimpsed the tears on her cheeks.

Aghast, she went to put her arms around her. "Vi, I'm sorry. I didn't mean—"

"It's okay." Violet dashed a hand across her eyes. "None of this is your fault."

"No, but I haven't helped, have I? If it's any consolation, I think I do understand just a little of what you've been through. It's not the same, I know, but when I found out about Joel ..." Olivia swallowed the lump in her throat.

"Look at us. We're a right pair." Violet gave her a quick hug before squaring her shoulders. "Come on, let's sort out these puddings."

A few minutes later, they entered the dining room bearing an enormous trifle, an apple crumble still hot from the oven, and jugs of custard and double cream. To Olivia's relief, the conversation was more animated than it had been all evening.

"He would certainly liven things up if he were here," Rafe was saying. "Always was the life and soul of the party."

"Like the last time we were here," Carla said, "do you remember? He mixed up these killer cocktails and had us all dancing into the early hours."

"That was Scott all over," Tim agreed. "I'll never forget him throwing up in the punch bowl at Liv and Joel's wedding."

Lottie and Adam doubled up with laughter.

"Ugh," Emma squealed. "Uncle Scott didn't really do that, did he?"

"He certainly did." Violet set the trifle on the table, a faraway look in her eye. "I was there."

"Those both look scrumptious," Rafe said. "How can I choose?"

"Have a bit of each," Olivia urged. "There's plenty to go round. Help yourselves to cream and custard, everyone."

Once she had served and resumed her place, the talk returned to Scott and his numerous antics. Below the level of the table, Olivia pressed a hand to her stomach. Did anyone but she remember another who should have been with them today, the other life that was snuffed out too soon?

"I wish I could remember Uncle Scott," Lottie said. "He sounds so cool."

Tim grinned. "I suppose he was pretty cool, forever getting into scrapes, but the most generous person you could ever meet."

"And he thought the world of you kids," Violet added. "But then, he was a big kid himself."

"Oh, yes." Olivia smiled at a sudden recollection. "The last time your Uncle Scott was here, Lottie, he and Aunt Vi played catch with you for hours. He was rather the worse for wear after too many cocktails the night before, and I have this picture of you throwing the ball to him and it hitting him on the head."

"Really?" Lottie's expression flickered between amusement and frustration. "I just wish I could remember."

"You were only little," Joel said, "and it was a long time ago."

Unable to ignore his brusque tone, one he rarely used with their daughter, Olivia glanced over to see him frowning at his barely touched crumble. Plainly he still found the memories too raw to dredge up. Olivia stifled a rush of empathy.

"God, but he was gorgeous, wasn't he?" Carla sighed. No one else seemed to have noticed Joel's mood. "And he had the most incredible blue eyes. No idea where he got them."

Rafe guffawed. "Wherever it was, they certainly made him a favorite with the ladies. I can't remember a time when he didn't have a pretty girl in tow, often a different one for every night of the week."

"Until he met Violet," Tim reminded him.

"Hmmm." Carla gave Violet an appraising look. "Before that, Scott never struck me as the settling down type. Do you remember — ?"

"Stop it!"

Olivia started at the cry, her spoon falling from her hand. Phoebe stared at them all with terror in her expression, fists clenched, eyes dark against her deathly pallor.

"Stop it," Phoebe screamed again. "Stop it, stop it, stop it!"

"Phoebs?" Carla put out a hand to her friend, but Phoebe shoved her away.

"Don't. I can't bear it." Knocking her chair to the floor, she fled the room in tears.

Carla looked at Rafe, clearly expecting him to step in. When he merely resumed eating his pudding, she threw him a glare and stood. "I'd better go and calm her down. Excuse me, everyone."

She swept into the passage, leaving an awkward silence draped over the table. Olivia picked up her spoon, then put it down again; she wasn't hungry. She glanced around the table, desperately seeking a topic of conversation to relieve the tension. *Come on, someone, help me out here.* Her family only exchanged uneasy glances, pushing their dessert around their bowls. She tried to catch Violet's eye, but checked at her sister's expression. She was observing her family's discomfort with undisguised interest, and the smile tugging at the corners of her mouth was triumphant.

***

"We can't. Someone might see," Lottie hissed, resisting Adam's attempt to pull her close. She kept her eyes trained on the stairs, heart hammering. Emma had gone into the bedroom, leaving them alone on the landing, but an adult could come up at any moment.

"Please." Adam tightened his grip on her hands. "I've wanted to do this all evening. Thought that meal would go on forever."

"I know." Forced to sit opposite Adam at the table, trying not to meet his eye or blush when his leg rubbed against hers under cover of the tablecloth, had been torment.

Unable to withstand the combined pressure of Adam's plea and her own yearning, Lottie allowed herself to be drawn against him. They kissed long and fiercely, until their breathing grew ragged and Lottie could barely stand.

"I have to go," she said. "Emma will wonder what we're up to."

"You will come up, though, once everyone's asleep?"

35

"I'll try." Lottie kissed him, hurriedly this time. Then, legs as unstable as marshmallow, she pried herself from his arms and wobbled into her room.

"What were you two whispering about out there?" Emma asked, removing her make-up in front of the dressing-table mirror.

Lottie turned her back to Emma and pulled her top over her head. "Just talking about Aunt Phoebs."

"Yeah, wasn't it awful? I thought she was having a nervous breakdown or something. Still, Mum will have calmed her down."

"I hope so. She and Uncle Scott must have been really close."

"Mum's never given me that impression," Emma said, unzipping her dress, "but no one talks about Uncle Scott much, do they? I'm not surprised Aunt Phoebs is screwed up, though. Who wouldn't be, married to Uncle Rafe? Did you see the way he kept looking down my front?"

"Gross." Lottie pulled on her fleecy pajamas, shuddering. "He gives me the creeps. How can you encourage him?"

"Because he's so fun to wind up. When I bent down to pick up my fork and my boobs popped out, I thought he was going to have a heart attack. I almost died trying not to laugh."

"I don't suppose Aunt Phoebe found it very funny."

"No," Emma conceded, extracting a lace nightie from her suitcase. "Poor Aunt Phoebs. I wonder how she ever ended up with a disgusting letch like Uncle Rafe. I doubt she's the sort to marry for money, so perhaps he's just amazing in bed. Yuck!"

Emma prattled on, taking an agonizingly long time to get ready for bed. Lottie crawled under her duvet and lay there, squirming with desire, awaiting the moment when she could slip up the attic stairs to join Adam.

***

Emerging from the bathroom, Joel came face to face with Carla. Before he could prevent it, their eyes connected and they shared a look heavy with understanding. He tore his gaze away with an effort.

"How's Phoebe?" he asked, voice level.

"As you would expect." Carla matched his tone. "And you?"

Joel laughed without mirth and made to move past her. "As you would expect."

"Joel, wait." She put out a hand to stay him. "We need to talk."

He flinched. "I have nothing to say to you, as you well know."

"Please, Joel. This hasn't anything to do with … with you and me. It's about Tim."

"And why would you think I'd be remotely interested in what you have to say?"

"This is ridiculous," Carla snapped. "Tim cares about you, damn it, and all this hostility's really getting to him."

"My heart bleeds. Tell him he should've thought about that before—" Joel broke off and glanced around the landing.

Carla pounced. "Before what?"

"I don't want to talk about it," Joel said, walking towards his bedroom. "Tim knows what he's done. You both do."

"But if you would just talk to—"

Joel closed the bedroom door, cutting short her appeal. Shaking from suppressed tension, he sank onto the edge of the bed. *God, what an evening. What a bloody horrendous evening.* How was he expected to get through another two whole days? All he wanted was to be alone with Olivia, to talk things over and try and save his marriage. After all, she had defended him to Rafe at the dinner table. That had to count for something, didn't it? Clinging to that one shred of hope, Joel dropped his head in his hands and waited for her to come upstairs.

***

"Here." Violet pressed a large Bailey's into Olivia's hand. "I'd say we both deserve it."

"Thanks," Olivia said, accepting the glass, "although I've had far too much to drink already. Let's find somewhere more comfortable before my legs give out."

She led the way to the sitting room off the hall, where they settled in armchairs on either side of the dying fire. *It's just like my marriage*, Olivia mused, watching the flames gradually flicker out. A terrible void opened up in her heart. She sipped her Bailey's, welcoming the creamy warmth that trickled down her throat.

"So," Violet said, "what's all this about Joel having an affair?"

Olivia kept her gaze on the glowing embers. "I've known about it for over two weeks now. The usual signs. Countless dropped phone calls, Joel acting shifty and not meeting my eye, putting the phone down whenever I come into the room, that sort of thing. Gosh, it's all such a cliché."

"And what does Joel have to say for himself?"

"He denies it, but what else would you expect? I've asked him again and again, if he's not having an affair, what's going on, but he just shakes his head. It's like he can't even be bothered to invent a plausible story. Probably realizes there's no point. I know him too well."

"The cheating bastard," Violet spat. "He should be strung up. What will you do?"

"After he's been hung, drawn and quartered, you mean?" Olivia smiled, though she was blinking back tears. "I just don't know. How can I trust him again? Yet, the idea of us not living together, here in this house … it's not something I ever imagined I'd have to think about. Well, I can't think about it now, anyway, with the house full of people."

"Why the hell didn't you tell me?" Violet said. "I would never have pushed you into this if I'd known."

"I couldn't. Admitting it out loud would have made the whole thing so much more real."

"That's all very well, but now I feel terrible."

"Vi, you're hardly telepathic. Besides, this is something you need to do. I understand that." Olivia regarded her anxiously. "How are you bearing up?"

Violet shrugged. "Better than Phoebe, it would seem."

Alerted to the satisfaction in her sister's expression, Olivia frowned. "Why do I get the impression there's more going on here than you're telling me?"

Violet opened her mouth, then appeared to change her mind. "Not now. It's late and we're both tired. We'll talk tomorrow."

Olivia was tempted to argue, but the frantic day of preparations and the Bailey's soporific effect weakened her resolve. "I'll go up then," she said, draining her glass. "Coming?"

"In a minute. I'll just finish my drink."

Taking the hint, Olivia left her to it and climbed the stairs. *Please, let Joel be asleep. I can't cope with another confrontation on top of everything else.* However, when she pushed open the bedroom door, one look at his tense stillness beneath the duvet told her she was out of luck.

"Liv?" His voice reached her through the darkness.

Ignoring him, Olivia crossed to her side of the bed where she quickly undressed with her back to him and pulled on the baggy T-shirt she'd taken to wearing since learning of the affair. If she hadn't been so desperate to shield Lottie from their troubles for as long as possible, she would have banished him to one of the spare rooms.

"Liv," Joel said again as she slid under the covers, "we need to talk."

She turned away from him, almost falling onto the floor in her effort to avoid contact. "Not now. It's been a long day."

He began to protest, but she overrode him. "I said not now. Please, Joel, I've had just about as much of today as I can take."

Joel fell quiet. The mattress shifted under his weight as he rolled onto his side. They lay in the silent blackness, balanced at the extreme edges of the bed, the few feet of space between them as unbreachable as the Grand Canyon. Olivia held herself rigid, restraining the impulse to reach out to him. Yet no amount of will power could keep the images from crowding her mind: she and Joel walking hand-in-hand through the snow, curled up together on the sofa by a roaring fire, talking late into the night before falling asleep in each other's arms. Lying beside the man she loved and being unable to touch him, desiring him while knowing he desired another, was unbearable.

Olivia closed her eyes, allowing the tears to trickle soundlessly into the pillow. Unchecked, her thoughts drifted back to that summer twelve years ago, the last time the family was together under this roof. How different everything had been then. As though she were sifting through a stack of photographs, pictures exhibited themselves before her eyes: herself, aglow with the new life thriving inside her and excited about showing off her new home; Joel proud of his position in Cameron's and looking forward to spending the weekend with his brothers; Violet and Phoebe both bright-eyed with the promise of love; and Scott, so handsome and vitally alive. Olivia lay awake long into the night, and, when she eventually plunged into an uneasy sleep, her dreams were haunted by memories.

Five

Fresh from the shower, Olivia wanders into the garden to let her hair dry in the afternoon sunshine. Stepping from the patio, she crosses the stretch of ankle-deep grass to flop onto the rug where her husband and daughter have their heads bent over a storybook.

Joel smiles at her. "Look, Lottie, here's Mummy. And I thought she was far too busy to sit with us."

"The beds are made up and Vi should be here soon to help with the food, so I'll have you know I'm pretty organized."

"Organized? You? That's a first."

Olivia swipes at him and Joel catches hold of her hand, drawing her into his side.

"Mummy," Lottie says, "Daddy's reading me the one where the wolf pretends to be the mummy sheep and eats all the baby sheeps and then they have to cut the wolf open to get them out."

"Joel." Olivia casts him a despairing glance. Surely he knows better than to tell her that one. She had nightmares for weeks the last time.

"It's okay," Joel says. "We had a little chat first so Lottie knows there's nothing to be scared of. Isn't that right, pet?"

Lottie nods and pats the open page impatiently. "Go on, Daddy."

As Joel resumes the story, Olivia picks up the newspaper lying on the rug and scans the headlines: interest rates held at fifteen percent for the tenth month running … unemployment on the rise … a cup-winning horse killed in a terrible fire. Nothing but doom and gloom. She tosses the paper aside. The purpose of this weekend, apart from giving her the chance to show off their new home, is to provide a much-needed escape.

"Mummy." Lottie tugs the skirt of Olivia's pale-green sundress. "Is that how the doctors are going to get the baby out? Will they have to cut your tummy open like with the wolf?"

"Gosh, I hope not. Although, on second thought, it might be less painful."

"Does it hurt lots when you have a baby?"

"I should say so, if your mum's anything to go by," Joel says. "She screamed the place down while she was having you."

"I did not! Don't listen to him, Lottie. Anyway, I forgot the pain as soon as you were born and I saw how beautiful you were."

Lottie frowns as though in deep thought. "I don't think I'm going to have babies."

"Probably wise," Olivia agrees, "if the way you mistreat poor Dolly is anything to go by."

"But Dolly is always being naughty because he's a boy. I would only have girl babies."

"And of course girls are never naughty. I'm so glad your little brother will have you to show him how to behave."

"Not fair," Joel protests. "I'm a boy, and I'm always good."

"That's only because you have Mummy to keep you in order."

Lottie is so adamant that Olivia and Joel burst out laughing, leaning into one another for support. It's wonderful to hear Joel laugh. With recession crippling the country and so many businesses going into liquidation, he is in an almost constant state of anxiety. If anything, since returning home last night to help her prepare for the weekend, the lines of strain about his eyes have deepened. A couple of days relaxing with his brothers away from the stresses of work is just what he needs.

Still chuckling, Olivia rests her head on Joel's shoulder, his hand on her swollen stomach. Lottie clamors for another story, and Olivia lets Joel's voice wash over her as she gazes out over the endless lawn. Even more than the farmhouse itself, the moment she glimpsed these grounds from the window of the master bedroom, she knew this was where she wanted to raise her family.

Secluding the house from the outside world is an acre of wild grassland, oak-fringed paths and tumbledown outhouses. There is a swimming pool screened behind a tall hawthorn hedge, into which Joel has fitted a wrought iron gate to keep Lottie away from the water. Like the house, the grounds were in a general state of neglect when they moved in and their efforts have done little to tame them. It's as though their land is an extension of the surrounding countryside, rather than an imposition upon it.

The doorbell chimes through the house, pulling Olivia from her reverie. "That'll be Aunt Vi," she says, and, hauling her bulk up with some effort, goes to answer the door.

***

"Wow," Violet says when Olivia shows her into the drawing room, "this is a bit different from the last time I saw it. I admit I did wonder whether you'd lost your mind, buying a moldering old ruin like this."

"Liar," Olivia teases. "You were just jealous because I got there first."

"You sussed me." Grinning, Violet waves to Joel through the open patio doors. He waves back, hands black with charcoal from cleaning the barbecue.

"Seriously, Liv," she says, "what a transformation. Okay if I have a nose around?"

"Mind? I've been dying to show it off."

Beaming with pride at her handiwork, Olivia ushers her across the hall to the cozy sitting room, then along the passage past the dining room and her own study where she can write by the window that overlooks the grounds. It's hard to imagine the wreck it was when they first moved in. Between them, she and Joel ripped out the moldy carpets to reveal the original boards, stripped off the '70s wallpaper and scrubbed the fireplaces until the stonework gleamed. Finally, they were left with a blank canvas to do with what they wished.

"Magnolia?" Joel had examined the tins of paint stacked in the hallway, his eyebrows raised. "Where are the purples, the garish reds?"

"You'll see," Olivia said.

Once the walls were painted cream, she hung them with abstract watercolors she daubed herself, draped vivid curtains at the windows, piled the sofas high with cushions, strew rugs over the newly varnished floorboards and set vases of flowers on every mantelpiece. It was hard work turning the neglected old place into a family home, but Olivia loved every minute of it.

"Shame Phil couldn't come," Violet says, peering into the small room assigned to Lottie's toys. "Where has he jetted off to this time?"

Joel's father, having left Cameron's in the capable hands of his four sons and taken early retirement, is forever traveling to exotic destinations with the most current of his lady loves.

"The Maldives." Olivia picks up a couple of stray Lego blocks and returns them to their box. "With a Russian ballet dancer called Natasha. Far more exciting than spending the weekend with us, but we'll miss him."

Phil Cameron, for all his womanizing and outrageous vanity, is always good fun and ready to enthrall with hilarious tales of his latest antics. How different from their own father. Olivia invited him out of duty and was mightily relieved when he declined, being already booked to play an amateur golfing tournament in Scotland. It's a standing joke between herself and Vi that their dad could dampen the mood of a funeral.

"Wow," Violet says again, entering the kitchen at the end of the passage. "No more gruesome pink cupboards. Oh, and this table's to die for. I hate to think how much all this must have cost."

Olivia grimaces. "So do I. Probably not the best time to overstretch ourselves with interest rates so high, but at least now I might be able to help with the bills. My agent's in talks with the publisher as we speak, and I'm keeping my fingers crossed for a good advance."

"Great news! Just remember your big sister when you're rich and famous."

"If anyone's going to be rich around here, it's you. Lawyers are paid far more than my writing's ever likely to be. Still, perhaps you'll find time in between cases to drop in on my lowly book signings. In the meantime, are you ready to get your hands dirty making kebabs?"

"Just so long as I can freshen up first. My car was like a sauna."

"Go ahead." Olivia leads her back into the hallway, where Violet collects her bag and follows her up the narrow stairs. "I've put you in the room at the end. You're going to have to share with Carla's friend Phoebe, hope you don't mind."

"That depends. What's she like?"

"Hard to say. I've met her a few times at various birthdays, but she never said much. Shy, I suppose. She's certainly nothing like Carla."

"In that case," Violet says, "I like her already."

***

"Daddy," Lottie calls, running onto the patio, "can we go swimming?"

"Not now, pet." He straightens from the barbecue to wiggle his shoulders. He has a black smudge on his nose like the chimney sweep in *My Naughty Little Sister*. "I need to get everything ready, but I promise we'll go in the pool tomorrow with your cousins."

Lottie sticks out her bottom lip, which makes Daddy laugh, but doesn't argue. Mummy must have asked Daddy to clean the barbecue, and Daddy always has to do what Mummy says.

Running off in search of something else to do, Lottie spreads her arms wide and swoops over the lawn like a bird. She loves the garden at her new house. The garden at her old house was tiny, with only one short path for her to ride her bike up and down. Here, she can play outside all day, setting up camp in the stables, lying in wait amongst the trees to ambush the enemy, and putting on her Care Bear rucksack to venture into dangerous territory where no girl has been before. Why do her cousins have to come and spoil everything? Emma might look like a princess from a fairytale, but she's always bossy, and their games are never any fun. No point playing with Adam, either. He's just a stupid boy, who likes calling her names and pulling her hair.

Panting, Lottie stops at the foot of the Magic Faraway Tree. A rope ladder swings from its branches, daring her to climb. She pauses only to make sure no one is watching, then scrambles up it. The tree house was here when they moved in, but Mummy and Daddy have told her she mustn't use it, that it's too dangerous. What do they know? This is the Magic Faraway Tree and, at the top, all sorts of enchanted lands wait to be explored.

From the wooden platform, she can see the whole garden, see all the way to the patio where Daddy is still cleaning the barbecue, and over the hedge to the swimming pool sparkling in the sun. She lies on her back and stares up at the leafy roof, happy in her private green world. Probably best not to tell Emma and Adam about the tree house. They'll only snitch. This way, she can come up here whenever she wants without anyone knowing where she is.

***

Squashed between the children in the back seat of Tim's car, Phoebe gazes out at the Denninshire countryside scrolling past the window. In the distance, the river runs through the landscape like a strand of silver, while early evening sunshine dapples the meadows and gentle hills with gold. But even her pleasure in the scenery can't quell her doubts.

"You're absolutely sure they don't mind me coming?" she asks again, unable to shake off the notion of gate crashing a private family gathering.

"How many times?" Carla flings her an exasperated look from the passenger seat. "I checked with Olivia and she said the more the merrier. Tell her, Tim. She obviously hasn't taken any notice of me."

"Carla's right." Tim smiles at Phoebe in the rearview mirror. "Liv adores entertaining. Besides, you and Carla have known each other for so long, you're practically family."

Phoebe returns the smile, though the knots in her stomach tighten at his words. She stares down at her hands twisting together in her lap. How she wishes it were true and she really were part of this family. Only she knows how much she has riding on the coming weekend, how many of her hopes and dreams are tied up in it.

"Are we there yet?" Adam whines for the thousandth time. "I need the toilet."

"Me, too," Emma says, "and I want a drink. I'm boiling."

Carla sighs. "Please don't start. We're all hot and thirsty, but we'll be there soon."

"But I need the toilet now!"

Scenting a tantrum, Phoebe pulls herself together. "Why don't we play I Spy?"

"Yay!" Adam brightens at once. "You go first, Aunt Phoebs."

"Okay, then." Phoebe glances out of the window to hide a desperate longing. Perhaps, one day, she really will be aunt to her best friend's children. "I spy with my little eye, something beginning with—"

***

"Hello, my darlings." Olivia embraces her niece and nephew as they charge through the front door. "How are you both?"

"I'm going to wet myself," Adam says. "Mum made me hold it for ages."

"I'm thirsty," Emma adds. "Can I have a drink?"

"Please can I," Carla scolds, kissing Olivia's cheek. She looks flushed and irritable, not at all her usual self. "That was a pig of a journey, I don't mind telling you. Beats me why you had to move to the back of beyond."

"It is pretty quiet after London," Olivia admits, "although we're only a fifteen minute drive from Denbury. Hello, Phoebe." She shifts her smile to the young woman with the cloud of dark curls standing a little behind Carla. "I'm so glad you could come."

"Thanks for inviting me." Phoebe returns her smile shyly. "The countryside around here is so beautiful."

Emma hangs on Olivia's arm. "Where's Lottie, Aunt Liv?"

"In the garden, I expect. Why don't you go and find Aunt Vi in the kitchen? She'll show you where the toilet is and sort you out with drinks. Then you can explore."

The children race off in the direction she indicates, their excited whoops echoing in the flagstoned passage.

"They're a bit hyper, I'm afraid," Carla says. "Been cooped up in the car too long."

"Luckily, we had Phoebe to keep them entertained on the journey," Tim adds, struggling towards them with a suitcase in each hand. "Liv, you're looking well."

"Like a beach ball, you mean." Olivia laughs. "Can you believe I still have three months to go? Goodness knows how big I'll get before this little chap's ready to be born. Joel's out the back, by the way, getting the barbecue going."

Tim grins. "In that case, I'd better go and give him a hand before he burns your new house to the ground. All right if I take this lot upstairs first, though?"

"Of course. Come on in and I'll show you where you're sleeping." Closing the front door, Olivia precedes them up the creaking staircase.

"I have to say," Tim says, "you've done an amazing job on this place."

"We're both thrilled to bits with it." Olivia beams at him over her shoulder. "You'll want to watch your heads up here. The ceilings are quite low."

"Can't see the appeal of these old houses myself," Carla says, running a dismissive eye over the beams. "Far too dark and poky. Give me an apartment with open-plan living any day."

"Yes, but that isn't for everyone, sweetheart," Tim reproves.

"It's lovely," Phoebe says. "How romantic to live in a place and know it's been standing for hundreds of years."

"I think so." Olivia smiles at her, wondering what can have drawn together two such different personalities as Phoebe and Carla. Clearly friendship works in mysterious ways.

***

"Is he coming?" Violet asks later when she and Olivia are alone in the kitchen. Murmured conversation wafts through the open window from the patio, and the smoky tang of charcoal flavors the air.

"Who?" Olivia doesn't look up from her task of spearing pieces of onion and spiced chicken onto kebab skewers.

"Scott. Who else?"

"Oh, well, your guess is as good as mine. He promised he'd be here but that's no guarantee. You know what he's like."

"Yes, I know."

Warned by a change in her sister's tone, Olivia glances up. Violet is staring down at her hands as they shred a lettuce for the salad, and her expression is softer than it has ever been. Olivia's stomach sinks. Her sister and brother-in-law have always got on well despite their seeming incompatibility, sharing a rapport that still baffles their families. This is different. Something must have happened in the month or so since the family was last together.

Returning her attention to the kebabs, Olivia keeps her voice casual. "You haven't happened to see Scott lately, have you?"

"We may have bumped into each other once or twice."

Olivia's stomach drops another notch. Violet's offhand tone doesn't fool her one bit and, knowing Scott's reputation as she does, she has a good idea what 'bumping into' means.

"Vi," she ventures, "I hate to interfere, and you'll probably think it's none of my business, but you will be careful, won't you?"

Violet cocks an amused eyebrow. "Hark at my little sister, the relationship expert."

"I'm serious. I couldn't bear it if you got hurt, and Scott—"

"Scott will only break my heart. That's what you think, isn't it?"

"Can you blame me?" Olivia twirls a wooden skewer between her fingers, picturing the youngest of her brothers-in-law: wild, charming, affectionate, gut-wrenchingly handsome, and the very last man she would have expected sensible, career-minded Violet to fall for.

"Don't get me wrong," Olivia says. "I love Scott to pieces. He never sets out to break anyone's heart. He just can't help himself." She smiles in an effort to soften the words. "I don't mean to lecture. I want to look out for you, that's all, the way you've always done for me."

"I know," Violet assures her, "but there's no need. This is one girl who can take care of herself."

Olivia opens her mouth to argue but the doorbell forestalls her.

"I'll get that," Violet says, eyes bright with anticipation, and hurries from the kitchen.

Six

"You're so lucky," Emma tells Lottie, twirling on the endless lawn with her arms thrown wide as if to catch everything around her and hold it. "Wish we had a big garden like this. We only have a stupid balcony thing."

"And Mum shouts if we don't put our toys away," Adam says, "or if we get crayon on the table, but Aunt Liv doesn't care."

"Mummy hardly ever gets cross." Lottie's chest swells with pride at her new home. "Shall we play exploring?"

"I want to be a pirate," Adam says, "like Long John Silver."

"And we'll be princesses you want to take prisoner." Emma holds out a hand to Lottie. "Come on, find us somewhere to hide."

Lottie hesitates. Should she tell Emma about the tree house? Adam would never find them up there. She stifles a giggle. How funny to watch from between the leaves as he runs all over in search of them. But, no, the tree house is her very own special place; her cousins would only spoil it. Mouth stretched in a wide grin at being the one in charge for a change, she takes Emma's hand and the two of them dart away into the grounds.

***

"What's up?"

Joel straightens from the barbecue to find his twin regarding him with concern. "How do you mean?"

"Hmmm, I wonder. You clearly haven't heard a word I've said for the past five minutes and you look like you haven't slept for a week. So, what's up?"

Joel wavers. It would be such a weight off his mind to acknowledge the dread which has been lodged in his stomach these past few days, cold and irrefutable as a bullet. Such a relief to get it out in the open and let Tim allay his fears as only he can. Carla's musical laugh disturbs his thoughts. His gaze flickers to where she and Phoebe are lounging at the table beneath a yellow and white striped umbrella, heads converging over their drinks, fair hair entwining with dark. No, this isn't the time for messy confidences. Not when Liv so wants them all to relax and forget work for a while.

"It'll keep," Joel says. Hoping to distract his brother from further questions, he calls, "And what are you girls whispering about?"

"That's for us to know and you to only guess at," Carla mocks, awarding him the same provocative smile that ensnared his twin more than ten years before.

Tim and Carla met during their first semester at university, while studying for the same economics degree. In the library one afternoon, carrying out research for their latest assignment, their fingers brushed as they reached for a particular book and they got talking. Abandoning their research in favor of a nearby pub, they ended up going for dinner and a moonlit stroll by the Thames. From then on, it was rare to see one without the other. Before they even graduated, Carla fell pregnant with Emma and Tim proposed.

"Earth to Joel." Tim's voice brings him back to the present. "Wouldn't you say this barbecue's about ready?"

"You're the expert." Joel returns to the matter at hand and takes up the tongs.

They work in companionable silence, placing sausages and burgers on the smoking coals, until Carla's laugh once more floats towards them.

Tim looks over at her, his face soft. "You know, even after all these years, I can't quite believe my luck."

Joel rolls his eyes. "Don't start on that again."

"But it's true. How did a guy like me end up with the brightest, best-looking girl on our course? Carla could have done anything she wanted, and yet she married me."

"Idiot. It's precisely because Carla's so bright that she knows a good thing when she sees him." Joel fights to conceal his irritation. Why must Tim always behave as though he's somehow unworthy of Carla? If anything, it's the other way around. Oh, he can't doubt Carla's love for Tim; it's evident in her glances and the proprietory way she slips her arm through his. Yet, he sometimes wonders whether she would have indulged in more than a casual romance if it weren't for Tim's assured position in the family business. As for sacrificing a career of her own, she makes up for it through her interest in Cameron's. Joel has long suspected that Tim's most creative ideas for moving the company forward come straight from his wife.

"Thanks for the vote of confidence." Tim smiles, though his expression is wistful as he gazes out over the grounds. "You're so lucky to have found this place. What I wouldn't give to move out to the country, to have somewhere to escape at weekends."

"So why don't you?"

"I think Carla would have something to say about that, don't you? Can you imagine her being stuck out in the middle of nowhere? She'd go crazy without Oxford Street on her doorstep and her smart friends to go to lunch with."

Joel bites his tongue and glances once more at his sister-in-law, so beautiful and composed in her cream linen dress. It's easy to see why she has such power over his twin; a less generous man would have trouble resisting that smile. All the same, Joel wishes, for once in his life, Tim would put his own happiness first.

***

"He is coming, isn't he?" Phoebe asks for the umpteenth time, her gaze straying longingly towards the house.

"He'll be here," Carla says. "He isn't going to pass up the chance to spend a whole weekend with you, is he?"

Phoebe bites her lip. "You really think so?"

"I know so." She smiles at her friend over her wine glass. Though Phoebe is unrecognizable as the ugly duckling she'd been at eleven, inside she's as unsure of herself as on the day Carla met her seventeen years before.

Her own beauty and self-confidence have always made Carla a magnet for those coveting a share of her popularity and, in the first weeks of secondary school, she was inundated with bribes from fellow students hoping to be chosen as her best friend. Only Phoebe, too timid and awkward to approach her, remained a mystery. Intrigued, Carla sought her out one lunchtime and, from that first swapping of secrets and chocolate bars, the two became inseparable. In Phoebe, Carla discovered what she had unconsciously been looking for: someone weaker than herself who needed her protection.

Renowned at school for being a plain Jane with her skinny legs, thick-lensed glasses and bushy hair, Phoebe was used to boys pushing her aside as they vied for Carla's attention. Eventually, when the girls reached their late teens, Carla took her friend in hand. She replaced the hideous specs with contact lenses to reveal her cocoa-brown eyes, relieved her pallor with make-up, and exchanged the shapeless leggings and sweatshirts for flowing skirts and blouses that disguised her bony legs while emphasizing her slimness. Yet, despite the improvements in her appearance, Phoebe's painful shyness made talking to men an ordeal and she soon lost their interest. Until she met Rafe.

During their first encounter at Carla's twenty-seventh birthday party a year before, Rafe seemed taken with Phoebe, flirting openly with her and insisting she sit next to him at dinner. Unaccustomed to such attention, least of all from someone so handsome and self-assured, it was natural Phoebe should respond to it, and their subsequent meetings have only caused her to fall deeper in love with him. Much as it thrills Carla to see her so happy, cheeks rosy with new promise, she can't subdue a stirring unease. Rafe is so brash, even arrogant. Can he really be serious about gentle, unassuming Phoebe?

Noticing her friend cast yet another hopeful glance towards the house, Carla squeezes her arm. "He'll be here," she promises. *And if he dares break her heart, he'll have me to answer to.*

***

Violet flings open the front door, heart racing, a smile of welcome on her lips.

"Oh." Her excitement dies at the sight of the stocky figure on the step. "It's you."

Rafe lets out a booming laugh. "Look who it is. Our very own answer to Joyce Davenport. So, when do I get to see you in action?"

"I'm sure you'll have your chance when I'm prosecuting you for possession of an offensive ego."

"God, I love a feisty woman. Feel free to cross-examine me any time. Now, are you going to leave me standing on the doorstep all evening?"

"If it were down to me, I would, but my sister wouldn't approve." Violet steps aside to allow him into the house, hating him for his smugness and lecherous eye, and, most of all, for not being Scott.

***

Olivia returns to the patio with two fresh bottles of wine. Dusk shrouds everything in a lavender haze and moths flutter against the roof of the umbrella. Every now and then the children run past, embroiled in some game of their own invention, their shouts carrying on the sultry air.

"You've been holding out on us, Liv," Tim says as she refills his glass.

"Oh? How's that?"

"Two little birds tell me we're going to have a famous writer in the family."

"Thanks for that." Olivia shoots the culprits an exasperated look. "Those little birds were supposed to keep their beaks shut until I had a firm offer from a publisher."

Joel holds up his hands. "I know, I know, but we're just so proud of you, we couldn't resist spilling the beans. Isn't that right, Vi?"

"Exactly right," Violet says, though her mind seems far away, doubtless with Scott, wherever he might be.

"All the same." Olivia continues around the table, replenishing drinks. "There's still so much that could go wrong. I'm terrified of jinxing my luck."

"Ye of little faith," Tim says. "Nothing wrong in believing in yourself. A year from now, I have no doubt the world will be queuing up outside Waterstone's to buy your book."

Laughing, Olivia drops into her chair beside Joel. A warm

contentment settles over her. Here she is, on the verge of achieving her dream, and with her family enjoying themselves in her new home. She has every reason to be happy, recession or not.

"Carla never told me you're a writer, Olivia," Phoebe says, eyes shining with admiration. "What do you write?"

"Contemporary romance, or, as my husband so aptly calls it, sentimental twaddle."

"Phoebe's a writer herself," Carla says. "She writes the most stunning poetry, but of course insists on keeping it hidden away."

"I didn't know we were in the presence of a literary genius." Rafe toys with Phoebe's curls, smiling into her eyes. "But then I imagine there are many hidden depths I have yet to discover."

Phoebe's cheeks glow in the gathering darkness. "Carla's exaggerating, really. They're just scribblings."

"And you're determined to put yourself down," Carla retorts. "Didn't our English teacher say your poems were the best he'd ever seen from a student?" She turns to the group. "I just know Phoebs could make a career out of her poetry if she didn't spend her life running around after Mr. Bradshaw. He's the accountant she works for. She's meant to be his personal assistant, but he treats her more like a slave. The other day, the lazy sod sent her out to buy his daughter's eighteenth birthday present, can you believe?"

"I didn't mind," Phoebe says. "It's nice that Mr. Bradshaw feels he can rely on me."

"Creative *and* efficient." Rafe's tone is warm with admiration as he slides his arm along the back of her chair. "An irresistible combination. This Mr. Bradshaw better watch out; I might get it into my head to poach his most valuable employee."

Phoebe beams and nestles against him. Glancing away from them, Olivia catches Carla regarding Rafe speculatively. The same question must be in both their minds. Is he serious about Phoebe, or will he only break her heart? Olivia hopes it's the former; Phoebe's a sweet girl and doesn't deserve to get hurt. Yet, though his affection seems genuine, it's impossible to tell what Rafe really feels behind the practiced charm.

"Well, I say we propose a toast." Tim raises his glass. "To Liv becoming a best-selling author and supporting us all in our old age."

"To Liv," they chorus, clinking glasses, and she turns away to hide her blush.

"It must be nice having time to pursue one's hobbies," Carla says, sipping her wine. "Since marrying Tim, I haven't had a moment to myself."

"I can imagine," Rafe drawls. "All those trips to the beauty salon and the hairdresser's must be very time-consuming, and that's before the endless shopping excursions and long lunches."

Carla flicks her hair over her shoulders. "For your information, being married to an investment banker is extremely hard work. How would Cameron's be without my support, I wonder? Many a deal has been struck during one of my dinner parties."

Olivia shares a grin with Joel. There has never been much love lost between Rafe and Carla, little wonder considering their strong personalities, and no family gathering would be complete without their needling.

"Speaking of Cameron's," Rafe says, "Liv chose just the right time to land herself a publishing deal. If things carry on like this, Joel's going to need a wealthy writer to support him."

Olivia's smile fades as anxiety creeps back into her heart. Whenever she brings up the subject of Cameron's future, Joel assures her there's nothing for her to worry about, but his recent abstractedness and the dark circles beneath his eyes tell a different story.

"Are things that bad?" she asks Rafe.

He chuckles. "Lord, no. I was only teasing. Cameron's has looked after the country's investments for over a hundred years. It'll take more than a recession to finish it off." He glances at his watch. "Where the hell's that brother of ours got to? He did say he was coming, didn't he?"

Joel shrugs. "What Scott says and what he ends up doing rarely amount to the same thing, as you well know."

"I'm sure he'll turn up," Olivia says, needing to believe it for Violet's sake. "He probably just got held up."

"That'll be it," Tim agrees. "In fact, I'm betting he's meeting with this mysterious new client of his, sealing the deal over a few whiskies."

Joel grins. "Wouldn't surprise me. I've never understood how Scott can work half the hours we do, hardly ever gracing the office with his presence before lunchtime, and yet still bring in more money than any of us."

"That's our little bro for you," Rafe says. "Always did have the luck of the Irish, or should that be the devil?"

The brothers laugh at the well-worn joke. Many siblings with such a brother as Scott would surely have envied him. He forever outshines them in all aspects of life, winning the most sporting trophies at school, attracting more adoring women than the rest put together, and generally cruising through life with indecent ease. Some might even have resented his very existence, seeing as their mother died giving birth to him. But no one hearing the Cameron boys talk of Scott could doubt their love for him. He has that effect on most people, ensnaring men and women alike with his roguish charm. He is also the handsomest man Olivia has ever met. With such a lethal combination, it's little wonder he's stolen her sister's heart.

Olivia glances over at Violet, who has scarcely spoken all evening. Paying scant attention to the conversation, she twists the stem of her wine glass round and round between her fingers as her eyes wander continually towards the house. *Don't let Scott have stopped off in a pub somewhere and forgotten where he's supposed to be. Don't let me have to see the hurt and disillusionment in her eyes, especially when things are going so well for me. That would be too cruel for words.*

***

Finally unable to stand the meaningless chat any longer, Violet leaves the balmy twilight and retreats to the kitchen. She begins loading the dirty things into the dishwasher; perhaps the rhythm will numb her disappointment. How can she have failed to notice before that her family is made up entirely of couples? Olivia and Joel, Tim and Carla, even Rafe and Phoebe, although what Phoebe sees in Rafe she can't imagine. Watching them together, the intimate glances and handholding, brings home how very single she is, how empty her life with no one to share it.

Violet stares down at the wine glass in her hand, trying to recall what it's doing there. She has built up so much hope around this weekend, let it seduce her with its promise, and now it has all come to nothing. Her eyes burn but she feels too hollow even to cry.

"You don't have to do that," Olivia says behind her. "You did your fair share earlier, helping me with the food."

Violet turns, glass in hand, making no effort to hide her desolation. "He's not going to show, is he?"

"I don't think so." Olivia shakes her head, expression full of helpless sympathy. "I'm so sorry, Vi."

Seven

"Lottie," Olivia calls from the kitchen doorway. She can just make out her daughter, a splash of pink in the twilight. "Time to come in."

"But we haven't finished our game."

"Too bad. It's way past your bedtime."

"No one's telling Emma and Adam to go to bed."

"I think you'll find they are," Carla says, breaking away from a heated discussion with Rafe. "Emma, Adam, inside now, please."

"But, Mum, we're not even tired."

"Can't we stay up a bit longer? Pleeease."

Before Olivia can put her foot down, the telephone rings. "Joel, round them up, would you?" she implores, then hurries through the kitchen and along the passage to pick up the extension in her study.

"Liv, thank Christ I got you."

"Scott?" Though slurred, the husky voice is instantly recognizable. Catching sight of Violet in the doorway, eyes bright with hope, Olivia can't suppress a surge of irritation. Does her brother-in-law have any idea the turmoil he's caused? "Where are you? We'd given you up for lost."

"Don't be cross. I would've been there hours ago but got held up. Any chance of giving a weary traveler a lift?"

"A lift? Where's your car?"

"Long story, and my money's going to run out any second. You'll come and rescue a poor soul in distress, won't you? I'm at Denbury station."

He sounds so forlorn that Olivia's heart softens. "Okay, sit tight. Someone will be there in fifteen minutes."

"Liv, you've saved my life. I can't tell you how —" A series of beeps end Scott's protestations as the money in the pay phone runs out.

Olivia replaces the receiver. "It seems the prodigal brother is going to show, after all, though he has apparently mislaid his car. He was calling from the station, says he needs a lift, but we're all over the limit. I suppose I'll have to call a cab."

"I can go. I only had one glass." Face radiant, Violet is already heading for the front door. "See you in a bit."

"Drive carefully." Smiling, Olivia wanders back out into the garden to find the children shrieking with laughter as Joel chases them over the lawn. She shakes her head in exasperation. Now Lottie will be thoroughly overexcited and refuse to settle for ages. Still, it's a small price to pay for her sister's happiness.

"Okay, kids." She raises her voice over the hilarity. "First one inside gets to choose a bedtime story."

***

Violet spies Scott slumped on a bench outside the station entrance and draws up to the curb. Heart sputtering, she fumbles in her haste to buzz down the window. "Your carriage awaits, my lord."

Head jerking up, Scott blinks as though in confusion. After a brief hesitation, he seems to pull himself together and ambles to meet her, black hair tousled and flopping over his forehead. His jeans and baggy T-shirt are rumpled as though they've been slept in and hang off his body, undernourished from an overdose of nicotine and too few decent meals. Violet can't tear her eyes from him.

"Vi." He hovers by her open window, looking embarrassed. "I wasn't expecting ... I thought Liv—"

"I'm the only one sober enough to drive," she says. Just the sound of that deep, smoke-roughened voice turns her limbs to blancmange. "Aren't you pleased to see me?"

"Course I am." Scott's eyes, a brilliant blue, sparkle as he smiles. "Honestly, Vi, you're my savior."

"Happy to be of service." She pretends not to notice his awkwardness, the forced twist to his smile. He's here now. Nothing else matters.

Once Scott has flopped into the passenger seat, Violet eases away from the curb and heads back through the town crowded with people enjoying the summer evening. A crescent moon paves the road ahead with silver and outlines the distant spires of Denbury Cathedral. She drives slowly, wanting to prolong the journey and distrusting her hands, unsteady on the steering wheel. Simply breathing in Scott's familiar smell, Christian Dior mixed with cigarettes and Jack Daniel's, makes her light-headed.

"So," she says to bridge the silence, "going to fill me in on why you took so long getting down here? Where's that flash Porsche of yours?"

Scott fiddles with his cigarette lighter. "I, er, seem to have misplaced it."

"Misplaced it?" Violet throws him an incredulous look. "How much did that car cost again? Surely even you couldn't lose something that big and expensive."

"I can explain. Here's how it happened. Yesterday evening, I drove straight from the office to meet a ... a friend in a bar. I only meant to stay for a quick pint, but you know how it goes. One thing led to another and we ended up in a club. By the time I staggered out at God knows what hour, I was completely sloshed and couldn't think for the life of me where I'd left the damn car. I was too drunk to drive, anyway, so I got a cab home and hoped I'd remember in the morning. Needless to say, I didn't."

Violet shakes her head, mentally joining the dots. Was he with a girl last night? Did he take her home, fall with her onto the bed where she herself had lain only a few weeks earlier? Her insides wrench at the thought. *For pity's sake, stop torturing yourself. Scott made you no promises. Besides, going all possessive will only drive him away.*

"Okay," she says, "that explains why you didn't drive down, but why not get a cab from the station?"

Scott looks sheepish. "Now, don't go off on one, but I kind of got chatting to this guy on the train. Turns out the poor sod's just been made redundant and his wife's due to give birth to their second child any day. I felt so sorry for him, I gave him everything I had."

"And how much was that?"

"Not sure. A couple of hundred, maybe."

"Scott, when will you learn?"

"Come on, Vi, have a heart. I had to help him out. I mean, what about his wife and kids? I couldn't let them suffer, could I?"

"If they even exist, which I doubt."

"You weren't there. You didn't see how desperate he was." Scott turns away.

An awkward silence descends. Soon they leave the town behind and emerge into open countryside, magical in the moonlight. Scott lights up a cigarette, rolling down the window to let out the smoke. Ashamed, knowing this is out of consideration for her, Violet keeps her eyes on the road. She shouldn't have been so dismissive, but people so often take advantage of Scott's kindness, his naivety, and it makes her protective. In an effort to ease the tension, she slides a CD into the stereo and 'Hard Day's Night' fills the car.

"Wow," Scott says, "this is my all-time favorite album. Never knew you were a fan."

"Ah, but there are a lot of things you don't know about me, Scott Cameron."

"As there are about me. For instance, I bet you didn't know I'm rather talented in the singing department." He adds his rich, gravelly voice to John Lennon's. "There is nothing in this world I'd rather do, 'cause I'm happy just to dance with you."

"You're full of surprises," Violet says. "Look, about the money. I'm sorry. Didn't mean to nag."

Scott shrugs. "No worries. I know I'm a gullible fool."

Violet falls quiet, unable to ignore her growing unease. A casual eavesdropper would have heard only the light banter of two good friends, but she is all too aware of the silences and unspoken questions. Where is their easy intimacy of a few weeks ago, the laughter and passion that sizzled between them? Has she misunderstood the significance of their encounter? She shoves the thoughts aside, blotting out everything but the music and the feel of the breeze toying with her hair. Scott starts to sing again and Violet imagines he intends the words for her.

"Bright are the stars that shine, dark is the sky. I know this love of mine, will never die."

***

"Nice of Scott to honor us with his presence," Carla remarks, once Olivia has herded the children up to bed. "I was beginning to think his family was too dull to tempt him away."

"I can't believe I've never met him," Phoebe says. "What's he like?"

Carla grins at her husband. "Divine, but as reliable as the rail network in snow."

"And what would the Lady Carla know of such a common mode of transport?" Rafe drawls. "There was me thinking you go everywhere by chauffeur-driven Rolls."

"We weren't all born with a diamond-encrusted spoon in our mouth, you know. Some of us had to work for what we have."

"While others were lucky enough to find a rich fool to marry them."

"Watch who you're calling a fool." Laughing, Tim turns to Phoebe. "Scott was always the one getting into scrapes when we were younger. Although, if he put his mind to it, I'd wager he's brighter than the rest of us put together."

"He's also a magnet for women," Joel adds. "They just can't seem to resist him."

"Gets his charm from his eldest brother." Rafe smirks, smoothing his hair. "Although he failed to inherit my own sense of commitment." He squeezes Phoebe's shoulder, then stands. "Just nipping to the loo. I've drunk enough wine to flood a vineyard."

As he makes his way indoors, a little unsteady on his feet, Carla pursues him with her eyes. She has watched all evening as he makes a play for Phoebe, casting her farther under his spell. Yet, even though she detects no falsehood behind his flattery, she can't rid herself of the fear that he's merely toying with her. Well, now's her chance to find out.

"I'd better make sure the children are behaving for Liv," Carla says. Hurrying through the kitchen and along the passage, she waylays Rafe at the foot of the stairs.

"In here." She seizes his arm to pull him into the poky sitting room.

"We are keen," Rafe says as she closes the door. "I mean, I'm used to women jumping on me, but most don't dare with their husband in the same house. Not that I'm complaining. Why don't we try out that comfortable-looking sofa?"

Carla folds her arms across her chest, glaring at him. "I wouldn't touch you if you paid me."

"Trust me, babe, you're the one who'd be paying me. So, if you're not after a bit of rough-and-tumble, what can I do for you?"

"You can take note of this, because I'm telling you, Rafe, if you break Phoebe's heart, you'll have me to deal with."

"How touching, I'm sure. Still, I imagine Phoebe can look after herself."

"What would you know? You didn't have to watch while the girls at school teased her, or comfort her when she cried her eyes out because she thought she was ugly and no man would ever want her. It's taken me years, yes, *years,* to help her build up some semblance of confidence. I won't have you shatter it with your selfish games."

Rafe considers her, head on one side. "If I didn't know better, Carla, I'd say you were jealous." And moving her aside as easily as if she were a child, he opens the door and saunters upstairs.

***

"Rafe seems pretty smitten with you," Joel says, smiling across the table at Phoebe.

She blushes. "I hope so … Joel, isn't it? Sorry, but you're so alike. I still have trouble telling who's who."

"It's easy," Tim says. "Joel's the ugly one."

"Get out of it." Joel punches him on the arm, grinning at Phoebe. "Most people find it hard to tell us apart at first, but you'll get the hang of it. I'm the one with the scar." He taps his left cheekbone. "See?"

"Only just. How did you get it?"

"Scott and I were having a sword fight with a couple of sticks—we must have been about eight—and Scott sliced my cheek open with the sharp end."

"Ouch."

"Quite. After I'd been stitched up at A and E, I wanted to break Scott's nose, but Susie—she was our nanny at the time—wouldn't let me rearrange his perfect features."

"It must have been fun," Phoebe says, "all growing up together. I had two sisters, but they're much older than me."

"We did have a laugh," Tim agrees. "I only wish Emma and Adam got on so well, but they wind each other up most of the time."

Phoebe looks wistful. "You both have lovely children. You're lucky."

"I know," Joel says. How different Phoebe is from Rafe's usual girlfriends, pretty secretaries with little of substance between the ears, who he indulges for a few weeks before dismissing them as unsuitable wife material. This gentle young woman with the sweet smile and lovely eyes might be just what his brother needs.

***

"The end." Olivia closes the book and gets off the foot of Lottie's bed. "Okay, time to shut your eyes now."

"Not fair," Lottie whines. "Don't like that story. I want to choose one."

"You can choose tomorrow," Olivia promises, returning *Alex's New Clothes* to its shelf. "Time to go to sleep now."

Adam, shunning the idea of sleeping on his own in favor of a bed next to his sister on Lottie's floor, pokes his head out from the pile of duvets and sleeping bags. "But we're not even tired."

"Don't be difficult for Aunt Liv," Carla scolds, coming in. "It's way past your bedtime already."

"But we're too excited," Emma says. "We haven't seen Lottie for ages."

Sensing a mutiny on the way, Olivia intervenes. "How's this for a deal? You can listen to a tape, so long as you promise to pack down."

This sparks another argument as to which tape they should listen to. Eventually, Olivia slips *Fantastic Mr. Fox* into the cassette player, and she and Carla kiss their offspring goodnight before heading back downstairs.

Carla sighs. "Kids! Who'd have them?"

"This is supposed to be the easy bit," Olivia says. "Wait till they're out partying all night."

Laughing, they reach the hallway just as headlights flash through the front windows. The women exchange a look.

"Finally." Carla's eyes dance. "Let the fun begin."

***

With every mile, Scott seems to retreat farther inside himself. He glowers out of the window, shoulders rigid, fists clenching and unclenching on his knees. Watching him from the corner of her eye, Violet's heart grows heavy. Her initial joy at seeing him again descends into a dull acceptance. At any moment he will disclose what's on his mind and blast her hopes to shrapnel.

A few minutes later, Violet pulls up on the sweeping driveway and kills the engine. Without the music, the silence is thunderous. Scott shakes his head as though emerging from a trance. For an age he simply gazes up at the house, breathing deeply as though psyching himself up

62

for an ordeal.

At length, he reaches for the door handle. "Well, cheers for the lift."

With the reflexes born of her days on the school netball team, Violet shoots out a hand to stop him. "Don't rush off. We have to talk."

"Not now, Vi. Everyone's expecting us."

"Please, just five minutes. You owe me that much."

"Okay." Scott leans back in his seat, tone wary. With the porch light casting his face into relief, Violet notices for the first time how tired he looks. Purple shadows stand out like bruises beneath his eyes and his skin has an almost grayish tinge. The result of strain, or merely too much sex and booze? Is she already forgotten, obliterated by a string of other bodies more beautiful and just as willing?

Violet stares down at the steering wheel, stomach churning. How to say what is uppermost in her mind without sounding like some nagging wife? Does it make a difference what she says? Perhaps it's too late. Get a grip, Vi, this isn't the courtroom. You're not on trial now.

"It's just—" She stalls, then wades in. "Well, I thought I might have heard from you after the other week."

Scott looks away. "Sorry about that. I meant to call, but things have been crazy."

"We're all busy, Scott, but most people find the time to answer their phone."

"Yeah, well, there's been a glitch with the line, friends calling and not getting through. Only just got it fixed."

A chill closes over Violet's heart. Trained to read the body language of witnesses, she knows when someone's lying. Did that wild, magical night mean so little to him? Violet won't forget it for as long as she lives: how they met by chance in a bar one evening and stayed long after their friends had left; how they went dancing till dawn, before tumbling into Scott's bed in a haze of wonder and discovery.

"Look at me," Violet says. When he remains unmoving, she seizes his face in her hands and forces him to meet her gaze. "Come on. Look at me and say it meant nothing."

He doesn't reply, but the mingled longing and helplessness in his eyes tells her everything she needs to know. Still holding his face between her hands, she leans forward and kisses him. Scott stiffens, but only for an instant. Then his arms slide around her, pulling her close, and Violet's senses once again roar to life at his touch.

"I love you," she murmurs against his mouth. "I've loved you from the moment I saw you throwing up in the punch bowl at Liv and Joel's wedding."

Scott winces. "You mustn't say that."

"Why not? It's the truth. I don't make a habit of telling men I love them, you know. In fact, you're the first."

Scott shakes his head, looking upset. Violet opens her mouth to speak, but he presses a finger to her lips and pulls her against him, staring over her shoulder so she can't see his expression. She lets him hold her, drinking in the warmth of his neck against her cheek as their hearts beat in time. For the moment, it's enough simply to have him close.

"We'd better go." At last, Scott pushes her gently from him and opens the car door. "We'll talk later, I promise."

"I'll hold you to that," Violet says, though too softly for him to hear. "You won't get rid of me that easily."

Eight

A cheer goes up as Olivia leads Scott onto the patio, and a moment later he is surrounded.

"You made it!" Tim drapes an arm over his shoulders. "We'd virtually given up on you."

Joel slaps Scott on the back, grinning. "What happened? Misread the timetable and catch the train for Dundee instead?"

"Nah," Rafe says, "he stopped off for a quickie with Rita from reception. Amazed you could tear yourself away, Scott. She's a cracker."

"As if he'd miss the chance to see his favorite sister-in-law." Carla leans in to kiss Scott's cheek. "I must say you're looking as sexy as ever."

Scott opens his mouth but no sound comes. Amidst their excitement, the others seem oblivious that anything's amiss. Only Olivia, alert for clues as to how things stand between him and Violet, notices his unusual silence, the dazed, almost sheepish expression in his eyes as they dart from one smiling face to the next. Not good signs. With a sinking heart, Olivia's gaze seeks out her sister on the fringe of the group. Her earlier sparkle has dimmed and she looks serious and thoughtful. *Oh, don't let Scott have hurt her.*

Knowing she can't question Violet in front of the others, Olivia moves closer to her brother-in-law to murmur in his ear. "You okay?"

"Fine." Gathering himself, Scott flashes her the famous smile that could melt the polar ice caps. "And how's my new nephew?"

"Probably wondering who on earth this nutter is that's turned up to disturb his peace and quiet." Olivia laughs through her anxiety as he pats her swelling stomach. Perhaps she's being over sensitive and his preoccupation has nothing to do with Violet. Perhaps he's just worried, as are they all, about Cameron's.

Scott winks. "Good practice for when I take him out on the town."

"Which won't be happening for at least eighteen years," Joel says. "We considered making you Godfather, but weren't sure you'd be a suitable influence."

"He'd probably add vodka to the baby's bottle," Carla agrees. "The poor child would be an alcoholic before his first birthday."

"You never know, the little chap might keep me on the straight and narrow." Scott turns to the young woman standing slightly apart from the rest and takes her hands. "And you must be Phoebe. How did Rafe land himself such a stunner? Remind me to give you my number so you can call me when you've had enough of him."

Phoebe giggles, flushing scarlet.

"Oi, hands off," Rafe says, sliding an arm about Phoebe's waist.

Joel thrusts a glass into Scott's hand. "Here, get this down you. You're a bit behind."

"I'll soon catch up, don't you worry." Scott gulps the champagne in one and pulls a face. "What sort of poncy drink is this? Still, never fear, for I am here. Liv, does this magnificent place of yours house such a thing as a drinks cabinet?"

"In the drawing room." Olivia gestures to the open patio doors. Before she can ask what he has in mind, Scott tosses his glass to her and hurries inside.

"Told you he was gorgeous, didn't I?" Carla sighs to Phoebe.

Catching her sister's eye, Olivia mouths, "Everything okay?"

Violet grimaces, but Olivia can't probe further as Scott rejoins them with his arms full of bottles.

"What are you doing?" Olivia asks.

"You'll see." Scott lines the bottles up on the low wall that flanked one end of the patio and disappears back into the house, re-emerging with an ice tray and several cartons of fruit juice.

"Just knew my wedding present would come in handy one of these days," he says, brandishing a cocktail shaker, and proceeds to arrange his apparatus.

"Are you sure you know what you're doing?" Carla sounds skeptical.

"I resent that. I'll have you know I worked in a cocktail bar for three years to top up my student loan. You know what a tightwad Dad is. He insisted we pay our own way through uni, and he actually did me a favor. The experience I gained behind the bar has proved far more effective in winning over the ladies than anything I learned during my studies."

"Well, I'm afraid this girl isn't so easily impressed," Carla mocks. Nevertheless, she moves to his side to watch.

"Is that so? What would you say if I were to offer you a screaming orgasm?"

"I'd say sounds lovely, but I think my husband would object."

"Too right he would," Tim says, laughing.

Carla grins at him and pokes Scott in the ribs. "You're having me on, though, right? There isn't really a cocktail called a Screaming Orgasm."

"There is, and I'm about to demonstrate how it's done. Gather round, ladies."

Infected by his charm and enthusiasm, Olivia joins the other women in forming a semi circle with Scott at its centre. Glancing over to where the brothers have settled at the table to watch their wives and girlfriends fall under their younger brother's spell, Olivia smiles at Joel. He gives her the thumbs-up.

"So what's in this one?" Violet asks Scott as he sets to work.

"This? It's a potent blend of vodka, Bailey's and kahlua." His tone is light, but Olivia notes the way he avoids Violet's gaze.

"Voila!" With a final flourish of the cocktail shaker, Scott fills their glasses. "Trust me, this is gonna blow your minds."

"I shouldn't," Olivia says, as he presses a drink on her. "The baby."

"One drink won't hurt. It'll be good practice for his student days."

Laughing, she takes a sip and almost chokes. "Christ, Scott, I don't know about blowing my mind. Blowing my head off, more like."

"Drink up, everyone," Scott encourages, distributing cocktails among his brothers. "Then I'll make you a Little Devil. First, though, let's have some music to liven things up."

"You'll wake the children," Tim protests, but makes no move to follow him into the house.

While the others discuss the merits of Scott's cocktail, Olivia sidles over to Violet. "Are things all right with you two?"

"Hard to say." Violet's eyes are troubled. "But I'm working on it."

Olivia opens her mouth to commiserate, and almost drops her cocktail as The Rolling Stones shatter the night stillness.

***

"Are you awake?" Lottie whispers into the silence.

No answer. Hardly daring to move, she raises her head a fraction off the pillow and peers through the darkness. She can just make out the two duvet-covered mounds huddled at the foot of her bed. Her stomach tightens with disappointment and fear and she drops her head back to the pillow. She thought she would feel safe, sharing a room with her cousins, but somehow their sleeping presence only makes her feel all the more alone. If they're asleep, how will Emma and Adam protect her from the wolf?

Dreading what she'll see but unable to prevent her eyes from moving upwards, Lottie stares, transfixed, at the hunched form on top of the wardrobe. The wolf is there, she knows, lurking in the shadows, just waiting to spring on her and gobble her up like the seven lambs in the story. She lies very still, rigid with terror, the duvet pulled up around her ears. If she looks away, even for a second, the wolf will pounce. Should she wake her cousins? No, Emma's been so nice all evening. Best not to risk annoying her. Should she try and make a dash for it? Lottie's gaze flickers to the door. Can she do it? Can she reach the safety of the landing before the wolf gets her? Moreover, does she dare?

***

67

Violet stands at the edge of the patio and stares up at the stars sprinkling the sky like seeds from a dandelion scattered on the wind. Drunken laughter explodes from the nearby table, mingling with 'Hard Day's Night' now blasting from the stereo. She feels apart from it, trapped behind a barrier of uncertainty. The stars sway and blur before her eyes. She has drunk too much, far more than she is used to, in her need to stop the doubts from imprisoning her heart. Scott promised they would talk but has scarcely spoken a word to her all evening. Had that simply been a ploy to get away? Are the instincts assuring her he feels the same no more than wishful thinking?

As if in response to her yearning, a hand slides into hers. "Dance with me?" Scott murmurs against her ear.

"What?" Violet looks at him, hesitating.

"Dance with me." He tugs her hand, and, laughing despite her fears, Violet allows him to draw her onto the black lawn.

"I don't need to kiss or hold you tight," Scott sings, twirling her around. "I just wanna dance with you all night."

Whooping their encouragements, the others follow suit.

"But I can't dance." Phoebe's protests carry over the music.

"Ah, but I can," Rafe says. "Hasn't anyone told you I'm the reincarnation of Fred Astaire?"

Carla snorts. "Fred Flintstone, more like."

"Yabba dabba doo!" With a cry, Rafe spins Phoebe around until she shrieks with laughter.

As the song melds into the slow bars of the next, Scott pulls Violet close. At once, it's as if everyone around them has been swallowed by the darkness, leaving the two of them alone. She is aware of nothing but his arms holding her tight and the rapid tattoo of their hearts.

"Bright are the stars that shine," he croons into her hair. "Dark is the sky. I know this love of mine, will never die."

"Lottie?" Olivia says, and Violet raises her head from Scott's shoulder to see a small figure emerge from the house. "What are you doing out of bed?"

"I was scared. The wolf was going to get me. Can I stay down here with you?"

"All right, but only for five minutes." Olivia sighs, and Violet hears her add in a hiss to Joel, "Didn't I tell you not to read her that story?"

"Uncle Scott," Lottie squeals, hurtling over the lawn. "Uncle Scott, you're here."

"Hello, beautiful." Scott releases Violet and kneels to scoop the child into his arms. "How's my bestest niece then?"

"All right now the horrid old wolf's gone. Can I dance with you and Aunt Vi?"

"Course you can." Smiling, Violet takes one of Lottie's small hands in hers and holds the other out to Scott. Together they spin around and around, faster and faster, until the stars blur above them and Violet's worries spiral into the darkness.

***

"What a night," Joel says much later, collapsing into bed. "Don't know what Scott put in those little devils, but they got everyone going."

"Hmmm." Already sleepy, Olivia nestles against his chest as his arm encircles her and their unborn son. "Although I bet you're in for a big devil of a hangover."

"It'll be worth it. How long is it since we went dancing?"

"Gosh, too long to remember. Didn't I get horribly drunk one night in my distant past and disgrace myself by ordering an incredibly handsome man to dance?"

"Before passing out at his feet and making him fall instantly in love with you." Joel squeezes her middle. "Scott was on good form, didn't you think?"

"As always." Olivia debates whether to mention the strain she detected in him when he first arrived. No, pointless to worry Joel. He already has more than enough on his plate. Besides, other than that initial awkwardness, Scott seemed his usual self, so maybe she imagined it.

"Wonder if everything's okay between him and Vi," she muses instead.

"You saw them dancing together." Joel yawns, his breath warm on her neck. "Trust me, Scott's crazy about her."

"I hope you're right," Olivia says, "I really do."

***

Stretched out on the bed, Tim watches Carla brush her hair before the dressing-table mirror. Even with his head spinning from Scott's killer cocktails, he reads her anxiety reflected in the glass. "What's on your mind?"

Carla turns to face him, expression troubled. "Promise not to be angry?"

Tim smiles. Clad in nothing but a camisole of cream lace, her hair falling in a silken shawl about her shoulders, Carla could be a succubus of the devil sent to lead men into temptation.

"I could never be angry with you, as you are well aware."

"It's just—" She stares down at the brush as she twists it in her hands. "Well, I know Rafe's your brother, but I can't help worrying. He really cares about Phoebs, doesn't he? He's not just stringing her along?"

Tim holds out a hand, touched as ever by Carla's protectiveness towards her friend. "Stop fretting and come to bed. Believe me, I've never seen Rafe so keen on a girl."

"You'd better be right," Carla says, mouth set, "because if Rafe hurts Phoebe, he'll regret it."

***

Giddy with alcohol and anticipation, Phoebe lets Rafe draw her into the shadows of the landing. She looks up at him, heart pounding so hard she fears it will burst through her ribcage. How handsome he is with that strong jaw and dark coloring. Can this charming, successful man really want her, Phoebe Graham, the girl boys only noticed at school to make fun of?

"Thanks for this evening," Rafe says, lips millimeters from hers. "I really enjoyed myself."

"Me, too." Phoebe catches her breath as Rafe trails his hands up her arms and over her shoulders to cup her face. Her head swims. Pleasure turns her insides to molten lava. She can't breathe. No one has ever touched her like this.

As Rafe's mouth lowers to hers, panic nudges at her desire. What is she doing? Beyond that one nightmarish incident, long ago blocked from her memory, she is as innocent as any Victorian bride on her wedding night. How can she possibly excite Rafe, so obviously a man of the world? What if he finds her wanting, is appalled by such a lack of experience in a woman of twenty-eight? What if …

His lips touch hers and the doubts float away. Giving herself over to instinct, her hands creep around his neck to hold him closer, body melding into his. Rafe presses her against the wall, hands sending electric currents through her as they slide under her blouse, stroking, exploring. Phoebe's knees buckle; only he keeps her from falling. When he eventually draws back, she moans, resisting.

Rafe chuckles. "Who would have thought you were such a firecracker? I'd better go before you lead me astray. Wouldn't want Miss QC to catch us."

"Okay." Phoebe curves her trembling lips into a smile. "See you in the morning."

"Can't wait." Brushing her mouth with the gentlest of kisses, Rafe holds the bedroom door open for her. "Sleep tight."

Dazed with happiness, Phoebe undresses and climbs into bed. Hugging herself in the darkness, she lets her imagination run riot. She sees herself standing at the beautiful bay window in a grand drawing room, Rafe's hand warm in hers as they watch their dark-haired children frolic on the expanse of perfect lawn. On the antique writing desk beside her is a leather-bound notebook, in which she has spent a happy afternoon composing poetry for her latest anthology, eagerly anticipated by the literary world. Phoebe falls asleep with a smile on her face and doesn't hear Violet come to bed.

***

Violet's words hang between them in a darkness thick with tension. All at once, she is perfectly sober. Arms folded on the table, now cleared of glasses, she keeps her gaze trained on Scott, standing at the edge of the patio with his back to her. Still he says nothing. Dragging on his cigarette, he stares out over the grounds as though unaware of her presence. Only the stiff set of his shoulders, outlined in the glow from the kitchen window, reveals his strain.

At last, Violet can bear the silence no longer. "Scott, did you hear me?"

"Yes." His tone is even and he doesn't look at her. "I heard."

"Well, then, I meant what I said."

"So what do you want me to do about it? I told you already—"

"Not to say it? Yes, you made that clear earlier." Anger propels Violet to her feet. "Okay, so you don't want to hear that I love you, you'd rather I just kept it to myself, but that doesn't change anything. My feelings aren't any less real because I don't say them out loud. What do you want me to do? Turn them off and pretend they never existed?"

"That's exactly what I want."

"I see. Well, sorry to be an inconvenience, but, unlike you, I can't turn my feelings on and off at will."

Finally, Scott turns to look at her. Despite the amount he's drunk, his expression betrays no emotion. "You have no choice. It's never going to work between us. I'm not right for you."

"Who are you to tell me who is and isn't right for me? I love you. Nothing else matters."

"Your career matters. I drink too much, smoke weed, throw my money away in casinos and lap-dancing clubs. Do you really think I'd make a suitable partner for a lawyer?"

"Aren't you listening to me?" Violet slams a fist into the table. "I didn't fall for you because I thought you'd make good marriage material. I suppose you'd have me end up with a fellow lawyer, or maybe an accountant. Someone safe and reliable, whose idea of a night out is a cigar and a glass of port at his club. Well, I don't want that. I want you, suitable or not, and anyone who doesn't like it can go hang." She takes a step towards him, gaze intent on his face. "Don't you love me? If you don't, if you can look me in the eye and say it, I promise I'll never ask you again."

"All right," he says. Throwing his cigarette to the ground, he crushes it viciously underfoot. "If that's what it takes. No, Violet, I don't love you."

She grows still. Though mid summer, the breeze ruffling her hair carries the threat of winter. "What about the night we spent together?"

"That was just sex." Scott walks past her towards the house. "I was at a loose end and you were available, not to mention willing. Get real, Vi. I can have any girl I choose. Why would I tie myself down, least of all to you?"

Violet blinks against the sting of tears; she mustn't break down. "I don't believe you really mean that."

"You'd better believe it." Scott pauses at the kitchen door, face hard. "You asked for the truth and I gave it to you. It's not my fault you don't like what you hear." With that, he stumbles into the house and crashes the door behind him.

Part 2
Saturday

Nine

She crouched on a small, wooden platform, its sides open to the elements, a post at each corner supporting a sloping roof. Dense foliage wrapped itself around her hiding place, painting her limbs a ghostly green. A breeze rustled the leaves; goose pimples prickled up her arms. This place was as familiar as her own body, though she felt sure she had never been here in reality.

Anticipation quickened her pulse. Fear crawled down her throat, contorting her stomach into icy knots, paralyzing her to the spot. Inevitably, inexorably, her eyes were drawn to a gap in the branches. She didn't want to look, dreaded what she would see, but was unable to stop herself. That's when it hit her, the horror, the terrible realization that sent her reeling backwards. She opened her mouth to scream, and then she was falling ... falling ... falling...

Lottie awoke with a start, heart pounding, pajamas sticking to her sweat-drenched skin. No matter how often she visited the mysterious dream world, the terror of it never diminished. Always it ended with the stomach-lurching sensation of falling, and each time she shot awake to dread chilling her blood, though she could never say afterwards what had frightened her. Lottie breathed deeply, trying to calm her rampaging pulse. It had been so long, several years, since the nightmare last troubled her. She'd even dared hope she might have grown out of it. Why, then, should it return now?

Gradually, as the dream faded to be replaced by the familiar surroundings of her room, the fear loosened its hold. Rolling over, she glanced at the clock on her bedside cabinet. Fourteen minutes past three. *Oh, my God!* Lottie sat up so quickly her head swam. How could she have fallen asleep? She was supposed to wait until everyone went to bed and then slip up the attic stairs to be with Adam. Now he would think she'd chickened out.

What to do? The remnants of the nightmare clung to her and the prospect of company, of seeking comfort in Adam's arms, tugged at her resolve. She threw back the covers. No harm in taking a peep at him, just in case he was lying awake. With a glance at Emma to make sure she was asleep, Lottie stole across the room and onto the landing. Closing the bedroom door softly behind her, she turned towards the stairs.

"Lottie?" A low voice spoke from the shadows, and Lottie whipped around.

"Sorry." Aunt Vi came to put a hand on her shoulder. "Didn't mean to make you jump. What're you doing up?"

"Bad dream."

"Oh, poor you. Want to tell me about it over a hot chocolate? I was just going down to make some."

Lottie hesitated, longing to be with Adam. Still, she could hardly risk slipping up to the attic with an adult on the prowl, and it would be nice to spend some time with the aunt she so rarely saw.

"Okay," she said, and they headed down the darkened stairs to the hall.

In the kitchen, Lottie spooned hot chocolate into mugs while her aunt heated a saucepan of milk.

"So, tell me about this dream," Aunt Vi said, once they were seated opposite one another at the table.

"It's hard to describe." Lottie sipped her drink; the hot sweetness soothed the last of her unease. "It isn't all that clear. I used to dream it all the time, but it stopped happening so much as I got older. Tonight's the first time in ages."

"What's it about?"

Haltingly, and with as much accuracy as possible, Lottie detailed what she could remember of the dream: her crouched position on the wooden platform, the strange, greenish glow, the sick feeling of dread. She paused, struggling for words to describe the nameless terror.

Aunt Vi leaned towards her, expression sharp with interest. "What happens next?"

"I don't know. I see something … something horrible, but I can never remember what. Then I'm falling, and I wake up."

Her aunt was silent for some time. Chin in hands, she frowned into the distance as though figuring something out.

"What do you think it means?" Lottie asked. "Why do I keep having the same dream?"

"Actually, I don't think it's a dream, at all." Her aunt's tone was far away. "I think it's a memory."

"A memory? How can it be? I mean, surely I'd recognize the place, but I've never been there in my life."

"You have. A long time ago. I think you're dreaming about the tree house."

Lottie stared at her. "What? We don't have a tree house."

"You did once. It was in that big oak near … near the memorial garden your parents planted for Uncle Scott. You weren't supposed to go up there; your mum and dad thought it was too dangerous, but naturally you did."

"So, why isn't the tree house there now?"

"Your dad tore it down after the accident." Her aunt paused, perhaps debating how much to reveal. "You were up in the tree house when you fell. Cracked your head open on the trunk and ended up with severe concussion."

A picture flashed into Lottie's mind: herself lying in a hospital bed, her head swaddled in bandages. "Mum and Dad said I was climbing a tree. When was this?"

"Twelve years ago, the last time we were all here together." Aunt Vi studied her face. "That's why you can't remember anything about it. The blow impaired your memory of the days leading up to the accident."

Like a fire bursting to life in a darkened cave, realization flooded Lottie's brain.

"Why didn't anyone tell me? Why all the rubbish about me being too young?"

Her aunt hesitated. "That was your parents' decision. You'll have to ask them."

Lottie fell quiet, sipping her hot chocolate. Did Mum and Dad still think of her as a child, their precious little girl, too fragile to be told the truth about her own family?

Some time later, she asked, "So why couldn't you sleep, Aunt Vi? Were you thinking about Uncle Scott?"

Her aunt nodded. "This house is full of memories. It reminds me of both the best and worst time of my life."

"You loved him, didn't you?"

"More than anything in the world."

"And did—?" The words were out before Lottie could stop them; she blushed.

Her Aunt smiled, though her eyes were sad. "Did he love me? I think so. At least, I have to believe he did, or I'd have no reason to get up in the morning."

Lottie nodded, and for the first time saw beyond the aunt she knew, the successful lawyer and witty companion who had introduced her to the sights of London, taken her to her first show and treated her to afternoon tea at Harrods. Beneath the brusque confidence, she glimpsed the woman within, a woman still tormented by grief for the man she had loved.

"Aunt Vi, can I ask you something? About you and Uncle Scott?"

"Course you can. What is it?"

"Well, how can being here remind you of both the best and worst time of your life?"

Again, her aunt paused. "I'll probably get into trouble, since your parents chose to keep it from you."

"Yes, well, according to Mum and Dad, I'm not even allowed to know about my own accident." Lottie scowled into her empty mug. "Please, Aunt Vi. If they're angry, I'll tell them it was my fault."

"I'll hold you to that." Her aunt took an audible breath. "Okay, the reason it's so hard for me to come back here, and why I don't do it too often, is because this is where Scott died."

Shock punched the air from Lottie's lungs. "Uncle Scott died here? He died here, in this house, and no one bothered to mention it?"

"Your parents' choice, as I said. They probably thought it would upset you."

"What, more than finding out they'd kept it secret all these years? How did it happen?"

"I've said too much already. No." Her aunt raised a hand to silence her. "Don't press me. Speak to your mum and dad about it."

"I will," Lottie said. The sense of betrayal settled heavy in her stomach. How could her parents have kept something so important from her? Okay, so she might have been a child when it happened, but that was no excuse for continuing the pretence once she grew older. From the meaningful glances Emma and Adam exchanged in her bedroom last night, she'd wager her horse they knew about it and had been told to keep quiet. Her insides boiled. Why should she be the only one left in the dark?

Lottie was still seething when she climbed into bed a while later. She lay there, staring up at the steadily lightening ceiling, unable to sleep for the questions assaulting her brain. Finally, when a patch of white between the curtains announced the arrival of another snowy day, she went to have a shower.

After pulling on her most comfortable cords and sloppy jumper, Lottie left Emma still fast asleep with the covers drawn up around her chin, and padded onto the landing. Shutting the door, she turned and almost collided with Adam. Her heart lurched. Dressed in faded jeans and sweatshirt, his hair rumpled and flopping into his eyes, he was even more handsome than he'd been the previous evening.

"Hey," Adam said. They shared a smile, heady with the pleasure of waking up in the same house and of a whole day to spend together.

"Sorry about last night," Lottie said as they descended the stairs. "I was on my way up when I ran into Aunt Vi." *And a good job she had, or she would never have found out the truth.*

"Don't worry about it." Adam slid his hand into hers. "I fell asleep. Anyway, we have all weekend. Wish there was somewhere we could go where no one would bother us."

"I know just the place," Lottie said. Her body tingled at the prospect of being alone with him. First, though, she had to tackle her parents.

***

Shooting awake from another disturbing dream, Phoebe opened her eyes to a cold, gray dawn. Her head pounded from lack of sleep, and every muscle ached, having been pulled taut throughout the endless night when the faintest sound set her heart into a frenzy and brought her out in icy sweat. Was that someone whispering on the landing, or merely the wind sighing down the chimney? Once, she swore she heard a floorboard creak outside her room. A member of her family also kept awake by memories, or ... or something worse?

The arrival of daylight gave her little relief. There were still two whole days to endure, two days in which to jump at shadows and fear she was going mad. How could she have let Rafe persuade her to come back to this house where she had vowed never to return? Evil lurked in every corner, oozing from the walls like asbestos, suffocating anyone who dared cross the threshold. Unable to lie there any longer, Phoebe slipped out of bed to sit by the window. She watched the sky brighten through the gap in the curtains as images flickered across her vision, the identical images that had haunted her dreams these past twelve years and poisoned her every waking moment. Would she ever be free of them?

"What're you doing?" Rafe's drowsy voice made her start.

She cast him a nervous glance. "I'm so sorry. Did I wake you?"

"You know my body clock's set to go off at dawn," Rolling over, he studied her through the dimness. "I hope there won't be a repeat of last night. If the rest of us can cope, so can you."

Phoebe looked down at the carpet. "It won't happen again, I promise. You should try and go back to sleep."

"What, with you sitting there like a nurse at my death bed?" Rafe threw off the covers. "I can hear someone in the kitchen. Let's go and grab a cup of tea."

Phoebe watched, unmoving, as Rafe padded across the room to unhook his dressing gown from the back of the door. He hesitated, then took hers down as well.

"Here," he said, draping it round her shoulders, "you must be frozen. What use are you to me if you catch a chill?"

"Thank you." Phoebe clutched it about her shivering body and took a deep breath. "Rafe, can we go home?"

"What're you talking about? Liv has invited us until New Year. How would it look if we upped and left?" Rafe must have seen her stricken expression for his voice softened. "Look, I know it's hard for you being back here. It's hard for me, too, but it won't be for long. Just try and be a brave girl. You can do that for me, can't you?"

Phoebe nodded, eyes filling with tears. Rafe was so generous, sticking by her despite her failure to give him a child. And the worst thing was, she didn't deserve it.

***

Escaping outside after breakfast, Joel crunched through the freshly fallen snow, a crisp wind on his face and the sun bright in his eyes. A memory surfaced—himself as a small boy, fooling around with his brothers in the garden of his childhood home, their laughter carrying on the chill air as they pelted each other with snowballs. An ache gnawed at his gut. Who would have thought that just thirty years later, one of them would be dead and the rest sitting over a breakfast table with nothing to say to one another?

Joel kicked a mound of snow; a powdery white cloud drifted upwards and blew away on the wind like smoke. God, that had been hell, forcing down a helping of bacon and eggs while trying to avoid Tim's attempts to catch his eye, asking Olivia to pass the ketchup as though everything was normal between them. *Well, look on the bright side. Only another forty-eight hours of torture to go.* New Year couldn't come fast enough. As for what it would bring for himself and Liv, he refused even to contemplate.

When Joel entered the sanctuary of his greenhouse, its damp warmth greeted him and he breathed the familiar earthy smell. The tightness around his chest eased for the first time since his family's arrival. He moved along the wooden benches, checking the progress of the various plants, administering water where needed. He loved the simple honesty of his work, so different from the impersonal coldness of the financial world, and the routine calmed his frayed nerves.

A blast of cold air whipped across his back as the door slid open and closed behind him.

"Joel," Tim said, "we need to talk. We can't go on like this."

Joel kept his head bent over his pot, feeling the soil for dryness. "Like what?"

"Please, don't insult me by denying it."

"And don't insult me by pretending you've no idea what this is about."

"I'm not," Tim said. "I haven't a clue. I'm guessing it has something to do with Carla, but I can't imagine what she can have done to upset you."

Joel looked up at his twin with scorn. "She's changed you, you know that? You used to have principles. You used to value ethics and loyalty more than money, but not anymore. Carla's modeled you into the perfect little businessman, concerned with nothing but making the maximum profit."

Rare anger flashed in Tim's eyes. "Give me some credit. If I have changed, it certainly isn't Carla's doing. I may have done my best for my wife over the years, tried to be the sort of man she can be proud of, but I'm still me. I've never put the business before my family, and I've never changed how I feel about you."

"Could've fooled me. What happened to trust, Tim? I thought I could tell you anything. I would have trusted you with my life, but you threw it back in my face."

Silence dropped between them, filled only by the snowflakes pattering on the glass roof.

"You've lost me," Tim said. "When have I ever given you reason to doubt my trust?"

Joel turned his back on him, on the confusion in his expression. "If it means so little that you can't even remember, there's no point discussing it. I just thought you valued our friendship too much to go blabbing my problems to your wife. Now, leave me alone."

"But I don't under—"

"I said go. I've got nothing more to say." Joel gripped the edge of the workbench and waited. Tim made no immediate move, clearly wanting to say more, but then his footsteps retreated and the door closed softly behind him. Joel dropped his head in his hands, eyes squeezed shut. How had everything gone so terribly wrong?

***

Loading the breakfast things into the dishwasher, Olivia watched from the window as Tim left the greenhouse and trudged through the snow. Head bowed, he seemed not to care where his feet carried him. Poor Tim. Whatever words had been spoken, they'd done nothing to heal the breach. If only Joel had felt able to confide in her, perhaps she could have helped mend things between them. *It's not your problem,* Olivia told herself. *Joel forfeited any right to your sympathy the moment he defected to another woman's bed.* She sighed. Whatever her head might say, her heart ached for the twins and the bond they had lost.

She jumped as the kitchen door clicked behind her. "Hello, sweetheart." Olivia turned with a smile, but faltered at her daughter's grim expression. "What's the matter?"

Lottie folded her arms across her chest, a gesture unnervingly reminiscent of her Aunt Violet. "Why didn't you tell me about Uncle Scott?"

An icicle formed in Olivia's stomach. "What about him, exactly?"

"About where he died. I mean, everyone else knows. How come I'm the only one being treated like a child?"

Olivia closed her eyes. She had known this moment would come, that she would one day have to explain, but the suddenness of it shook her.

"Who told you?"

"Aunt Vi. She accepts I've grown up, even if you don't."

"Violet?" Olivia had expected the culprit to be Emma or Adam, letting it slip in an unguarded moment, but her own sister? The betrayal tasted sour in her mouth. "She had no right telling you when I asked her not to."

"Don't blame Aunt Vi," Lottie said. "Neither of us could sleep last night and I guessed something was wrong. I went on at her until she told me. She didn't even say that much. Not how Uncle Scott died, or anything. She said I should ask you."

"Did she, indeed?" Olivia's mind whirred, seeking a means of escape. Finding none, she sighed. "You'd better sit down then. I'll make us some coffee."

While Lottie pulled out a chair at the table, Olivia used the time it took to boil the kettle to think through her approach. How much should she say? Was honesty the best policy here, or would it be kinder to lie? If only she could talk it over with Joel, but that was no longer an option. She was on her own.

"So." Olivia set the coffee on the table and sat opposite her daughter. "You want to know how Uncle Scott died."

Lottie nodded.

Olivia paused, tempted to go with an easy lie about Scott simply having a heart attack. She dismissed the idea. Better that Lottie hear the truth from her.

"The thing is, sweetheart." She reached across the table to squeeze her daughter's hand. "Your Uncle … he drowned."

"Drowned?" Lottie gazed about in obvious confusion, as though expecting a well to spring up in the middle of the kitchen floor. "How?"

"There used to be a swimming pool here, years ago. You know Uncle Scott's memorial garden? Well, that's where the pool was. We had it filled in after the accident."

"We had a swimming pool? Wow, I never knew that. But I still don't understand. How could he drown?"

Olivia sipped her coffee, extracting comfort from its warmth. "Let's just say he had rather too much to drink. The post mortem suggested he went swimming while drunk and passed out in the water. By the time anyone found him, it was too late."

"How horrible," Lottie breathed. "Poor Aunt Vi, being reminded of that whenever she comes here." Her eyes widened. "And that's why Aunt Phoebs got so upset last night when we were talking about him."

"Hardly surprising," Olivia said. "She was the one who found him. Anyway, you see now why we haven't invited the family here for so long."

"I put it down to Dad and Uncle Tim not getting on. I never imagined anything like this. You should have told me."

"Your dad and I did what we felt was best. There seemed no point dragging it all up and upsetting you, especially when you were too young to remember."

Lottie's eyes flashed. "But that's not true, is it? Aunt Vi told me. She said I hit my head falling out of the tree house, the tree house I never even knew about."

"Oh, did she?" Anger forced Olivia upright. How nice to know her sister had such respect for her wishes.

"Why shouldn't Aunt Vi tell me? I can sort of understand why you didn't want me to know about Uncle Scott, but this is different. It's my own memory we're talking about."

"Yes, and at the time of your accident, the doctor made it clear we weren't to pressure you into remembering. It would happen on its own, when you were ready. He assured us it's quite common to suffer partial amnesia after a blow to the head, and drawing attention to it would do more harm than good. The fact that you're so upset now only proves his point."

"I'm not upset that I can't remember," Lottie protested. "I'm upset because my parents never thought to mention it. Anyway, if the doctor said my memory would come back on its own, how come it hasn't?"

Olivia gazed into her almost empty mug. "The doctor also said there was a possibility you would never regain your memory of the days leading up to the accident, especially as the hours directly before it were so traumatic." The instant the words left her mouth, she could have cut her tongue out.

Lottie pounced. "Traumatic? You mean Uncle Scott's death?"

"Among other things. Although you were only little, you must have felt something was wrong that day. It's no wonder you've blocked it out all these years. I'm betting there are times when Aunt Vi would give a great deal to forget."

Fury swamped her momentary compassion. For reasons Olivia couldn't fathom, her sister had deliberately gone against the wishes she and Joel laid down all those years ago. Pushing back her chair, she snatched up the empty mugs. The jangle of china broke the silence as she added them to the dishwasher.

"Mum," Lottie said, "if the family hasn't been here since Uncle Scott died, why get together now?"

"That would be your aunt Violet's doing." Olivia retrieved a dishwasher tablet from the cupboard under the sink. "She seemed to feel it was time we put the past behind us."

Lottie was quiet, perhaps warned off by the acid in her mother's tone.

At last, she ventured, "Don't be too cross with Aunt Vi, will you? She meant well."

"Don't worry." Olivia slammed the dishwasher shut with her hip. "You leave your aunt to me."

Ten

"Finally," Adam said as they headed outside after lunch. "Thought we'd never get away."

"I know." Lottie had tried to get Adam alone on the pretext of introducing him to Gypsy, but Emma put paid to that plan. Moping because she had been unable to track down her boyfriend so he could dish out the gossip on 'the party of the century', her cousin developed a sudden enthusiasm for horses and tagged along to the stables. Not until lunch was over and Emma left the table to try Jerry again did she and Adam manage to escape.

As she waded through the snow, Lottie's eyes strayed to the distant hawthorn hedge marking Uncle Scott's memorial garden. To think he had died there and she'd never known. An image seared across her mind: a young, dark-haired man floating face down in a sea of turquoise water. She shivered. How cruel that someone so alive as her uncle should have met such a pointless end. Even in photos, his handsome face radiated vitality and mischief.

Poor Aunt Vi. For Uncle Scott to have died at all was awful enough, but for it to happen so soon after he and her aunt fell in love was beyond heartbreaking. Lottie tried to imagine how she would feel if Adam were discovered drowned just when they had found each other. Dread caught hold of her heart. It didn't bear thinking about. The knowledge that the tragedy took place here, in these very grounds, made it all far too real.

A snowball shattered against the nape of Lottie's neck. Icy water trickled inside her jumper and she squealed, whirling round.

Adam grinned. "That'll teach you for not giving me your undivided attention."

Poking her tongue out at him, Lottie scooped up a handful of snow and aimed. It hit Adam squarely in the chest. "And that'll teach you for being a narcissistic— Aagh!"

She dodged Adam's next missile and fled, giggling as she skidded in the snow. A look over her shoulder told her he was hot in pursuit, and she ducked as he aimed another snowball at her back. Pausing briefly to retaliate, she ran on, her route drawing him away from the house. Eventually, breathless and shaking with laughter, they tumbled into the stables.

"Not fair," Adam panted. "How come you're so fast?"

"Fanatical games teacher," Lottie said. Sidestepping Adam's attempts to draw her against him, she nodded at the mare who had raised her head from the bucket of oats to watch. "Not in front of Gypsy. Anyway, I've got something to show you."

Lottie climbed onto an empty crate that stood in one corner and reached up to tug on a handle in the ceiling. A ladder descended, revealing a square opening.

"Neat," Adam said.

Lottie smiled. "And a great place to come when you don't want to be found. After you."

Waiting until Adam had vanished from sight, Lottie followed him up the creaking ladder and hauled it up behind her. The trapdoor fell into place with a thump and they were alone in wood-scented darkness. Lottie pulled off her boots before unzipping her coat and spreading it over the hay-strewn floor. Beside her, she felt Adam do the same. Then his arm slid around her and his mouth brushed her ear.

"Lie down," he said, his breath tickling her skin.

Powerless to resist the gentle pressure on her shoulders, Lottie sank back into the hay. Adam leaned over her, close but not touching; the heat of his body filled her senses. Her heart went into a stampede, excitement charging through her veins. She had never been so nervous. Then, Adam's lips found hers as his hands sought out the bare skin beneath her jumper and she forgot everything but him.

***

Even lounging by the drawing-room fire, Rafe couldn't ignore the tension. Though he tried to concentrate on the *Daily Mail* crossword, he was conscious all the while of Carla flipping through a magazine on the sofa opposite. If only he could talk to her, share a few words away from prying ears. Fat chance. Lowering the paper a fraction, Rafe peered over the top to eye the impediment. Seated in the armchair on the other side of the fire, Violet seemed engrossed in her book. Rafe had the uncanny sense that she was following their every move. Did she suspect something? But even if she did, why should she care? With the exception of Scott, Violet had never expended much energy on his family.

"Anyone seen Lottie and Adam?"

Glad of the interruption, Rafe smiled up at Emma in the doorway. She reminded him so forcibly of Carla at nineteen, same provocative pose and confidence in her own desirability, that the shock stole the air from his lungs.

"Not for a while," Violet said, turning a page. "Think they went outside."

"You look stressed," Rafe told his niece, recovering. "Want to give me a hand with the crossword?"

Emma flopped next to him on the sofa and tucked her feet beneath her. "Still can't get hold of Jerry. I just know he got off with someone last night."

"Good riddance," Carla said. "On the one occasion I had the misfortune to meet him, he was stoned out of his head and could hardly string two words together."

"Trust me, Mum, it's not his conversation I'm interested in. He's just sooo sexy. If he dumps me, my heart will be broken forever."

"Sure, until the next one."

Emma looked mutinous and Rafe patted her thigh. "I'm sure this Jerry of yours is just sleeping off the excesses of last night. Anyway, it's his loss if he's been up to no good. He'd need his head tested to throw away a stunning girl like you."

"Thanks, Uncle Rafe." Emma gave him the heart-dissolving smile, which carried both her father's sweetness and her mother's seductive charm. "Let's see this crossword."

She leaned closer to read over Rafe's shoulder. Her silken hair swung forward, tickling his neck, and her flowery perfume teased his senses. He sucked in a breath. The force of his longing caught him unaware. His gaze wandered to her breasts straining to escape the cashmere, then to the firm, denim-clad thighs millimeters from his own. He looked away hurriedly and met Carla's stare. The ferocity in her eyes told him she knew exactly what was on his mind and the fate that awaited him if he dared even think it.

Oblivious, Emma studied the crossword. "Seven down, 'understanding', eleven letters. No use asking Mum. That's not something she knows much about."

Rafe stifled a chuckle. "I thought it might be 'sympathetic' but that doesn't fit."

"How about 'considerate'?" Emma's eyes scanned the page. "Yes, look, the third letter's an 'N' and the second to last is a 'T'."

"Nice one." Resisting the temptation to smile at her in case it triggered another glare from Carla, Rafe filled in the answer.

"I saw Aunt Phoebs going outside earlier without a coat," Emma said. "Do you think she'll be all right?"

"She'll be fine. Doesn't feel the cold much, your aunt." Rafe spoke casually to mask his growing anxiety. What had got into his wife lately? Ever since he'd mentioned the planned reunion, she'd been a nervous wreck. Naturally it was hard for her coming back here. Rafe was certain that last image of Scott must be imprinted on all their memories, just as it was on his own. Still, at least the rest of them were attempting to put the past behind them. Phoebe wasn't even trying.

Clearly sharing his concern, Carla got to her feet. "I'd better go and check on her."

"It's okay," Emma said. "Uncle Joel went out after her."

"All the same, I'd like to see for myself." Carla continued towards the door. If anything, Rafe thought she looked even more apprehensive. Then again, she had always been ridiculously overprotective where Phoebe was concerned.

Once her mother had left, Emma leaned in again to study the crossword. "Twelve across, 'evil', ten letters, first and third letter 'I'. What do you think, Uncle Rafe?"

"No idea," Rafe croaked. With Emma's breasts grazing his arm, he could focus on nothing but the evil thoughts racing through his mind. Even the way her slightly crooked front teeth nipped at her lower lip held him entranced. He had the crazy urge to press her back on the sofa and kiss her until she begged for mercy. She's your niece, scolded the sensible half of his brain. Yes, argued the less coherent part, but she's so very like Carla.

"Iniquitous," Violet said.

"What?" Rafe started. For a terrible moment, he thought she had read his mind.

"Iniquitous. That's the answer to twelve across."

"Oh, right." Rafe penciled it in, though his hand shook so much the word was almost illegible.

Beside him, Emma stretched and stood. "I'm going to see if I can find Lottie and Adam. See you later."

"See you." Rafe couldn't tear his eyes from her retreating figure, mesmerized by the sway of her hips, imagining those incredible legs wrapped around him. She paused at the door to fling him a smile over her shoulder, giving Rafe the unsettling impression that she knew the effect she had on him and was enjoying his discomfort.

***

The wrought iron gate creaked open at his touch. Joel slipped through the gap in the hawthorn hedge and into Scott's memorial garden, which he and Olivia had planted to mark the first anniversary of Scott's death. They'd hoped it would be a place where Violet might come to remember Scott, but in the end it was mainly Joel who sought solace there. The process of creating it had in itself been a kind of therapy, penitence, even, as though every blister and drop of sweat would atone for his mistakes.

A scream pierced the quiet. Joel almost stumbled backwards into the hedge and his gaze flew to the figure huddled on the bench. Phoebe gaped at him, expression livid with terror, face whiter than the snow on the lawn.

"It's okay." As fast as the snow allowed, Joel hurried to sit beside her.

"It's only me. I didn't mean to frighten you."

"I thought—" Phoebe clutched his arm, eyes huge and staring. "I thought it was—"

Joel shook his head, aghast. "I'm so sorry. I saw you come out here from my bedroom window, wanted to make sure you were all right."

One look at her told him she was far from all right. Dressed in only a flimsy skirt and jumper, she shivered convulsively as her eyes darted in ceaseless panic. Hating the way she was twisting her hands together, as though she might rip the fingers from the knuckles, Joel took them both in his. They were colder than those of an ice sculpture.

"You're frozen," he said. "Come back inside and I'll make you a hot drink."

Phoebe seemed not to hear. "I see him, you know. I see him everywhere, watching, blaming, even when I close my eyes at night. There's no rest for the wicked."

"There." Joel rubbed warmth back into her fingers, trying to conceal his alarm. Phoebe wasn't just scared, she was half-crazed. "I won't let anything hurt you."

Phoebe let out a harsh laugh that made him jump. "What can you do? What can anyone do? What's done is done. There's no rest for the wicked."

The last words, spoken like a mantra, sent goose pimples up Joel's spine. "Stop saying that. You couldn't be wicked if you tried."

"Oh, but I am." Phoebe's mirth died and her eyes filled with tears. "I was thinking about … about him before you came. Then the gate opened and all I could see was the dark hair, and I thought … I thought it was him come back to—"

"I'm so sorry." Joel didn't know what else to say. "You should never have had to come back here. I wish—"

"There you are!"

They both started. Joel looked up to see Carla, as ill-dressed for the cold as Phoebe, almost running towards them. He dropped Phoebe's hands as though they had become white-hot.

Shooting him a suspicious glance, Carla took Phoebe's hands in her own. "What're you doing out here without a coat? You're like ice. Let's get you inside before you catch pneumonia."

Phoebe made no protest. She merely permitted Carla to pull her to her feet and slide a supporting arm about her waist.

"How could you let her stay out here?" Carla snapped at Joel. "You know how delicate she is."

Joel's anger flared. "I did ask her to come in, but I couldn't exactly force her."

"Couldn't, or wouldn't?" Carla gave him another hard look, then turned to lead Phoebe away.

***

"You okay?" Adam asked

Lottie nodded, unable to describe her inner chaos. All at once, she felt shaky and sore and elated and totally, utterly changed.

"Good." Adam drew her closer and kissed her. "I'm glad I was your first."

A shadow fell across Lottie's contentment. "This wasn't your first time, though, was it?"

"It was in every way that counts."

Pictures of Adam with another girl danced across Lottie's vision. Envy wrenched at her gut, an unfamiliar sickening sensation that left her weak and trembling. "Who was she?"

"No one. It was just a game of truth or dare that got out of hand. I was too pissed to remember much. It didn't mean anything."

Lottie only nodded.

"Silly," Adam teased. "Haven't I told you you're the only girl I've ever loved?"

Smiling, Lottie snuggled closer. "You know how forgetful I am."

They lay in blissful silence for a while, basking in each other's nearness.

"I saw our dads talking in the greenhouse earlier," Adam said. "Then my dad came out looking like yours had sentenced him to death."

"I don't get it." Lottie trailed her fingertips over his chest. "Your dad's the nicest person I know. How could anyone fall out with him?"

Adam closed his eyes, heart thudding beneath her touch. "Beats me. In a way, though, it's lucky our dads don't get on."

"How come?"

"Because then we would've been brought up like normal cousins and might never have fallen for each other."

"I don't believe that," Lottie said. The notion that she could have spent time with Adam and not tumbled headlong in love with him was inconceivable. "I wouldn't have cared who you were. I would still—"

She broke off as Adam pressed a finger to her lips. The creak of the stable door drifted up from below and they kept very still, hardly daring to breathe.

"Lottie?" Emma called, her voice indistinct through the trap door. "Adam? You in here?"

Silence. Lottie looked up at Adam, his eyes wide, mirroring her own horror. If they were discovered like this…

"Come on, you two. This isn't funny." Emma paused, perhaps

expecting them to leap out at her from a shadowy corner. Finally, she muttered, "Sure I heard something," and then the door banged behind her.

Lottie and Adam stared at one another through the gloom, then began to laugh. Once they started, they couldn't stop. Lottie leaned into Adam for support, shaking with silent mirth until her stomach ached and the tears rolled down her cheeks.

***

"Can I give you a hand, Liv?" Tim asked as she got up to collect the after-dinner-coffee mugs.

"Thanks," Olivia said, "but Vi will help me."

At a look from her sister, Violet rose from the table without a word and followed her along the passage to the kitchen. Ever since her earlier talk with Lottie, she had known it was coming, that Olivia would be furious with her. Well, let her be angry. There was more at stake here than her sister could possibly imagine.

Deciding to jump in before Olivia could go on the attack, Violet closed the kitchen door. "She had to know."

Olivia dropped the mugs onto the worktop with a clatter. "If you don't mind, I'll be the judge of what my daughter does and doesn't have to know."

"Lottie isn't a child anymore. You can't go on protecting her forever."

"And what would you know about it? You might be one of the best lawyers in the city, but you know sod all about being a mother."

Violet flinched. Images of the children she had long ago hoped to have with Scott paraded before her eyes, taunting her. The pain must have shown in her expression, for her sister's face softened.

"I'm sorry, that was a cheap shot. I just don't understand what you thought to achieve. Why dredge it all up again, especially as Lottie can't even remember it?"

"But I think she can," Violet said. "Deep down. You know she dreams about being up in the tree house before she fell?"

"Yes, I know. Lottie's been having these dreams for years, but as long as that's all she thought they were, no harm could come of them."

"And you think that's healthy? You don't think it would be better for her to remember things as they really were?"

"Better for who?" Olivia challenged. "Lottie, or you?"

Violet dropped her gaze for an instant, conceding the point. "You agree with me then? You think Lottie might have seen something that day before she fell?"

Olivia sighed and folded her arms across her chest. "Why else do you think I've been so anxious for her not to remember? If she did see something, if she actually witnessed her uncle's death, surely you can understand why I'd rather she forgot."

"Of course I can, but what if there's more to it than that?"

"More? How do you mean?"

Violet hesitated. This was the moment to put her trust in her sister and reveal the terrible suspicion that had been growing within her for months.

She sucked in a breath. "I don't think Scott just drowned." She met Olivia's gaze. "I think he was murdered."

Eleven

"What do you think's going on?" Emma hissed as Lottie led her and Adam into her bedroom. "Your mum and aunt have been shut in the kitchen for ages."

Lottie flicked on the light and went to draw the curtains, guilt prodding her conscience. She hadn't meant for Mum and Aunt Vi to fall out. Still, she didn't regret pushing for the details. She had a right to know what went on in her own family.

"It's partly my fault," she said, turning back to her cousins. "Aunt Vi told me about Uncle Scott, and Mum's not too thrilled about it."

"But that's great!" Emma threw herself onto the camp bed. "It's been so frustrating not being able to talk to you about it, compare notes."

"I guessed you must already know. When did you find out?"

"Oh, years ago. Well, we only learned the full story more recently, but we've always known how Uncle Scott died here."

Perhaps sensing Lottie's feelings, Adam smiled at her. "We wanted to talk to you about it, but Mum said we'd be grounded for a year if we breathed a word. She reckoned your mum thought it might upset you."

"Right, and I'm not upset now, at all."

Adam laughed and stretched out on her bed, his grin challenging her to join him. Lottie hesitated. Could she be trusted to sit near him without giving them both away? Deciding not, she perched on the foot of Emma's bed.

"So," Emma urged, "what did your mum tell you?"

"Well, it was obvious she didn't want to tell me anything, but in the end she admitted Uncle Scott got really drunk and drowned."

"Committed suicide, more like."

Lottie gasped. "Are you serious?"

"We can't know for sure, can we?" Emma said, shrugging. "It's not like he left a note, or anything. Our parents certainly told us it was an accident, but we heard them talking one night when they thought we weren't listening and suicide was mentioned."

"I don't get it." Lottie's thoughts went to Aunt Vi. "Why should Uncle Scott kill himself?"

"That's where Mum and Dad were a bit vague," Adam said. "They obviously don't like talking about it."

"But from what we can make out," Emma put in, "there was a massive family bust up. We haven't been able to find out what started it, but, later that same day, Uncle Scott was dead."

Lottie fell quiet, replaying in her mind the earlier conversation with her mother.

"The doctor also said there was a possibility you would never regain your memory of the days leading up to the accident, especially as the hours just before it were so traumatic."

"Traumatic? You mean Uncle Scott's death?"

"Among other things."

What other things? Was that what Mum had meant? A quarrel so terrible that it had resulted in her uncle taking his own life? An image of Aunt Violet at the kitchen table, her face etched with grief, came back to her.

"I don't believe Uncle Scott committed suicide," she said. "He couldn't have done that to Aunt Vi." *Any more than I could to Adam.*

Lottie permitted herself the luxury of gazing at him. Only a few hours earlier, they were wrapped around one another in the hayloft. Her body throbbed all over at the memory. She could cope with anything, just so long as he went on loving her. As though reading her mind, Adam caught her eye and smiled, and she glanced quickly away, heart swelling. How could Emma be oblivious to the heat sizzling between them?

Emma flopped back against her pillows with a sigh. "You might be right. I don't suppose we'll ever really know."

"No," Lottie agreed, grateful to be distracted, "but at least I now know why I can't remember anything about that weekend."

"Weird, though, isn't it?" Emma said. "I've heard of people losing their memory for a bit after hitting their head, but you'd have thought yours would've come back by now."

"The doctor warned my parents it might not, and, since no one ever bothered to fill in the blanks for me, it's not that surprising."

As she said this, a picture flared before her eyes — a rectangle of water dappled by sunlight and the shadow of the hedge surrounding it. She blinked and it was gone. Had that been a true memory, or simply an image conjured up by what she'd been told?

"What I don't get," she said, "is why my parents didn't tell me about the tree house."

Adam frowned. "What tree house? Weren't you climbing a tree when you fell? That's what Mum and Dad said."

"Really?" Lottie's spirits lifted. So her cousins didn't know everything. "That's what I've always thought, too, but it turns out I was actually up in the tree house. You don't remember it, then?"

Emma shook her head. "You never showed it to us, or I would. It explains where you used to disappear to when Adam and I couldn't find you."

"But why all the secrecy? Okay, so my parents have clearly been determined to keep everything from me, but yours at least told you about Uncle Scott. Why would they lie about my accident?"

Adam's frown deepened. "Don't know. Where exactly is this tree house?"

"Dad dismantled it after my fall, Aunt Vi said, but it used to be in that big oak. The one near Uncle Scott's garden."

"Where the swimming pool used to be, right?" Adam got off the bed and began to pace. "So if you climbed it, you'd have a good view of the pool and most of the grounds."

"Yes, but—" Lottie caught her breath. She and Emma exchanged flabbergasted looks. "Adam, you don't mean—"

"That Lottie might have seen what happened to Uncle Scott?" Adam turned to face them. "It makes sense."

Lottie's head spun. Could Adam be right? Had she witnessed something no child should ever have to see? Was this the reason behind her parents' secrecy? It couldn't be true. Even as her brain rebelled against the idea, she recalled her dream, saw herself peering down from the platform through a curtain of leaves, and felt again the sense of horror that paralyzed her just before she fell.

***

It took a moment for the full impact of Violet's words to sink in. When her brain finally grasped their meaning, Olivia had to quell the impulse to laugh. Surely this was some sort of joke. One look at her sister's grim face convinced her otherwise. In any case, Vi would never speak lightly of the event that had so destroyed her life, which left only one other explanation: her sister had lost her mind. Her grief at losing the man she loved, so long buried, had at last stolen her sanity.

"I can see what you're thinking," Violet said. "You think I'm crazy."

Olivia trod with care. "No, but what you're saying is crazy. You must see that."

"Why must I? From where I'm standing, it makes perfect sense." Violet crossed her arms in the familiar gesture. "I was in pieces after it happened. I couldn't think straight. I certainly wasn't up to questioning the coroner's verdict. For years afterwards, I couldn't even bear to think about him. Instead, I threw all my energy into my career. I told myself if I worked hard enough, the pain would go away."

"I know." Exasperated as she was, Olivia's heart went out to her sister. "You've had a terrible time of it."

Violet shook her head. "I'm not saying all this so you'll feel sorry for me. I'm just trying to explain why it's taken me so long to see. The thing is, it's only recently that I've been able to think about what happened, and the more I do, the less anything adds up."

"Vi," Olivia said gently, "don't you think you might be letting what you see in your work cloud your judgment? No one could blame you. Coming into contact with criminals on a daily basis is bound to have an effect, but don't you think it's possible you're seeing a crime where none exists?"

"No, I don't. If my job has taught me anything, it's that there's rarely such a thing as a coincidence. People don't generally die of their own accord when there's a motive for bumping them off, and, whatever else you say, you can't deny there were several who stood to gain from Scott's death."

"Because of Cameron's?"

"Obviously. Come on, Liv, you can't tell me it doesn't fit. One minute the business is on the verge of ruin, the next, Scott's dead and the problem is solved. Convenient, huh?"

"Convenient?" Olivia couldn't quite believe she was having this conversation. "Vi, think about what you're saying. You can't honestly think one of us, one of the family — "

"I don't know why you look so shocked. Two-thirds of murders are committed by someone known to the victim."

"Which would include me, I suppose. You think I might have sneaked down to the pool in secret, invited Scott to go for a swim with me and held his head under the water?"

"Course not. You can't even swat a bluebottle, but there were plenty of other people who I'd say were more than capable of murder that day. Rafe, for one, would go to any lengths to protect his precious Cameron's, and I'm betting there's not much Carla and Phoebe wouldn't do for the men they love. As for Joel and Tim, they might not seem the type, but you'd be amazed how people can turn when their livelihood is threatened."

"How dare you!" In her anger, Olivia forgot to keep her voice down. "There isn't a better man alive than Tim, and have you any idea how cut up Joel was after Scott died? What you're suggesting is monstrous! I know my husband and he could never, ever do anything so ... so—" Words failed her.

Violet raised an eyebrow. "You wouldn't have thought he could cheat on you, but he has. Who's to say what else he's capable of?"

"Scott's death was an accident, Violet, or else he killed himself. Why are you so determined to ignore the truth?"

"Because I don't believe it. Scott would never have killed himself. Not when he knew how much I loved him."

"But did he know that? The way I see it, we all turned against him that day."

Violet's face drained of color; she looked stricken. "Scott loved life too much ever to throw his away."

"And you don't think his family loved him, too? You don't think they would have put up with any amount of hardship if only they could bring him back?"

Her sister made as if to protest, but Olivia had run out of patience. She didn't need this. Not on top of everything else. All the pain and misery of the past weeks surged up inside her, spilling over in a torrent.

She jabbed a finger in Violet's face. "This isn't about Scott, is it? This is about you. You and your guilty conscience. It suits you to think Scott was murdered, so you refuse to hear reason. You'd rather believe anything, even that Scott's own brothers wanted him dead, because you can't accept you might have been to blame."

***

Joel found Rafe alone in the sitting room, sprawled on the sofa in front of the fire. "Okay if I join you?"

His brother glanced up from his newspaper with obvious pleasure. "Come on in. You and I haven't had a chance to catch up yet. Actually, I got the impression you'd rather we weren't here."

"Sorry about that." Joel sank into the armchair by the fire, grimacing. "I know I haven't been much of a host."

Rafe regarded him with the shrewdness that had earned him such respect in the financial world. "Something wrong? You don't seem yourself."

Joel sighed. There was no doubt that his older brother's robust outlook would be a huge comfort just now, but he couldn't risk it. Coming clean would lead to dangerous questions, questions he could not afford Rafe to explore.

"This isn't an easy situation. Not for any of us."

"No." Rafe reached for his whisky on the coffee table. "Look, I owe you an apology, too. I didn't mean what I said yesterday about you being a coward for leaving the business. You know how I get when I'm nervous, and being back here—"

"You don't have to explain. Perhaps it *was* cowardly to leave when I did. Anyway, I didn't expect you to understand why I had to do it."

"But I do. I'm not saying I agree with your reasoning. I still think you were mad to throw away such security, but I can at least see your thinking behind it. You were always the sensitive one, even when we were kids."

Joel smiled. "Maybe, although then I had Tim to back me up."

"You mean before he had Carla to take charge of his life for him?" Rafe chuckled. "I'm guessing Tim would have liked nothing better than to shut himself away in the country and grow vegetables, but can you imagine how Carla would have taken it?"

Joel's smile faded. "She would have locked him up first. A husband who spent his days up to the elbows in soil wouldn't have fitted in with her life plan at all."

"Hardly. Think yourself lucky you ended up with a woman like Liv. She's one in a million."

"I know." *And like the fool I am, I went and threw it all away.*

They were silent for a while, the only sounds those of the flames crackling in the grate and the rustle of Rafe's newspaper.

Seeming to cotton on to Joel's mood, Rafe said, "You never did tell me why you and Tim fell out. I've asked Tim, but he claims not to know."

"No, well, he and I clearly have different ideas of what constitutes trust." At least, Joel thought, since Carla came into their lives. He had believed the bond between him and Tim was stronger than anything else, that their friendship would endure no matter what. Then Tim met Carla and thereafter loyalty to everyone else took second place.

In a rare display of tact, Rafe didn't press for details. He simply continued turning the pages of his newspaper until Joel broke the silence.

"Were we wrong, do you think, inviting you all back here?"

"Not at all. It was never going to be a stroll in the park, but you have to take control of your demons or they'll take control of you."

An image of Phoebe's face as it had been that afternoon, ghostly pale, eyes haunted and dark with fear, swam into Joel's mind. If he'd ever seen anyone pursued by demons, it was his sister-in-law. In fact, he suspected she was on the verge of a nervous breakdown.

"Rafe, where's Phoebe?"

"Nanny Carla sent her to bed with a hot drink. Phoebs is finding it particularly tough being back here. Not surprising, really. She's always been highly strung. Still, I told her she has to put a brave face on it, same as the rest of us."

"Don't you think you should take her home? She's really not coping."

"Certainly not," Rafe said. "It's just as important for Phoebe to face up to the past as it is for the rest of us, perhaps more so. No, I said we'd stay until the New Year, and that's what we're going to do."

***

"Take them," Carla urged, pressing the sleeping tablets into Phoebe's hands. "Please. They'll help you sleep."

"I'll never sleep." Phoebe stared at her with wild eyes, her face as white as the pillows propped behind her head. "I heard him, Carla. Last night. Heard him walking up and down outside my door. He's come back, I know it, come back to punish us."

Carla almost dropped the tablets. She took in her friend's rolling eyes and her hands gripping the edge of the duvet, the skin around the nails red and raw where she had bitten them. Was Phoebe going mad? Had her mind, fragile for as long as she'd known her, finally taken as much as it could deal with and shut itself down? No, she wouldn't allow it. She had worked too hard to keep Phoebe's mental health intact to let it disintegrate now. Carla took a deep breath. It was vital she remain calm.

"Phoebs, listen to me. There's nothing here to frighten you, I promise. Please, just take these." Again, she tried to force the sleeping pills into her friend's hand. "You're going to make yourself ill if you don't sleep, and you know how Rafe hates it when you're ill."

As she had hoped, the mention of her husband penetrated Phoebe's inner turmoil and she finally accepted the tablets. Relieved, Carla steadied the mug of cocoa in Phoebe's shaking hands and watched her swallow them. After all these years, Phoebe's loyalty to Rafe was undiminished. What had he done to inspire such devotion, other than to treat her like a glorified secretary-come-housekeeper and cheat on her in the worst possible way? No, he had done nothing to deserve Phoebe's love. Yet she gave it constantly and without condition.

"That's right," Carla said, as Phoebe's rigid body relaxed. "Rest now."

Phoebe nodded, turning her face away. Carla sat by her until her friend's eyes began to close. Then she stood and moved about the room, rearranging the bedclothes and switching off the overhead light in preference to the softer glow of the bedside lamp. Gradually, the fear receded from Phoebe's expression and it became smooth and untroubled, and she slept. After dropping a quick kiss on her forehead, Carla made her way along the passage to her own room.

"How is she?" Tim asked, looking up from his book.

Carla sank onto the bed beside him. "Sleeping. She'll be okay for a while. How about you?"

"Me? Oh, I'm fine."

"Liar." However much Tim might have her believe all was hunky-dory, he couldn't hide the deep-rooted hurt in his eyes, the great sadness weighing on his heart. Confronted with the distress of the two people she cared for most in the world, along with her children, Carla began to think this reunion was a terrible mistake. What good could possibly come of it?

"Is it Joel?" she guessed.

"You know me too well." Letting the book fall shut without glancing at the page number, Tim tossed it aside and looked at her. Confusion etched lines around his eyes and mouth. "I just wish I knew what I'd done to make him hate me."

"I saw you go and talk to him this morning. What did he say?"

"Nothing that made any sense. He kept going on about how I'd betrayed his trust. Seems to be under the impression I told you something he'd confided to me in confidence, but I'd never have done that."

Carla sat very still. A series of memories flitted through her mind: a snatch of conversation overheard from behind a hedge; herself pacing this very room, hands twisting together; Joel's face, full of shock at what seemed the ultimate betrayal. What should she do? She couldn't bear to see Tim so unhappy when she had the power to shed some light on the puzzle, but could she risk it? Would he hate her, blame her for twelve years of estrangement from the brother he adored? On the other hand, what if Joel blurted it out in a fit of anger? No, it would be better coming from her.

"Tim," she said, heart thudding, "please don't be mad at me. I've only just realized, or I swear I would have told you before."

"What is it?" Tim sat up and laid a hand on her back. "Why should I be mad?"

Carla took a fortifying breath. "Because I think this whole thing is my fault."

***

Once everyone had gone to bed, Violet unlocked the back door and slipped out into the night. Her boots creaked through the snow and she shivered, drawing her coat tighter against the bitter air. Nothing, however, could drive away the chill left behind by the row with her sister. Like a police officer examining CCTV footage for evidence, she replayed the argument over and over in her mind, trying to make sense of it. Was she really so immersed in iniquity that she saw crimes where none existed? Did she simply seek to find a reason for Scott's death because she couldn't accept the utter pointlessness of it? Worse still, was Olivia right when she said that she, Violet, would believe anything rather than admit she had been to blame?

Reaching the gate in the hedge, she pushed it open and crossed the garden to sit on the bench. Olivia and Joel had designed this place, she knew, in the hope that she might find some comfort here, but she had visited it only a handful of times over the years. The memories she worked so hard to suppress for fear that they would tear her apart inside were stronger here, his presence impossible to ignore.

Heedless of the wind biting her fingers, Violet traced the words Joel had carved into the bench's wooden back. "In loving memory of Scott Cameron. No matter how dark the sky, your star will always shine." As she sat there, a fragment of song she had avoided playing or even thinking about since Scott's death drifted down the years to haunt her.

"Bright are the stars that shine, dark is the sky. I know this love of mine, will never die."

Violet hugged her chest, heart splintering with an exquisite mixture of grief and longing. She raised her head to stare up at a sky dotted with stars, the very same stars that had twinkled down on her and Scott all that time ago. She hadn't been able to bear the sight of them, couldn't bear that they still continued to shine when Scott was no longer here to see them, but now she was unable to tear her gaze away. She drank them in, transfixed, until their brilliance blurred before her eyes.

"I'm sorry," she whispered, hot tears coursing down her cheeks. "I'm so sorry."

Twelve

Immersed in a dream where her book is made into a film starring Richard Gere, Olivia struggles up in bed. Dazed and disorientated, she focuses on the doorway and the small figure dressed in a pink and yellow spotted swimming costume, then squints at the clock. Seven-thirty. Heavens, she only fell into bed a few hours ago. No wonder she feels like she's recovering from jet lag.

"Mummy." Lottie sounds impatient. "I said, can we go swimming?"

Olivia collapses back onto the pillows with a groan. "Not now, sweetheart. It's the crack of dawn. You can go swimming later, I promise."

"But we want to go now." Bouncing into the room, Lottie taps a sleeping Joel on the head. "Wakey wakey, Daddy. You need to take us swimming."

"Don't do that to Daddy's head, pet," Joel mumbles and burrows deeper under the duvet. "It hurts."

Lottie looks up at her mother, forehead creased. "Is Daddy poorly?"

"He's fine. Just had too many of Uncle Scott's cocktails last night. He'll be okay later to take you swimming. Now, leave Mummy to have a little rest, there's a good girl. Then I'll come down and get you some breakfast."

"I can get breakfast," Lottie says, and rushes from the room.

The thought of her daughter let loose on the kitchen without supervision would normally have catapulted Olivia out of bed. In her current exhaustion, however, she merely listens to Lottie's excited voice calling to Emma and Adam and their shrieks as they charge down the stairs. Olivia winces. If she feels rough purely from lack of sleep, the others must be close to death after the amount they drank. They certainly won't take kindly to being woken at such an unearthly hour.

Olivia is melting into the arms of sleep once more, when an almighty crash yanks her back to reality and she shoots upright. "Oh, my God! What was that?"

"Best go see," Joel says, voice muffled by the pillow.

"Thanks so much for your support." Sighing, Olivia relinquishes any hope of snatching a precious five minutes more sleep and reaches for her dressing gown.

A few moments later, she staggers into the kitchen to find a shame-faced Lottie sitting at the table with her cousins and Violet on her knees with a dustpan and brush.

Her sister glances up, grimacing. "Sorry, should've been keeping a closer eye on them. Lottie dropped a bowl."

"Doesn't matter," Olivia says, too shocked by Violet's appearance to be exasperated. Her eyes are red and puffy as though she has been crying all night, and she's still wearing yesterday's jeans and T-shirt.

"I wanted to show Emma and Adam I'm grown up." Lottie's face crumples. "Don't be cross."

Olivia plants a kiss on her hair. "I'm not cross. Why don't the three of you go and play outside while I make breakfast?"

The instant she opens the back door, they tear into the grounds like puppies kept in overnight. Smiling, Olivia fills the kettle at the sink and puts it on to boil.

"Want to talk about it?" she asks, sobering as she turns back to her sister.

Violet collapses at the table and drops her head in her hands. "Not sure I can."

"Poor you." Olivia goes to hug her, but Violet pushes her away.

"Don't," she says in a tight voice. "You'll only set me off again."

Understanding, Olivia returns to making the tea. "Did you go to bed at all last night?"

"Couldn't face it, so I just curled up in the armchair in here. I think I dropped off eventually, but only for an hour or so."

No wonder she looks so pale and exhausted. Violet drank her fair share of cocktails the night before, but, unlike the others, hasn't slept it off. Not that she seems particularly hung over. Perhaps heartbreak works in the same way as Alka-Seltzer.

Before Olivia can probe deeper, Carla stalks into the room. "How am I supposed to sleep with all that screeching going on outside? What was that you were saying yesterday, Liv, about this being the easy part of bringing up children? At least teenagers tend to sleep all day, unlike this lot. I swear my head's going to explode!"

"We did rather overdo it. Sit down and I'll get you something to help the headache." Catching Violet's eye, Olivia mouths, "We'll talk later," then goes in search of some painkillers.

***

"This is great," Joel says later, as they tuck into plates of bacon and eggs on the sunny patio. To spare the adults' headaches, the children have been dispatched into the grounds with a picnic of bacon sandwiches and apple juice.

"There's nothing like a fry-up to cure a hangover," Rafe agrees. He turns to Phoebe. "Do try and eat, angel. You'll feel better afterwards."

She nods, wanting to please him. But, with her stomach churning from the combination of spirits and quivering every time he strokes her thigh under the table, she knows she won't be able to swallow a thing.

"Phoebs isn't used to drinking so much," Carla says.

Phoebe's insides tauten. Why does her friend always feel it necessary to speak for her? She's devoted to Carla, can't imagine how she would have got through the years without her, but sometimes her protectiveness is almost smothering.

Perhaps sensing her resentment, Tim smiles. "None of us are used to drinking that much. I won't be accepting another of Scott's cocktails in a hurry, that's for sure."

"Speaking of Scott," Carla says, toying with her food, "I don't see why he gets to have a lie-in. It's his fault we're all dying this morning, after all. Think I'll go and wake him up."

Olivia puts out a hand to stay her. "Leave him a while longer. You know what a grouch he is when he's tired. If he hasn't surfaced soon, I promise I'll go and drag him out of bed myself. More tea, anyone?"

In the confusion as cups are passed back and forth across the table, only Phoebe appears to notice the anxious glance Olivia casts her sister's way. Poor Violet. She looked so happy last night when Scott waltzed her over the starlit lawn. Now, as she pushes her food around her plate without eating, her pallor and the shadows beneath her eyes stand out starkly in the harsh light of day. Phoebe's heart cries out to her. No stranger to rejection, she hates seeing another's pain, especially when she herself is so on top of the world.

As though he has read her thoughts, Rafe's hand creeps into hers under the table and his breath caresses her ear. "Eat up. You and I have some unfinished business to see to."

***

Lounging on the grass in the shade of the hawthorn hedge, one eye trained on the children in the pool, Joel steels himself. Now that he has engineered this time alone with Tim, he can't find the words to begin. What if his twin doesn't understand, is furious with him? Worse still, what if he tells … The knots that have twisted his gut into a constant ache these past days strengthen their grip. *Come on, man, what's wrong with you? Just spit it out.*

"There's something I need to tell you," he says abruptly. "If I don't get it off my chest soon, I'll go mad."

Tim glances up with concern. "What is it?"

Unable to meet his twin's eye, Joel focuses on a blade of grass as he winds it around his finger. "You remember I had a meeting with Mr. Langdon earlier this week to discuss the future of his investment? Well, as it turned out, the true purpose of the meeting was to inform me he'd decided to withdraw his business."

"That's no great surprise." Tim's tone is calm, but his stillness betrays his tension. "We're losing clients left, right and center at the moment."

"Which is precisely why we can't afford to lose Langdon. We're dependent on his money to keep us ticking over through this damn recession. That's why I felt I had to do what I did." Still not looking at his brother, grateful for the shrieks of the children that mask his words, Joel tells him everything. Tim listens without interrupting and remains silent for a long time after he has finished.

"Let me get this straight," he says eventually. "You guaranteed Langdon a five percent return on his investment over the next year?"

"That's about the size of it. It's the only way I could stop him withdrawing his funds then and there."

"But a five percent return? Right now we're struggling to give clients any return at all. What sort of agreement was this? Did you sign anything?"

"What do you think?" Joel's fingers close on a fistful of grass, almost uprooting it. "You know Langdon isn't fool enough to commit his cash without a written contract."

"No, but I did hope you weren't fool enough to sign something we can't deliver on. What happens when the year's up and he wants to see how his investment's progressing? Worse still, what if he wants to withdraw his funds?"

Joel shakes his head. "What can we do? Either forge the statements or top it up with money from another client's account."

"Christ, Joel." The ground vibrates as Tim slams his palm into it. "What were you thinking? You don't need me to tell you how illegal that is. The authorities will hang us out to dry if they find out."

"Don't you think I know that? I've been beating myself up over it ever since, but Rafe said to hang on to Langdon at all costs."

"Oh, so you're going to tell Rafe about this little stunt, are you? You think he'll approve of you putting the company in jeopardy?"

Joel says nothing. Rafe is the last person he would want to learn of this and they both know it. Silence descends between them, and they watch the children take turns diving into the pool. At Emma's insistence, the cousins join hands and plunge into the water as one, sending up a shower of cold droplets. At once, the awkwardness evaporates.

"Watch it," Joel says, drying his face on his arm.

Tim puts a hand on his shoulder. "Sorry, didn't mean to come on so strong. I know you wouldn't have taken this decision lightly."

"No, I'm sorry. I've no right taking it out on you, and I shouldn't have put the company at risk like that. It just seemed the only way to save the situation."

"I know. Look, you're not the first person to bend the rules a bit, and I'm betting you won't be the last." Tim gives him a shake. "Come on, snap out of it. When we survive this crisis, you'll look back on this as one of the shrewdest business decisions you ever made. Besides, if this new venture of Scott's comes off, we'll be able to give Langdon his return without resorting to anything underhand, so there's no reason anyone should ever find out."

***

"Feeling better?" Rafe asks, leading Phoebe into the grounds away from prying eyes.

She smiles at him, her pale cheeks flushed by the sun. "Much. It's so peaceful here. How wonderful to live somewhere like this."

"Maybe you will some day." Rafe squeezes her hand and is rewarded by the hope in Phoebe's eyes. No need to tell her he hasn't any intention ever to leave the city, that he would hate to be so far from Cameron's, even at weekends. Besides, if his wife is closeted away in the country all week, who will take care of him? Still, best not to disillusion Phoebe so early in their relationship.

As they follow the uneven path that coils through the wilderness of ancient trees, overgrown hedges and weed-choked grass—clearly Joel and Olivia haven't yet had time to tackle the garden—Rafe is aware of Phoebe's adoring gaze. What a coup to have found himself such a suitable girl. In contrast to his previous conquests, of which there have been countless, she is quiet, efficient and reasonably intelligent, the ideal candidate for ensuring his life runs like clockwork. Phoebe would never make embarrassing remarks during an important dinner party, or forget to post vital mail.

The fact that she is so unassuming, both in manner and appearance, is a bonus. She might not be a trophy to flaunt on his arm, but he'll never lose sleep worrying what she gets up to all day while he's at work, whether the aerobics class penciled in her diary is in fact a disguise for something more clandestine. How Tim isn't driven mad fretting over the extra-marital activities of the gorgeous Carla, Rafe can't imagine. Then again, his brother has always been too trusting for his own good.

"Rafe." Phoebe's timid voice breaks into his thoughts. "Do tell me to mind my own business, but are things very bad for Cameron's?"

"Why?" Rafe drawls. "Are you only interested in me for my money?"

Hurt clouds Phoebe's eyes. "How can you say that? You know I think the world of you. It's just, well, I know how much Cameron's means to you."

"Not as much as you do," Rafe says, slipping an arm around her.

"Look, I won't patronize you by telling you business is booming, but it's only a blip. The economy goes through good times and bad. It's just a matter of riding out the storm until things pick up again. You certainly don't need to worry your pretty head about it." As if on impulse, Rafe draws her to a halt outside their destination. "Let's take a peep in here."

The door creaks open at his touch and they enter the cool, dark interior of the stables, welcoming after the brilliant sunshine.

"I always wanted a horse." Phoebe's gaze travels over the rusty tools and planks of wood littering the dusty floor. "Perhaps Lottie will have one when she's older."

"I see something far more exciting than a horse." Rafe leads her over to the corner, where he reaches up to haul on a handle in the ceiling. A ladder descends at their feet, revealing an opening above. "Must be a hayloft. Shall we take a look?"

Phoebe eyes the ladder doubtfully. "It might not be safe."

"I dare if you do," Rafe says, smiling into her eyes. "I'll go first to make sure."

Before Phoebe can protest, he climbs quickly to the loft and collapses on the bed of hay he prepared during his pre-breakfast stroll. After only the briefest hesitation, she follows.

"That wasn't too difficult, was it?" Rafe pulls her onto the hay beside him, then draws the ladder back into place.

"What are you doing?" Phoebe whispers in the sudden gloom. She sounds both nervous and fascinated. "What if—?"

Rafe silences her with a kiss. At once her lips part beneath his, eager and willing, and she puts up no resistance as he presses her back onto the hay. He moves his mouth downward, exploring the soft skin of her jaw, her throat, her shoulders. Phoebe moans, writhing under his touch. Rafe smirks. How flattering to be wanted so much. His pulse quickens. There is something intensely erotic about the hayloft, the smell of straw and sun-baked wood, the sense of being separated from the rest of the world. Undressing Phoebe in the darkness, it's easy to imagine her body is that of another, a curvy, voluptuous body that has so often taunted him in bikinis and revealing dresses. Still, if all goes as planned, the secret passion he has harbored for so long will soon be requited.

***

"I don't get it," Violet confesses as she and Olivia drink coffee at the kitchen table. "I really thought we had something, but now Scott doesn't want to know."

"I'm sure that isn't true," Olivia says; she would have said anything to erase the desolation from her sister's eyes. "We all saw the way he looked at you last night."

"It didn't mean anything. It was 'just sex', he said." Violet winces. "Well, it might have been just sex to him, but it was the most magical night of my life."

Olivia clenches her fingers around her mug. How can someone as generous and loving as Scott be so careless with the hearts of others? Reaching across the table, she lays a hand on her sister's. "I'm sorry, Vi. I really am."

Violet gives her a twisted smile. "It's my own stupid fault. I went into Scott's bed with my eyes open, and still managed to fool myself into believing it would be different for me. I should have realized I'm too dull to hold him."

"You're not dull, and you're definitely not stupid. It's obvious Scott cares about you, but, well, he's never been the commitment type, has he?"

Before Violet can reply, Carla drifts in through the back door looking distracted.

"Everything okay?" Olivia asks.

Carla glances towards the table without appearing to see her. "What? Oh, yes, it's just a bit hot out there. Thought I'd lie down for a while."

"Good idea." Olivia looks longingly after her. "I'll give you a shout when lunch is ready."

Once Carla has gone, Olivia gets up to pour more coffee.

"I can't stay, Liv," Violet says. "You see that, don't you? I hate to let you down, but I can't face Scott, knowing how he feels."

"I understand." Olivia sets a replenished mug before her. "But you'd better wait a while. Being caught drunk behind the wheel wouldn't be the best start to your career. At least stay for lunch."

Violet agrees, perhaps too weary to argue, and Olivia squares her shoulders. As soon as the chance arises, she intends to root Scott out and demand to know what the hell he's playing at.

***

Carla paces her room, too churned up to lie down. About to join Tim by the pool, she'd overheard his and Joel's conversation through the hedge. She didn't mean to eavesdrop, had merely caught the urgency in their low voices and was concerned. By the time she realized the exchange wasn't intended for her ears, that they would hate her to have heard, it was too late. Now their words spiral around her head, impossible to forget.

Of course, things are tough for the company at the moment; in the current economic downturn, it's only to be expected. Yet, while so many of their rivals are going bust, Tim has always maintained that Cameron's is strong enough to withstand the recession. What on earth was Joel thinking? After eight years of marriage to a financier, Carla understands enough to know that giving false guarantees is sufficient cause to close a company down, even land the guilty party in prison. For Joel, normally so upright and pedantic, to take such a step, the situation must be direr than the brothers are letting on. God, what if they lose the business? If Cameron's goes under, they'll lose everything: their security, their lifestyle … everything.

Pausing by the window, Carla grips the sill and stares out over the sunny grounds. Calm down. It won't come to that. The Camerons are so proud of the firm; there's no way any of them would put it in jeopardy. After his initial shock, Tim took Joel's revelation in his stride so perhaps she's worrying unnecessarily. Soon the economic crisis will be over and nobody need ever know the lengths to which one of Cameron's directors went to keep it afloat. Joel is a shrewd businessman and Tim a man of sound judgment. They must know what they're doing. Mustn't they?

Thirteen

Scott pries his eyes open, then screws them shut again as a blade of sunshine stabs through a gap in the curtains, piercing his aching head. As he recalls where he is, the awful reality of his situation slams into him. He groans and buries his face in the pillow, fighting nausea. What is he doing here? How could he come, knowing what he has done? His family wouldn't have given him such a warm welcome last night if they knew the truth, that's for sure.

Scott groans again. Panic churns in his gut. Christ, he's going to throw up. He should have come clean right away, had intended to, but, confronted by their obvious pleasure at seeing him, his nerve disintegrated. He couldn't disillusion them like that, couldn't bring himself to watch their smiles turn to looks of fury and horror. Instead, he fell back on what he does best: playing the fool and ensuring that everyone has such a good time that they don't notice anything's wrong. Still, he can't go on pretending indefinitely. He'll have to pour out the whole appalling business, and soon. Shit, what a God-awful mess.

The soft click of the door breaks into his turmoil. Most likely Rafe come to get dressed. Scott doesn't move. Of all his brothers, Rafe is the hardest to face, the one whose eyes he finds it impossible to meet. With any luck, his brother will assume he's still asleep and leave him be.

"Heavens, it smells like a brewery in here. It's no use pretending to be asleep, Scott, because I can tell you're not."

Relief smoothes the tension from Scott's body. It's only Liv. Unearthing his head from the pillow, he opens his eyes a crack to squint at her, fresh and pretty as ever in a jade-green dress that flows over her rounded stomach and her hair tied back with a matching scarf. She sets a tray on the bedside cabinet. Scott's stomach growls in response to the aroma of coffee and bacon.

He manages a smile. "Is this my favorite sister-in-law bringing me breakfast in bed?"

"I'm afraid you're a little behind the times. It's gone two o'clock. How you've managed to sleep through the racket the kids have been making, I don't know." Olivia drops an Alka-Seltzer into a glass of water and holds it out to him. "Drink this."

Scott makes a feeble attempt to sit up, before flopping back onto the pillows. "Sorry, Liv, can't move just yet."

"You can if you don't want this poured over you." Olivia tilts the glass in warning. "And if you want to have a chance of catching Vi before she leaves."

Vi. Scott winces at the sound of her name. Hell! His other troubles have so far kept thoughts of her at bay, but, at Olivia's words, his defenses crumble and they come crashing through. Struggling into a sitting position, steadying himself against the headboard when his surroundings slide past as if on a conveyer belt, Scott accepts the glass. He gulps down the fizzing liquid, grimacing at the taste, while Olivia flings open the window to let country air freshen the room.

"Watch what you're doing with those curtains," Scott begs. "My head isn't up to light just yet."

"I don't suppose it is, the amount you drank last night." Olivia draws the curtains together, shutting out the offending sunshine, and comes to sit on the edge of his bed. Returning the empty glass to the tray, she sets the plate of bacon sandwiches on his lap. "These should settle your stomach."

Scott toys with a sandwich, too agitated to eat. "What was that about Vi leaving?"

Olivia frowns. "Well, you wouldn't expect her to stay after last night."

Last night. Scott closes his eyes, trying to remember. A jumble of memories scroll across his mind: the gentle warmth of Violet's mouth beneath his, the coconut smell of her hair, her face softened by starlight and laughter, tears shimmering on her cheeks when he said he didn't love her ... Scott's eyes snap open, but, under Olivia's accusing stare, he drops his gaze to find the sandwich crushed to a pulp in his fist.

"I never meant to hurt her," he mumbles, "but it was for the best."

"You wouldn't say that if you'd seen the state she was in this morning. How could you do it, Scott? She really thought you cared about her. So did I, for that matter."

"I do. Christ, I care about her too damn much."

"Then tell her so."

Scott shakes his head, instantly regretting the motion as the room spins. "It's not that simple."

"Isn't it? You care about each other, don't you? What could be simpler than that? But perhaps this is nothing to do with Violet." She regards him shrewdly. "Perhaps it's more to do with you and your fear of commitment."

"That isn't it." Scott forces himself to meet her gaze, willing her to understand. "You have to believe me, Liv. It's Vi I'm thinking of. I'm trying to protect her."

"What? From being corrupted by your wicked ways? And what if Violet doesn't want to be protected? The fact is, Scott, she knows you as well as any of us and she still wants you. Surely that counts for something?"

But would she still want me if she knew the truth? Unable to explain without confessing the whole sordid story, Scott only grimaces. Some of his desperation must have shown in his expression, for Olivia's face softens.

"Do try and eat something," she says, standing up, "and at least think about what I've said. Just don't take too long, okay? I've persuaded Vi to stay for lunch, but she'll be gone soon. It's up to you to decide what you want."

***

Emma fidgets in her chair at the patio table. "Can we get down now?"

"You should let your lunch go down first," Tim says, "or you'll get indigestion."

"We won't." Adam leans across the table so that it wobbles precariously. "Mum, can we get down?"

"Watch what you're doing," Carla snaps, moving her teacup out of harm's way. "Daddy's right. Just sit still and behave for five minutes."

Her children look mutinous, but Lottie diverts their attention by showing them the face she has created on her plate with an assortment of crisps, cucumber slices and cocktail sausages. If only Emma and Adam could be as placid as her niece.

Sipping her tea, Carla watches Rafe and Phoebe across the table. Something has changed between them. She can't pinpoint what it is—the intimacy of Rafe's hand resting on her leg, perhaps, or the unfamiliar gleam in Phoebe's eye—but there's a connection between them that wasn't there at breakfast. It doesn't take a brain surgeon to surmise what's behind it, and Carla's heart grows heavy with unease.

"Where did you get to?" Joel asks Olivia, pulling out a chair for her as she emerges onto the patio.

She flops down beside him. "Tending to your little brother, who, I have to say, is feeling rather sorry for himself."

"Serves him right," Rafe says, "after the state he got us all into last night."

"Look, Mummy," Lottie pipes up, "I've made a face."

"That's lovely, sweetheart, but perhaps now you could eat some of those crisps."

Joel tweaks Olivia's ponytail. "I sense a certain amount of favoritism going on here. How come Scott gets tending to, while the rest of us just get bullied?"

Olivia slaps his hand playfully. "For your information, Scott had to endure his fair share of bullying."

"Come off it, Liv," Rafe scoffs. "You couldn't bully an ant."

"And don't we all love her for it?" Tim smiles at his sister-in-law, pushing a plate of food towards her. "Here, I've saved you something from these gannets."

"Thanks." Olivia takes a sandwich, her gaze traveling around the table. "Where's Vi? Not gone to pack already?"

"'Fraid so," Joel says. "You haven't persuaded her to stay then?"

"I've done what I can. It's out of my hands now."

And in the less than reliable hands of Scott, Carla muses. *Certainly not somewhere I would put my faith.*

"Can we leave the table?" Emma demands. "Our lunch has gone down now."

"Just as long as you take it eas—" Tim begins, but his warning is drowned as all three children scrape back their chairs with excited whoops.

"Wait for me," Lottie implores, but Emma and Adam are already streaking over the lawn and she has to run to catch up.

"Not so fast," Olivia scolds. "You'll make yourselves sick."

Scenting an opportunity to have a private word with Phoebe, Carla gets to her feet. "I'll go and keep an eye on them. Coming, Phoebs?"

Phoebe shoots Rafe a longing glance, but nevertheless stands up and allows Carla to slip an arm through hers. Together, they head for the open stretch of lawn where the children have started a game of piggy in the middle.

"Violet looked awful," Phoebe says, once out of earshot. "She must really like Scott."

"More fool her," Carla retorts. "It's not as if she didn't know what she was getting into. The first weekend Tim took me home to meet his family, Scott actually came on to me. He couldn't have been more than fifteen."

Phoebe giggles. "Still, he did seem genuinely fond of Violet. Hope she's okay."

"Violet can look after herself, which is more than I can say for some people." Pulling Phoebe to a stop a short distance from the children, Carla gives her a searching look. "How about telling me what's going on between you and Rafe."

"Not sure I know what you mean," Phoebe says, though her blush betrays her.

"Oh, I think you do. You've gone to bed with him, haven't you?"

"Well, not to bed, exactly."

"Okay, too much information." Carla grips her arm. "The point is, you've slept with him. I only hope you know what you're doing."

Phoebe regards her, unperturbed. "And I hope you're not about to give me a lecture on the facts of life. I am twenty-eight, you know."

"I do know. It's just—"

"Just what?"

Carla shakes her head, unable to put her nameless anxiety into words. "I'm trying to look out for you, that's all."

Phoebe squeezes her arm. "I know you are, and I appreciate it, but you can't hold my hand forever. I'm a big girl now." She smiles with a quiet confidence that has never been there before, a confidence Rafe has given her—one he can so easily snatch away.

Not wanting Phoebe to see her skepticism and think her churlish, Carla averts her gaze to watch the children. Emma and Adam are tossing the ball to each other, while Lottie jumps up and down between them in increasingly frustrated attempts to catch it.

"Not fair," she protests, close to tears. "You're too tall."

"Emma, Adam, play nicely," Carla warns. Reaching a decision, she turns back to Phoebe. "If things are really serious between you and Rafe, you'd better know how things stand with Cameron's."

Phoebe's brow creases. "How do you mean? I asked Rafe this morning if the business is in trouble and he said not."

"Rafe doesn't know everything that goes on in the company." In a low voice, Carla fills her in on the conversation she overheard that morning.

"The fact is," she says, "if the authorities ever found out what Joel's done, it could spell the end of Cameron's, and, if that happens—" Carla falters at her friend's expression.

Phoebe turns to her, eyes blazing in a face white with anger. "How could Joel be so stupid? Surely no client is worth putting the company at risk. How could he do it?"

"Calm down." Carla puts an arm around phoebe's shoulders. She has never seen her friend so het-up. "I doubt it'll come to that. Joel's a shrewd businessman. He wouldn't have signed the contract unless he felt it absolutely imperative to keep Cameron's afloat."

The rage subsides from Phoebe's expression as quickly as it arose. "I'm sure you're right. I just can't bear to think that Cameron's might go under. It would break Rafe's heart." She shakes her head. "I wish there was something I could do."

"You and me both," Carla says. If the business collapses, Tim will lose his livelihood and she the status of being married to a successful financier. At least she now has Phoebe to share the burden, for there can be no doubting her commitment to Rafe. What isn't apparent is whether he returns this loyalty. Carla resolves to find out.

"I'm not playing anymore," Lottie wails, as the ball flies over her head yet again. Before either adult can step in, she runs sobbing towards the house.

***

"That brother of ours is taking his time getting out of bed," Rafe says, once Olivia has gone indoors with the dirty plates. "I've a good mind to go and drag him out myself."

"Best leave him a while," Joel advises. "He might be sorting things out with Vi."

"Well, as long as he gets his skates on. I'm dying to hear more about this investment opportunity of his. I counter-signed the authorization for him last week but didn't press for the details."

Joel nods. Company policy requires two signatures before large funds can be withdrawn, but the brothers never question one another's transactions as a matter of trust.

"All pretty mysterious, isn't it?" Tim removes his sunglasses to wipe his brow. "Scott's said nothing to me other than that it's a really lucrative deal."

"And God knows we could do with one of those," Joel says. "If anyone can find a money-spinner in a recession, it's Scott."

"Speaking of money-spinners, Joel," Rafe says, "how did your meeting with Langdon go?"

Joel exchanges a look with his twin. The clatter of china from the kitchen and the children's distant shouts fill the brief pause. Rafe might sometimes bend the rules to fit his purpose but he expects the behavior of the company's employees, not to mention his brothers and fellow directors, to be beyond reproach. Though they are equal partners, as the eldest, Rafe considers himself the unofficial head of Cameron's and is certainly the most devoted to it. Anyone who risked the business' reputation, for whatever reason, would live to regret it.

Joel keeps his tone casual. "It went very well. I changed Langdon's mind about withdrawing his funds, persuaded him that the safest place for his money is with us."

"Which, of course, it is." Rafe leans back in his chair with a complacency Joel envies. "Excellent work. The way things are, I'd have hated to lose one of our best clients."

"Especially if you're thinking of settling down at last." Joel's gaze flickers to where Phoebe is deep in conversation with Carla.

Rafe smirks. "Great minds think alike. Reckon she'd make me a good wife, then?"

"She's a sweet girl," Tim says, "and she's obviously nuts about you."

"Bright, too," Joel adds, "unlike most of the girls you've fooled around with over the years."

Rafe inclines his head. "Undemanding, reliable, and not at all bad looking. I'm really coming round to the idea. I just didn't want to rush into anything and end up with someone totally unsuitable. Like you did, Tim."

"And what's that supposed to mean?" Tim asks.

Rafe holds up a placatory hand. "Now, don't get all defensive. Carla's a stunning girl. What man wouldn't be proud to have her on his arm?"

"You're talking about my wife like she's a trophy, something I can take out of the cabinet every now and then to show off. She might be beautiful, but that's not why I love her."

"Sure it isn't. Trouble is, most men aren't as honorable as you. The curse of being with a cracker like Carla is that you have to put up with knowing other men are lusting after her."

"Let them. Why should I waste time worrying about other men's fantasies?"

Rafe arches an eyebrow. "But how long before one of them is brave enough to do more than dream? Men can be very persistent when it comes to bedding a woman they have the hots for, take it from me. How can you be sure Carla won't give in to temptation?"

"That's enough." All at once, Tim's features are set in stone. "For your information, I happen to trust my wife, and I'll thank you not to speak about her like that again."

Joel stares at his twin, taken aback, but Rafe only shrugs. The awkward silence continues until Lottie hurtles onto the patio, bawling her eyes out.

"What is it, sweetheart?" Joel asks, scooping her up.

Lottie buries her face in his T-shirt. "Emma and Adam are being horrid. They won't let me catch the ball."

"Never mind. I'm sure it's a silly game, anyway. You come and sit with the grown-ups."

As Lottie snuggles into his chest, Joel peers over her head at Tim who is still granite-faced, then glances at Rafe. Though he has been forced to drop the subject of Carla, a curious glint lingers in his eye, almost a challenge, and Joel can't suppress a twinge of unease.

***

From the doorway of Violet's room, Scott watches her stow her few possessions—wash bag, pajamas, yesterday's clothes—in her holdall. This must be how Adam felt when Eve tempted him with the apple, aware he was about to do something forbidden but unable to resist the lure of the unknown.

He realizes now that it was the thought of seeing Vi again that drove him here, even while his instincts warned him to stay away. He has tried so hard to keep his distance, fighting the urge to answer her phone calls or drop in on her in the long evenings, distracting himself with other women and finding them all wanting. Then, in a single moment of weakness, maudlin with alcohol and the disastrous events of the last couple of days, he got on a train bound for Denbury and all his efforts fell by the wayside. Why put himself through several weeks of hell only to cave in at the first excuse?

"You don't have to do this," Violet says, not looking up from her packing.

Scott starts; he'd believed himself unnoticed. "Do what?"

"Say you're sorry about last night."

"Even if it's true?"

"Even then." Violet's composure fills Scott with admiration. Only her refusal to look at him gives her away. "I know you didn't say what you did to hurt me. I asked you to tell me where I stood and you did. If anyone should be sorry, it's me. I shouldn't have presumed what happened between us was anything more than a bit of fun."

"Don't say that." This calm acceptance is even harder to bear than her tears. "Like you have anything to be sorry for, other than a dubious taste in men."

"And there's not much I can do about that." Violet laughs shakily, making a great show of zipping up her bag. "Would you mind leaving me to say goodbye to the others? You'll only make this harder for me than it already is."

"What if that's what I want?" Scott asks. "To make it harder."

Slowly Violet straightens to look at him, the faintest glimmer of hope in her eyes. Scott's heart stutters. He can only gaze at her, at the gold flecks in her hair picked out by the sunshine flooding the room, at the expressive face that captivated him years before, and which is now so pale and drawn. Christ, she's lovely. *Turn around, Scott. Just get the hell out of here and let her carry on with her life.*

"What are you saying?" Violet's tone is even.

Scott takes a deep breath, readying himself to shatter her hope yet again. "I'm saying I want you to stay." The words are out before he can stop them, before he has a chance to think them through. Unable to help himself, he closes the distance between them and takes her hands, cold despite the warmth of the day. "Don't go."

She scours his face, expression still doubtful. "And what you said last night—"

"That was just talk. I swear, I never thought you'd believe me so easily. I was sure you'd know what happened between us meant, well, everything. I was just trying to save you from getting involved with someone so unsuitable."

"And what if I don't give a damn whether you're suitable or not?" Freeing her hands, she cups his face between her palms.

At her touch, the last threads of Scott's resolve snap and he draws her against him. "You know, that's precisely what concerns me."

Fourteen

This time, don't let him goad you, Carla instructs herself as she lies in wait on the landing. No matter what he says, just stay calm and find out what you need to know.

When the bathroom door opens, Rafe's eyebrows lift at the sight of her. "Fancy meeting you out here. If I had a suspicious mind, I'd think you're stalking me."

"It isn't for pleasure, I assure you. We need to talk." Seizing his arm so that her long nails dig into his flesh, she draws him along the landing.

"I detect a theme developing," Rafe drawls as she closes the bedroom door behind them. "First a sofa, now a bed. Really, Carla, I thought you had more subtlety."

A putdown springs to Carla's lips but she swallows it. She mustn't let him get to her. Putting as much distance between them as possible, she crosses to stand with her back to the fitted wardrobes and glares at him, arms folded.

"Whatever would Tim think if he walked in on us now?" Rafe persists. "You and me alone in your bedroom while everyone else is outside."

Heat rushes to Carla's face. "Tim wouldn't think anything. He happens to trust me."

"Funnily enough, that's what he said. But then, my brother has always been a trusting soul."

"What? When did Tim say this? Why were you talking about me behind my back?"

Rafe chuckles and leans against the closed door, facing her. "Someone's got a guilty conscience. I only pointed out the dangers of being married to such a beautiful woman as yourself. With all that temptation dangled in front of her, I said, how can you be sure she remains faithful? He got really shirty with me. I must have touched a nerve."

"How dare you!" Carla spits. "What gives you the right to tell Tim what sort of person I am? I've never so much as looked at another man since I met him, not that I expect you to believe that. You've never liked me, have you? Not from the first time Tim brought me home."

Rafe seems to consider, his eyes moving over her body in a visual caress. "Oh, I wouldn't say that."

Carla forces herself not to squirm under his gaze. Hugging her arms tighter to her chest as though to keep her resolve intact, she frowns at him. "I didn't drag you in here to discuss my marriage. We need to talk about Phoebe."

"Ah, yes, Carla the eternal protector. Don't you think it's time you stopped trying to control Phoebe and let her live her own life?"

"Not when she's involved with a bastard like you."

"Your friend doesn't seem to think I'm a bastard, and I promise you she was perfectly happy in the hayloft this morning when I ... how should I put it ... initiated her."

Carla's insides contort with revulsion, along with another emotion she can't identify. "Look, I really don't need to hear all the sordid details."

"No? Does imagining me with your best friend drive you wild with jealousy? Or did you simply want to be there to watch and hold her hand?"

"God, you're disgusting." Carla looks away. "All I care about is that Phoebe doesn't get hurt. She's had enough heartache already. So, are you really serious about her or just fooling around?"

Rafe cocks his head to one side. "What do you think?"

Carla's shoulders slump. So it's just as she fears. Rafe sees Phoebe only as a bit of sport, a hobby to pass the time and be given up when he tires of it, which will break Phoebe's fragile heart. *Oh, why did I let her within ten feet of him?*

"Of course," Rafe says, advancing, "you could always help me make up my mind."

Carla snorts. "You mean to say the high-flying businessman can't make up his own mind about a woman?"

"I think it would be fairer to say because I'm a businessman I like to know I'm getting a good deal." Rafe stops in front of her, so close that Carla has to press herself against the wardrobe. "I have no aversion to Phoebe. On the contrary, I'm sure she'd make me an excellent wife and I'm seriously considering asking her to marry me."

"Is that so?"

"Certainly. Phoebe's a good girl, and I know how much it would mean to her to have a family of her own. If I could only be sure of receiving a small compensation, I wouldn't even hesitate."

"Compensation? I don't follow you."

"Oh, I think you do." Rafe places his hands on the wardrobe either side of Carla, hemming her in, and gazes directly into her eyes. "You must know I've always wanted you and I think you feel the same about me."

Carla sucks in a breath. "You're mad."

"Am I?" Rafe moves until their bodies almost touch. "Am I imagining the chemistry that's been there ever since we met? The way we can't even be in the same room without the sparks flying between us?"

"Let me go." Overcome with claustrophobia, Carla shoves against his

122

chest. Her head spins. The masculine smell of him, aftershave mixed with fresh cotton, fills her senses until she can scarcely breathe.

Rafe laughs softly. "You see? It's no use denying the effect I have on you. Come on, admit it." Leaning towards her, he brushes his lips against her earlobe.

Carla flinches as though he has branded her and shoves him harder. "Don't touch me."

Rafe lets his mouth linger for a moment longer, then steps back, smirking. "Have it your way. Just don't come running to me when you don't like the consequences."

Carla clenches her fists to stop her hands from shaking. *He's bluffing. Don't let him rattle you.* Arranging her face into what she hopes is an indifferent mask, she merely watches as he blows her a kiss and saunters from the room.

***

"Vi," Scott calls, throwing the ball to her left.

Violet dives for it, a breeze ruffling her hair, the sun warm on her bare limbs. She can't remember when she last felt so carefree. Plucking the ball from the air just before it touches the lawn, she pokes her tongue out at Scott. "Hah, you'll have to do better than that to beat these reflexes."

"Aunt Vi!" Lottie giggles. "Mummy tells me off for sticking my tongue out."

"We'd better not tell her then, had we? I don't want to get into trouble." Violet smiles at her niece and gently tosses her the ball. "Catch."

Lottie hugs it to her chest in triumph. Then, with a look of great exertion, she grasps the ball in both hands and throws it. "Uncle Scott!"

Catching him off guard, the ball bounces off his head and flies over the lawn to land in a flowerbed. Lottie scampers off to retrieve it, shrieking with laughter.

"Seems my own reflexes could use sharpening up." Grinning, Scott comes over to take Violet's hand. "Must be dulled by all those cocktails."

"You're not the only one hung over, you know. You're unfit, that's your trouble."

Laughing, they watch as Lottie extracts the ball from the Busy Lizzies.

"She's a sweet kid," Scott says. "Not like those other little horrors." He nods towards the distant hedge, through which the 'little horrors' can be heard splashing about in the pool under the supervision of Tim and Phoebe.

"Guess they take too much after Carla," Violet agrees, "but I'm sure they'll turn out okay. Can't fail to with a dad like Tim."

Lottie rejoins them, the ball clutched in her arms. "Are you boyfriend and girlfriend?"

"I don't know." Violet keeps a straight face with difficulty. "Sort of, I suppose, although it's pushing it to call me a girl."

"I know, twenty-eight is positively ancient," Scott says.

Violet slaps his arm. "I'm three years older than you, Mister, and everyone knows you shouldn't cheek your elders."

"But you do love each other," Lottie persists. "You're holding hands, so you must."

"Can't argue with that." Scott squeezes Violet's fingers, smiling into her eyes in a way that makes her heart sputter.

"Are you going to get married?" Lottie's face is alive with interest. "Can I be a bridesmaid?"

Violet laughs. "I've no idea. Your uncle hasn't asked me."

"But you will, won't you, Uncle Scott? You will ask Aunt Vi to marry you?"

"Lottie, you can't force people into proposing. Your uncle might not want to marry me."

"But he must, or he wouldn't have kissed you in the kitchen earlier."

"We should probably listen to her," Scott says, drawing a blushing Violet to his side. "Lottie obviously knows far more about these things than we do." He grins down at his niece. "And when I do ask your aunt to marry me, you'll be the prettiest bridesmaid the world has ever seen."

***

"I never imagined two such hung over people could look so happy," Olivia says, pulling up a chair beside Joel's on the patio.

He glances up from his Ian Rankin with a smile. "I know. What did you say to Scott to make him see sense?"

"Nothing he didn't already know. I just helped him see things more clearly."

"Well, I'm pleased for them. I really think Vi could be the making of Scott, help him settle down."

"Tame him, you mean? Like you did me?"

Joel grins. "Something like that."

Olivia leans back with a sigh, relieved to take the weight off her feet. She puts a hand to her stomach in a now familiar gesture, feeling the shape of her growing baby. He seems to be getting heavier by the day. Even without the scan, she would have known it's a boy.

"How's he doing?" Joel asks, watching her.

"Resting, I think, thank goodness." Olivia pats her stomach fondly. "Probably worn out after all the shifting about he's been doing these past couple of days. Whoops, watch out, Scott!"

Laughing, they watch as the ball wallops Scott on the head and Lottie runs off in pursuit. Olivia glances sideways at Joel. How much more relaxed he looks, his eyes alight with amusement, the lines of tension smoothed from his brow.

"You seem better," she says, taking his hand. "Are you?"

Joel interlocks his fingers with hers. "Much. Things have been getting on top of me lately, but having some time out has really helped me put them in perspective."

"I'm glad." Clambering to her feet, Olivia kisses him before going inside to start on dinner. She casts a wistful glance back at the patio. If only she could sit a while longer. Still, if this get together gives Joel and the rest of the family a break from their worries, all her hard work will be worth it.

**

As she stands under the shower with hot water cascading over her skin, Phoebe's earlier anger withdraws to a distant recess of her mind. She overreacted, she knows. She was simply terrified by the idea of Rafe losing his beloved Cameron's and furious with Joel for putting it at risk. Still, Carla was right. Joel is a sensible man and wouldn't want to jeopardize the business any more than Rafe. It's his livelihood, too, after all. Besides, out here, surrounded by gorgeous countryside and far away from the chaos of city life, it's impossible to dwell on anything so bleak as the recession.

Phoebe tilts her face up to the spray, revelling in her previously unimagined happiness. She has spent a wonderful afternoon fooling around in the pool with Tim and his children. Tim is such a kind man, and Emma and Adam are too adorable for words. How lucky Carla is. For once, Phoebe acknowledges her friend's good fortune without envy. Perhaps, some day very soon, she will have a family of her own.

Rubbing shampoo into her hair, Phoebe can't prevent a smile as she relives the hour in the hayloft with Rafe that morning. He made love to her with such gentle consideration, not once drawing attention to her inexperience, all the while gazing into her eyes with such tenderness that it seemed impossible any woman had ever been so cherished. In that moment, Phoebe knew she would never want any man but him. Please, God, she prays, rinsing the suds from her hair, give me Rafe for the rest of my life and I'll do everything in my power to make him happy.

Turning off the shower, Phoebe wraps herself in her bathrobe and pads next door to her bedroom. She takes a lot of trouble drying her hair, combing and styling it as Carla has taught her, until the dark curls fall in a soft cloud about her shoulders. She then massages scented body lotion into her skin, the skin that earlier came alive at Rafe's touch, before slipping into the lilac skirt and sleeveless blouse, which Carla says so suits her. After applying her make-up, she examines her reflection in the mirror. Not exactly Miss World, but hopefully she'll do Rafe proud.

Insides fluttering at the prospect of an evening spent with Rafe and—she shivers in anticipation—perhaps another hour in the hayloft after dinner, Phoebe opens her bedroom door. The tempting aroma of garlic and herbs wafts up the stairs from the kitchen and her stomach rumbles. All that swimming with the children must have given her an appetite. About to set off along the landing, she glances up at the sound of feet descending the attic stairs.

"Hello," she says with a smile. "I was just thinking about you."

Behaving as though she hasn't spoken, Rafe brushes past and continues along the passage.

Phoebe follows, confused. "Rafe, is everything okay?"

"Fine," he says without looking round. "Why shouldn't it be?"

"No reason." Phoebe falters. What can have gotten into him? Oh, God. A horrible thought occurs to her. Surely he can't have found out about Joel and the illegal contract. Quickening her pace to catch up, she tries to take his arm. "Please, it's obvious something's up. You can tell me, whatever it is."

"I just said I was fine, didn't I? Give it a rest."

Phoebe snatches her hand away as though bitten. Why is he being like this? It's as if he can't even bear her to touch him. What's changed? In a flash of terrible clarity, the truth hits her. She freezes where she stands, cold with the inevitability of it. This is all her fault. There can be no other explanation.

"Rafe, wait." Blinking back tears, she calls to him as he starts down the stairs. "Please, what did I do wrong? Whatever it is, I'll put it right, I swear."

Halfway to the hall below, Rafe swings to confront her. "For Christ sake! I've got enough on my plate without listening to your whining. You're so wet, you know that? No wonder you've never found yourself a man."

Phoebe gasps, recoiling from the icy venom in his gaze. Her knees give and she puts a hand out to steady herself against the wall. She tries to speak, but no sound emerges. She can only watch as Rafe stalks down the stairs and out of sight. Oh, God. She moans, wrapping her arms about her chest. It feels as though her heart will tear in two. God, what have I done? Unable to see her way through a mist of tears, Phoebe uses the wall to guide her back along the landing to her room. Stumbling inside, she pushes the door to and collapses on the bed.

Face buried in the pillow, she sobs as she hasn't since her school days. How can she truly have thought Rafe wanted her? Why would someone as handsome and successful choose a plain nobody like her when he could have any girl he fancies? To think she actually fooled herself into believing he desires her, that he considers her beautiful. God, one look at her naked body and it's a wonder he hadn't fled. Doubtless only his consideration for her feelings forced him to carry on. What a bitter disappointment she must have been.

Oh, how can anything hurt so much? That time in the hayloft was so magical, a memory she would have treasured forever, but the realization that Rafe viewed it as nothing more than a trial to be endured turns it into something shameful, humiliating. Just like that other time. The dream she harbors of living out the rest of her days with Rafe, of bearing his children and sharing his bed, is simply that. A dream. Without it, her life has no meaning.

Fifteen

"Dinner's ready," Olivia calls, emerging onto the patio. Friends again after the ball incident, the children are clowning about on the lawn with Joel. "Come and sit up, please."

"What're we having?" Rafe looks up from the *Financial Times*. "Smells delicious."

"Chicken in white wine sauce. Hope it's okay. Speaking of wine, can I get anyone another drink?"

As she fills their glasses, Olivia detects an atmosphere and studies the group more closely. A little apart from the rest, Violet and Scott have their heads bent over Joel's puzzle book as they debate crossword solutions in low voices. Rafe, too, seems relaxed, leaning back in his chair with the paper. No, the blame for the awkwardness lies with the silent couple partway down the table, Tim staring into the distance, mouth set in a grim line, Carla gripping the stem of her wine glass as though she intends to snap it in two. *Please don't say they've had a row.* Carla's sulks, though rare since Tim is so amenable, are legendary for their power to chill even the most convivial mood.

"Dinner won't be a minute," Olivia assures the table at large, emptying the remains of the bottle into Tim's glass. "Does anyone know where Phoebe is?"

"Went up to have a shower when we came out of the pool." Tim takes a huge gulp of wine. "I thought she'd be down by now."

"I'll go and root her out," Carla says, and, looking more anxious than Olivia feels the situation warrants, hurries indoors.

Rafe watches her go with an amused smirk, then glances over the *Financial Times* at Tim. "Seen this article on one of our rivals going bust? It makes for interesting reading."

Tim doesn't look at him. "Unlike you, I don't take pleasure in the downfall of others, rivals or otherwise."

Rafe shrugs and returns to the paper. Olivia regards them curiously. It isn't like Tim to snap, least of all at his family. What can have upset him?

At a peal of hysterical laughter, she looks up in exasperation to see her husband still fooling about with the kids. "Joel, didn't I just tell you lot to come and sit up? Dinner will be ready in two minutes, and anyone who's not at the table by then will go to bed on an empty stomach, adults included."

***

The heart-rending sobs bring Carla up short. For an instant, it's as if she has been transported back in time, back to her first year of secondary school, when she came across Phoebe bawling her eyes out in the girls' toilets. Then, it was because some of their classmates had stamped on her glasses. Now, Carla fears what has been broken will be far harder to mend. Rushing into the room without knocking, she sits on the edge of the bed and pulls Phoebe into her arms.

"Sshhh," she says, rocking her gently back and forth. "It's all right. Everything's all right."

"It isn't." Phoebe is shaking so much her words are almost impossible to decipher. "N-nothing will ever be all right. Rafe doesn't want me, Carla. He doesn't want me."

"Of course he does. Only this afternoon you were telling me how good things are between you."

"Not anymore. I must have been an awful let down for him, being so ugly and having no experience. Now he finds me so disgusting he can't even bear to be near me. He said I'm wet, that it's little wonder no man has ever wanted me, and he's right."

Carla's arms tighten around her as the blood pounds in her ears. How dare he! How dare Rafe torture Phoebe like this simply because she, Carla, refused to give in to his demands. Hadn't he listened to a word she'd said about the fragility of Phoebe's confidence? Does he even care? God, what a stupid question. Of course he doesn't care. If he did, he wouldn't have tried to blackmail another woman into his bed.

Aware of Phoebe's tears drenching her shoulder, Carla makes an effort to speak calmly. "Phoebs, I know it feels like the end of the world but I promise you it's not. Rafe's a bastard who doesn't deserve you. You'll find someone else, someone decent who'll love you the way you should be loved."

"You don't understand." Phoebe pushes herself away to glare at Carla. With her swollen face and her eyes wild and brimming with tears, she looks deranged. "I don't want anyone else. I'll never love anyone the way I love Rafe. He means everything to me. Everything. How can I go on without him?"

A chill crawls over Carla's skin, carrying with it the memory of that terrible night. She shivers. During their first term of university, a guy on their course asked Phoebe to go out with him. She was reluctant at first, sure she would make a fool of herself, but Carla talked her round.

"You'll have a great time," she said. "Mike seems like a really nice guy and he obviously fancies you if he's invited you to dinner."

Eventually, just as she always did, Phoebe trusted Carla's judgment and went on the date. It almost cost her her life. Carla will never forget the image of her friend collapsed on the bedroom floor, the front of her dress covered in vomit, an empty bottle of pills beside her. Later, she learned the full horror of what happened: how the young man seduced Phoebe into his bed, only to taunt her afterwards that the whole evening had been nothing more than a bet between him and his mates. Carla vowed then that she would never again allow a man to hurt Phoebe. And I've failed, she thinks, despising herself for her carelessness, her stupidity. How could I have let Phoebe within ten feet of Rafe and his wandering hands? This is all my fault.

"Listen to me." Carla grips Phoebe shoulders, fear making her rough. "You mustn't do anything stupid. Promise me. Rafe's not worth that."

Phoebe says nothing. She simply gazes back at her, the mingled defiance and desperation in her eyes offering no comfort. Fighting panic, Carla tries to think rationally. She has to stop Phoebe resorting to anything drastic.

"Wait here," she says, standing up, "and don't you dare move a muscle until I get back."

Carla hurries to her own room where she kneels to pull her suitcase out from under the bed. At the bottom, she unearths the bottle of sleeping pills the doctor prescribed for those nights when her overactive mind won't let her rest. Tipping two into her palm, she stops off in the bathroom to fill a tooth mug from the tap, then returns to Phoebe. To her relief, she's still sitting exactly as she left her.

"Here." Carla presses the tablets and water into her hands. "Take these."

Phoebe shows no curiosity about the pills. She simply swallows them obediently, before allowing Carla to help her undress and get into bed.

"There, you'll sleep now." Carla smoothes the covers. "Things won't seem so bad in the morning."

Phoebe says nothing, her eyelids already beginning to droop. Carla sits on the edge of the bed to watch over her until she is certain Phoebe has fallen asleep. Soon, her ragged breathing grows even and oblivion wipes the lines of pain from her face. Satisfied, Carla leaves her and goes downstairs, wishing she could forget her own turmoil so easily.

***

Hefting the stack of pudding bowls, definitely heavier than usual, onto the draining board, Olivia leans against the worktop and closes her eyes. If only she could leave her family to fend for themselves and slip up to bed. Resting her head against the wall cupboard, she reaches round to rub her aching back.

Dinner, far from the relaxed affair of the previous evening, had been downright uncomfortable. After informing the group that Phoebe was feeling unwell and wouldn't be joining them, Carla spent the meal pushing her food around her plate and hardly speaking to anyone. Joel made a stab at mediating between Tim and Rafe but was soon forced to admit defeat, while Scott and Violet were too wrapped up in each other to notice anything amiss. Thank heavens for the children. With that egotism only the very young possess, they were blissfully unaware of any awkwardness and chatted away with blithe unconcern. Without them, Olivia can't imagine how they would have got through the evening.

"Liv?" Joel's anxious voice cuts into her thoughts.

Opening her eyes, she attempts a smile. "Just recovering from that ordeal."

"Wasn't it a nightmare?" Joel comes over to wrap his arms about her middle. "I felt like banging my brothers' heads together."

"Rafe must have really upset Tim for him to behave like that. What did he do?"

"Oh, the usual, putting the boot into Carla again."

"I should've guessed. Tim puts up with a lot of things, but he won't stand for anyone criticizing Carla. Nor should he. So, what was it this time? More about how she's allegedly planning to take control of Cameron's?"

"No, Rafe was actually having a go at her for being too beautiful, can you believe?"

"Cheek," Olivia says, laughing. "How dare Tim have the gall to fall in love with a gorgeous girl. What does Rafe think? That he should have passed her over for some plain Jane?"

Joel grimaces. "That's exactly what he thinks. Apparently, beautiful women are far more likely to cheat on their husbands because of all the temptation put their way."

"That's the most ridiculous thing I've ever heard! As if Carla would ever cheat on Tim."

"I know. It's just Rafe being Rafe. Should I talk to him, suggest that it might be an idea to apologize?"

"Please." Sighing, Olivia rests her head on his shoulder. "I don't think I can cope with another meal like that one."

Joel looks down at her. "Sure you're all right? You're a bit pale."

"I'm fine. Just my late night catching up with me." She disentangles herself from his arms. When Joel still looks anxious, she gives him her brightest smile. "You're such a worrier. Everyone will be gone tomorrow afternoon and then I promise to put my feet up."

***

Once the others have gone to bed, Scott takes Violet's hand to lead her through the starlit grounds. With her fingers warm in his and night air filling his lungs, its earthy freshness better than any drug, he can pretend he hasn't a care in the world. Just as he's been pretending all that brilliant afternoon.

"You're looking very serious," Violet says. "Care to share?"

Scott looks at her. The breeze toys with her hair, blowing a strand across her cheek, and her eyes are soft with love. Should he tell her? Is this the moment to confront her with what he has done, to wipe the happiness from her expression and watch it replaced with shock and disbelief? He opens his mouth to say the words, 'Vi, there's something I need to tell you,' but they don't come. He can't do it. Not yet. Let them have this one enchanted night together, untainted by anger or recriminations. He owes her that much.

Scott manages to smile. "I was only thinking how lucky I am to have you. Most people would have told me where to go after the way I treated you."

"Ah, but I'm not most people." Violet smiles, too. "So, no regrets?"

"What do you think?" Pausing beneath a large oak, Scott pulls her close and kisses her. "And you? Not having second thoughts?"

"If that's a subtle attempt to get rid of me, Scott Cameron, I'm afraid it won't work. You're stuck with me now, for better or worse."

"I'll hold you to that."

They continue walking, Scott's arm around Violet's waist, her head on his shoulder.

"It's a beautiful night," Violet says. "If my job didn't tie me to the city, I'd consider moving out here."

"Then that's what we'll do. When we both retire, probably when we're old and gray, we'll buy a little cottage with roses round the door."

"You old romantic. Aren't you being just a tad optimistic, though? You'll probably be tired of me long before I get my first gray hair."

"Now you're the one trying to get rid of me. For better or worse, remember?" With his free hand, Scott unlatches the gate in the hedge and leads Violet onto the lawn framing the pool.

"What're you doing?" she asks, laughing, as he flops onto the grass at the water's edge and draws her down beside him.

"I'll give you one guess." Scott pushes her gently back onto the lawn and kisses her.

"Hmmm, can't imagine. What would anyone think if they looked out of the window?"

"They'd be wildly jealous. I know I would be if I saw you with anyone else."

Violet lets out her breath in a sigh of pleasure, eyes closing as he begins to undress her. He takes his time, mouth never far from hers, spinning out the moment. When she finally lies naked before him, Scott catches his breath at the sight of her, lithe and supple as a dancer, skin glowing in the moonlight.

"How did I stay away so long?" he says, half to himself, stroking his way down her belly to the soft swell of her hips. "I'm so sorry."

"You're here now. That's what matters." Voice husky, Violet pulls him down to the grass. "Just look at those stars. They never shine like that in London."

"Bright are the stars that shine," Scott murmurs against her neck, "dark is the sky. I love you, Vi. Don't you ever forget it."

***

"Carla?" Tim's voice comes suddenly through the darkness. "What's wrong? You're fidgeting worse than the kids."

She starts. "Sorry, didn't mean to keep you awake. I just can't seem to settle."

"Poor you. Did you bring your pills?"

"They're in my suitcase. I'll take some in a bit. Think I'll go and check on Phoebs first, though, see if she's okay."

"I'm sure it's just a touch of sunstroke," Tim says. "We were in the pool for a good couple of hours this afternoon. Still, maybe getting up for a while will help you sleep."

"Bound to." Dropping a soft kiss on his mouth, Carla slips out of bed and wraps her silk dressing gown around her naked body. "No need to wait up for me."

Once on the landing, she pauses outside Phoebe's room to peer through the partially open door. Phoebe is sound asleep, her breathing deep and even, but Violet's bed is empty. With any luck she and Scott are still downstairs. Otherwise, they might be sharing the spare attic room originally intended for Adam. She'll have to tread carefully.

Casting a quick glance around to check no one's watching, Carla starts up the attic stairs. The ancient boards creak under foot and she halts at each sound, heart thumping. More than once, she almost loses her nerve and flees back to the safety of Tim's arms, but the image of Phoebe's stricken, tear-blotched face lends her courage. Rafe can't be allowed to shatter Phoebe's brittle confidence, the confidence Carla has worked so hard over the years to build up. She won't allow it, no matter the cost to herself.

And what about Tim? The question snakes into her mind, arresting her on the attic landing. *How would he feel if he knew what you're doing, or don't you care?* Pain shoots through her, so intense that she leans against the wall, fighting nausea. How can she even be considering doing this to

Tim, sweet, trusting Tim, her soul mate of the past eight years, who worships the ground she walks on? She spoke the truth when she told Rafe she's never so much as looked at another man. And now she's about to betray Tim in the worst possible way.

But what choice do I have? The desperate question echoes in Carla's head. Well, answers the rational part of her brain, for one thing, you could tell Tim the truth. Hope flares inside her. A way out. She imagines returning to her room and telling Tim the depths to which Rafe has sunk in order to trick his own brother's wife into bed, imagines a rage-maddened Tim confronting Rafe with the unforgivable betrayal, and Phoebe's devastation when she hears of it.

Carla's hope dies. She recalls again Phoebe sprawled unconscious on the floor of her university room, face drenched in sweat and tears, the telltale bottle of pills beside her. Carla had been to blame; she should never have pushed her into going on that date. Well, this time she won't fail her. If Phoebe ever learns how Rafe used her to get to Carla, her own best friend, it will destroy her. She's bound to do something drastic and this time she might not live to tell the tale. It's not a risk Carla is willing to take.

As for Tim … Agony deals her another blow to the heart. Tim can't be hurt by something he doesn't know about, and Rafe won't want to risk destroying their family any more than she. This is the only way to ensure no one gets hurt. Inhaling a strengthening breath, she calms her nerves. Best get this over with.

The door to her right stands open, revealing the room beyond to be empty. At least she doesn't have to worry about Scott and Violet overhearing. Rafe's door is closed, but the faint light seeping from beneath it suggests he's still awake. Darting one last glance down the stairs to assure herself she isn't being observed, Carla slips inside.

As the door clicks shut behind her, Rafe looks up from his book. Stretched out on his bed in only his boxer shorts, he raises his eyebrows. "Carla, what an unexpected pleasure. What can I do for you?"

"Don't play games, Rafe. You know why I'm here." Carla folds her arms, averting her eyes from his chest outlined in the glow of the bedside lamp. "How could you be so foul to Phoebe? You realize what this has done to her? She's in pieces."

Rafe shrugs. "I did warn you not to come running to me if you didn't like the consequences. Of course, if you've reconsidered my proposal …"

He lets the sentence peter out, but his unspoken words reverberate inside Carla's head. She clenches her fists. "I don't see that you've left me any choice."

"There's always a choice, Carla." Setting aside his book, he swings his legs off the bed and approaches. "Still, I knew I could count on you to make the right decision. I promise you won't regret it."

"I already do," she retorts. "Please don't imagine for a second I want to do this."

"We'll see." Depriving Carla of the chance to argue, Rafe lays his hands on her shoulders and kisses her.

The shock of another man's mouth on hers stuns her into immobility. All the strength seeps from her limbs; she can't move. Then, as Rafe's tongue expertly teases her lips apart and his hands slide inside her dressing gown, her body responds. Even as her brain is repelled and screams at her to stop, desire roars through her like a forest fire, wild, relentless, setting light to everything in its path. Of their own volition, her hands creep around his neck to pull him closer, fingers tangling in his hair, and her dressing gown tumbles to the carpet. His skin brushes hers and she stifles a moan.

"God, you're beautiful," Rafe breathes, voice ragged, as he trails kisses down her neck and over her shoulders. "Have you any idea how long I've wanted you?"

At the sound of his voice, common sense penetrates her desire. "Rafe, we can't. Not here, not now. Tim will be wondering where I am."

"Rubbish." His mouth travels down to her breast, gentle, teasing. "He'll be fast asleep, trusting soul that he is."

"But Scott. He could come in at any minute."

"What? When he has a sexy lawyer to keep him occupied? Nah, take it from me, he won't be sleeping in here tonight. Besides, we can't stop now." Rafe runs his hands down over her ribs and around her waist to draw her close. "Stop fighting it. Let yourself go."

Carla shakes her head, but, powerless to resist, she allows him to draw her down to the carpet and into the darkness of the unknown.

Some time later, legs trembling so much they can barely support her, shivering from the cold water used to remove all trace of Rafe from her body, she steals back into her own room. Just as Rafe predicted, Tim is sound asleep. For a while, Carla simply stands by the bed to study his face, the face that means more to her than any other in the world. Remorse and self-disgust roil in her stomach. How could she have betrayed him so abominably? Worse still, how could she have enjoyed it? Careful not to disturb him, she climbs back between the sheets and tilts her face from him. At least, if he should wake, he won't see the tears pouring down her cheeks.

Part 3
Sunday

Sixteen

This time the dream was clearer. She felt the wooden planks rough against her fingers, the dull ache of cramp pinching her legs from staying still too long. A breeze stirred the leaves that concealed her hiding place; it brushed cool fingers up her arms and over her face, and she shivered despite the warmth of the day. Most potent of all was the fear. Hot and cold at the same time, it coiled around her like a boa constrictor, crushing the strength out of her.

Unable to move, she peered through the gap in the branches at the swimming pool below, turquoise streaked with gold in the afternoon sunshine. A shadow loomed over the water, elongated and distorted, full of menace. She made out the two figures on the ground. What were they doing? Was this a strange game only adults understood? Yes, that's what it was. Just a game. But this wasn't right. Surely they should stop now. She tried to look away, didn't want to see. But terror held her in place. It's only a game. Only a game. Her breath came in ragged bursts. Someone would hear her. They mustn't. Had to be quiet. She couldn't be found. Not here. Not now. Where was Mummy? *Please, Mummy, hurry up and come.*

"Oh, my God!" A cry rent the stillness, sharp with horror. "Oh my God, what have you done?"

And then she was falling … falling … falling …

Lottie jolted awake. She was shaking as though racked by a fever, and she gulped in great lungfuls of air like a person saved from drowning. This time, the dream had been so much worse, so terrifyingly real, and the sense of horror took longer to let go. She stared into the darkness, trying to recall what she had seen in that dreadful moment, what could have filled her with such revulsion. It eluded her, lurking just out of reach.

Gradually, her heart rate slowed and she breathed more easily. She was safe now, safe in her own bed. There was nothing to frighten her here. Nevertheless, the certainty that she had witnessed something too awful to contemplate remained with her. But what was it? Why could she never remember? The answers were there somewhere, tangled up in her brain. She only had to unravel them. Then again, she wondered, rolling onto her other side to try and go back to sleep, did she even want to?

***

Olivia tossed and turned long into the early hours. Each time she tottered on the verge of sleep, guilt prodded her awake. No matter how hard she tried to shut it out, her final words to her sister, "You can't accept you might have been to blame," replayed in her head and she saw again Vi's stricken face. She shouldn't have said those things. True, Violet's theory was ridiculous; the fact that she could even entertain the idea that a member of Scott's own family had murdered him, utterly barbaric. Still, she shouldn't have lashed out when she knew her sister's state of mind was so brittle. Vi wasn't crazy, Olivia didn't believe that for a second, but keeping her grief locked away inside for all these years couldn't be healthy.

Beside her, the regular creak of bedsprings warned that Joel also lay awake, perhaps wrestling with his own guilt, or else taut with desire for the other woman, the one who had tempted him from the familiar and into the excitement of the unexplored. Olivia closed her mind to the thought, but not before it sliced yet another piece from her heart. She couldn't think about that now on top of everything else.

When the alarm clock's illuminated digits displayed three-thirty, Joel's voice floated out of the darkness. "You awake?"

She contemplated ignoring him, but what was the point? Her restlessness must be as evident as his.

"Yes," she said, swallowing the lump in her throat. His words brought back memories of times gone by, when she'd been unable to sleep for fretting over Lottie or a subplot in her latest novel she couldn't make work. Joel would hold her, talking softly and smoothing away her anxiety until she fell asleep.

Joel was silent for a while, as though considering his next words. At last, he said, "Liv, we can't go on like this."

"I know." The strain of playing the cheerful hostess, of pretending to her family that all was well, smiling at Joel across the dinner table when inside she longed alternately to slap him and throw herself into his arms, proved harder with each mealtime.

"We need to talk." Clearly sensing a chink in her armor, Joel applied the pressure. "We made a promise to each other, remember? If ever there was a problem, we said we'd talk about it, that we'd always keep the channels of communication open."

A problem? Olivia almost laughed. Surely he appreciated they were dealing with more than a minor hitch. And what happened to the promise Joel made her on their wedding day, that he would be faithful to her as long as he lived? For an instant, she was tempted to confront him with Violet's opinion of his character and how she suspected him of doing away with his own brother. Hurting as she was, she still couldn't bring herself to wound him deliberately.

"Not now," she said, weary to her bones. "I haven't got the energy. Just wait till New Year when everyone's gone home, and then I promise we'll sit down and decide where we go from here."

Olivia expected him to argue. However, perhaps realizing any protests would harm his cause, Joel did not speak again. An interminable time later, his even breathing told her he had finally fallen asleep. Olivia lay beside him for a while longer, but when the clock read a quarter past five she gave up. Slipping out of bed, she pulled on her dressing gown and fluffy slippers against the chill and crept downstairs to make a cup of tea.

"Oh." Pushing open the kitchen door, she paused at the sight of her sister huddled at the table in her dressing gown. "Hello."

Violet lifted her chin from her hands. She was as pale and puffy-eyed as Olivia felt. "Hello."

Olivia hovered in the doorway, assailed by a fresh wave of remorse. "Want a cup of tea?"

"Thanks, already have one." Violet indicated the mug before her.

Olivia came in and closed the door. As she passed the table on her way to the sink, she noticed the untouched contents of Violet's mug and the scum forming on its surface. "All the same, you look as though you could use a fresh cup."

Her sister made no move to stop her as she whisked away the mug and tipped the cold tea down the plughole. Olivia busied herself filling the kettle and dropping a teabag into the pot, all the while conscious of a silence heavy with the words that had passed between them and those still needing to be said. She hated falling out with Violet, but this was worse. And she knew she was mostly to blame.

Setting the mugs on the table, Olivia took a deep breath. "Sorry about last night."

Violet accepted the tea, eyebrows raised. "Are you?"

"Well, of course I am. You know I'd never set out to upset you. I was angry, that's all. Everything seems to be sliding out of my control." Sighing, Olivia flopped into the chair across from her sister and wrapped her hands around her own mug. "You do understand, don't you, why I've always tried so hard to protect Lottie?"

Violet nodded, gaze lowered.

"I'm not saying you weren't right," Olivia went on. "Perhaps it wasn't healthy to discourage Lottie from regaining her memory, but I just kept thinking, suppose she did see something that day? What if it's best she forgets?"

"Liv, you don't have to explain. I totally overstepped the mark, interfering like that. I'm sorry."

"Well, I suppose Lottie was bound to find out the truth sooner or later. Anyway, I do see why you had to ask, had to know."

"Still, that's no excuse." Violet sunk her chin into her hands, looking much older than her forty years. "I shouldn't have taken advantage of Lottie. It's just so hard sometimes not knowing, never being sure."

"You don't really believe Scott was murdered, though? Not really."

"I did. It all made perfect sense inside my head, but, out loud, I could hear how crazy it sounded. You certainly think I've lost my marbles, don't you?"

"I wouldn't say that. Perhaps just mislaid them temporarily."

A grin lit up Violet's face, the same wicked grin that must have captivated Scott all those years before. Thankful she had patched things up between them, Olivia smiled back.

***

Sitting up in bed, Carla watched Tim's face by the sunlight peeping through the curtains. Anxiety seemed to plague him even in sleep; it was evident in the frown corrugating his brow and the new lines fanning out around his eyes. Carla resisted the urge to smooth them away like wrinkles from a tablecloth. She despised herself, knowing she was in part to blame for his troubles. At least she had gone some way to repairing the damage. If only she could be sure Tim wouldn't hold it against her.

Oh, she knew what others thought of her, what Joel, in particular, thought. Even before the rift, he had never trusted her completely, believing she would take advantage of Tim's generosity and use it to her own ends. Acid burned her stomach at the injustice of it. What right had anyone to judge her? Okay, so she'd made mistakes, done things she could hardly bear to contemplate, but she had only ever wanted the best for Tim. She might bully him into giving more dinner parties than he would choose, might spur him on to reach greater heights within the company than would otherwise be possible, but Tim knew she did it solely because she wanted him to achieve his full potential. At least, Carla hoped he knew.

Tim's eyes fluttered open and he gave her the slow, sweet smile that still held the power to melt her heart. "You're looking grim. Have I sprouted warts in the night?"

"I did say I'd take you warts and all." Carla tried to smile, but couldn't quite manage it. Aware of Tim's gaze on her, she lowered her eyes to her hands as they twisted the duvet.

"What is it?" Rolling onto his side, Tim draped an arm across her stomach. "You're not still fretting over this thing with Joel?"

"Can you blame me? This whole stupid situation is my fault. If only I'd realized—"

"How could you? It was only yesterday that Joel gave me a clue as to what I'm supposed to have done. Anyway, you weren't to know. I'm surprised you can even remember. It was so long ago."

Carla tilted her head to look at him, still uncertain. "So you're not angry? No one could blame you if you were."

"Tell me, when have I ever been angry with you? The important thing is that I know now and can try to put things right. Come here." Tim drew her down beside him and held her close. "You look exhausted. If I know you, you've been lying awake all night worrying."

Carla nestled against him, fuzzy with relief. "I thought you might never forgive me."

"You silly thing. What did you think I'd do? Divorce you for withholding vital evidence?" Tim kissed her softly. "How about we have a lie-in this morning?"

"Suits me." With Tim's arms around her, reassuring her of his love, all was right with her world.

***

"Typical," Emma grumbled, staring out of the dining room window at the brilliant sunshine. "The only snow I get to see in years and it's melting."

"You were complaining yesterday that it was too wet," Adam said. "Make up your mind."

"Go and enjoy it while it lasts," Olivia advised, as she cleared away the breakfast things. "Put some color in your cheeks."

Her eyes rested on Lottie when she said this, and Joel had to agree his daughter looked almost as worn out as Olivia. A glance in the mirror above the fireplace told him his own sleepless night hadn't fared him much better. With the exception of Emma, who glowed with good health, his whole family bore the shadowed eyes and pasty complexions of too little sleep. Insomnia must be catching.

As Olivia added the last plate to the pile, the telephone rang.

"I'll get that," she said before Joel could move. "Lottie, be a love and take this lot through to the kitchen."

With a roll of her eyes Joel felt sure was for her cousins' benefit, Lottie pushed back her chair and hoisted the stack of plates into her arms. Aware that Tim had been attempting to catch his eye throughout breakfast, Joel gathered up several empty mugs and followed his daughter along the passage. Surely Tim couldn't want a repeat of yesterday's conversation. Hadn't they already said everything there was to say?

Dumping the mugs on the worktop, Joel draped his arm around Lottie's shoulders. "You okay? Mum told me you've been having bad dreams again."

Albeit reluctantly, he thought. Until now, he and Olivia had shared everything, believing there was no problem that couldn't be sorted out by talking it through. Last night, however, as they got ready for bed, she had filled him in on the latest developments with the air of a teacher on parents' evening informing him of his child's progress. The memory aggravated the ever-present pang in his gut. Still, at least Olivia's detachment had made Joel's alarm easier to hide. Could it really be that Lottie's memory was returning after all these years? Christ, anything but that. He and Liv had done all in their power to spare her from the horror she might or might not have witnessed, but what if their best efforts hadn't been enough?

"I had it again last night," Lottie said, recalling him to the present. "That's two nights in a row now. Why won't it leave me alone?"

Joel stroked her hair, concealing his unease. "I don't know. Perhaps because this is the first time we've all been together since your Uncle Scott died. Having everyone back here might be triggering something in your memory." *So thank God they would all be leaving the next morning, before their presence could do any further damage.*

"Maybe." Lottie peered up at him, eyes troubled. "Dad, I thought yesterday that I wanted to get my memory back, but now I don't think I do."

Joel hugged her tight. "Don't you go worrying about it. You'll make yourself ill. Everything will be fine. Look, Adam seems to be terrorizing his sister outside. Why don't you go and give him a hand?"

Lottie glanced out of the window to where Adam was chasing Emma through the snow, then at the pile of washing-up on the worktop.

Joel grinned. "It's okay, I know you're allergic to any kind of housework. I'll sort this lot out. You go and make the most of having your cousins here."

"Thanks, Dad," Lottie said, hugging him back, and dashed from the kitchen.

Joel's smile faded along with her footsteps. She would be devastated if he and Liv split up. Trying not to dwell on the unthinkable, he made short work of stacking the dishwasher in case Tim decided to corner him. Then, pouring a fresh mug of tea, he went with it into the hall where Olivia was still on the phone.

Her voice pursued him as he climbed the stairs. "Thanks, Jill, that would have been fun but I've got the family here for the weekend … yes, lovely to have everyone together."

Not for the first time, Joel marveled at his wife's ability to keep her emotions locked away. No one listening to her cheerful exchange would ever guess her heart was breaking. Oh, yes, Olivia was stronger than people thought, and, if he failed to patch up their marriage, he had little doubt she would cope a damned sight better than him. But he couldn't let himself think like that. She'd agreed to talk things over. That had to be a good sign. Clinging to this one shred of optimism, Joel made his way along the passage to poke his head around Phoebe's bedroom door.

"It's me," he said, hoping not to scare her. "Me, Joel."

Propped up against her pillows, Phoebe smiled at him. When Rafe had informed them at breakfast that she was having a much needed lie-in, Joel feared her mental state must have deteriorated. To his relief, however, Phoebe seemed calm. Though she still looked pale and tired, her eyes had lost their frantic terror.

"I've brought you a cup of tea." He advanced into the room. "Thought you might be in need."

Phoebe accepted the mug. "How kind, but you shouldn't have gone to any trouble. I don't want to be a nuisance."

"You could never be a nuisance," Joel said, perching on the edge of the bed. "How're you feeling? You look better."

"I'm fine. Just tired. Rafe insisted I rest, but I'll get up soon. Don't want to put anyone out."

"You won't, I promise. Stay in bed as long as you like. It'll be a late one tonight, remember, seeing in the New Year."

Phoebe nodded, though Joel wasn't sure she'd heard him. She was quiet for some time, staring into the contents of her mug.

"Joel," she said, "I'm going mad, aren't I? Tell me the truth."

Joel's throat constricted. Taking her free hand, he squeezed it. "No, you're not going mad. You're overwrought, that's all. Who wouldn't be? Just hold on till tomorrow and then you'll be able to go home and put your feet up."

Phoebe's smile said plainly, "Put my feet up, married to Rafe? That'll be the day." Joel looked at her, overcome with sadness. Much as he loved his brother, he couldn't help wondering whether Phoebe would have been better off with someone gentler.

He started, dropping Phoebe's hand as the bedroom door opened. Phoebe slopped tea down the front of her nightie. Even before he turned around, Joel knew who it would be.

"Well, well, well," Carla drawled. "This is becoming a bit of a habit, me walking in on the two of you. Anyone would think you're up to something."

"And anyone would think you're spying on us," Joel shot back.

Carla raised her eyebrows. "Now, why should I want to do that? For your information, Mr. Guilty Conscience, I was looking for Rafe, but since he obviously isn't here, I'll leave you to it." And, spearing them with a significant look, she closed the door behind her.

Seventeen

Carla climbed the stairs with a sense of deja vu. She had waited all morning for the chance to get Rafe on his own, and finally, as they sat with Violet and Olivia in the drawing room after lunch, Rafe excused himself. Seeing her chance, Carla gave him a couple of minutes' head start, then followed. As she marched along the landing, she remembered the occasion years before when she had trodden these very floorboards. This time, however, she would be the one in control.

Rafe opened the bathroom door just as she reached it. His mouth twitched at the sight of her, and Carla knew the irony of the situation was not lost on him.

"Couldn't stay away, huh?"

"Not here." Carla glanced pointedly towards the nearby bedroom where Phoebe was still resting before starting up the attic stairs. She didn't need to look over her shoulder; curiosity and the lure of being alone with her would pull him as irresistibly as a fish on a line.

On the landing, she couldn't prevent her eyes from straying to the room which had been Rafe's during their last stay. Behind that closed door, this whole nightmare had begun. Shuddering at the memory, she turned her back and opened the door to her son's room. Once Rafe had preceded her inside, taking the opportunity to brush against her in the confined space, she closed the door and leaned against it, arms folded.

Rafe moved towards her, one eyebrow cocked in amusement. "You really shouldn't look so fierce. You know how it turns me on." He reached out to touch her cheek.

She stiffened. "Don't even think about it."

"What's wrong?" He dropped his arm to his side, looking confused. "I thought this was why you brought me up here."

"God, you haven't changed a bit. Only a man with your over-inflated ego would delude himself into believing I'd want you anywhere near me. What did you think? That I'd give in to my passion right here on the bed where my son will later be sleeping? You make me sick."

Rafe's expression tightened. "Well, since it obviously offends you to be in the same room as me, what can I do for you?"

"You can stay away from my daughter."

"From Emma? You've lost me. Why shouldn't I spend time with my own niece?"

"Don't play the innocent with me, Rafe Cameron. I know better than anyone what you're capable of." Carla advanced, backing him into a corner, and brought her face within an inch of his. "Do you think I haven't seen the way you look at her, that I don't know what's going through your depraved little mind? Well, I won't allow it, you hear me?"

"Sounds to me as though you're jealous," Rafe said. "You needn't be. Tempting though your daughter is, give me an experienced woman any day."

Carla swung her hand back and slapped him across the face. "How dare you! Do you honestly think, given the choice, I'd have let you lay so much as a finger on me? Did you really imagine I enjoyed it with you? God, you're more deluded than I thought. Well, you may have tried to destroy my life, but I won't let you do the same to Emma."

Rafe dropped his gaze, one hand to his reddening cheek. "Don't be like this. I mean Emma no harm, I swear. I might admire her from afar, but can you blame me? She's a stunning young woman, and she reminds me so much of you. It's been so long since we were last together, over two years."

"Yes, and if I remember rightly, I made it clear at the time it wouldn't happen again." Carla stepped away, but Rafe caught hold of her wrist.

"Please, don't do this. I love you, Carla. I've been going out of my mind without you."

"If you love me, you'll do as I ask." Wrenching herself free, she headed for the door. "Stay away from me and my daughter, or I won't be responsible for my actions."

Rafe trailed after her. "Don't go. Not like this. We can work this out, I know we can. You can't seriously want to throw away everything we have. We're so good together."

"About as good as ice cream and gravy," Carla retorted without looking round. "You've put a strain on my marriage for long enough. It's over."

Rafe didn't respond. Had he finally got the message? Hardly daring to hope, Carla reached for the doorknob.

"You're very brave all of a sudden," He said. "Have you forgotten our bargain?"

Carla fixed him with a cold stare. "No, Rafe, I haven't forgotten the way you blackmailed me, how you threatened to leave Phoebe and tell Tim I seduced you if I ever confessed the truth. I just don't believe you're fool enough to act on it. You've had plenty of opportunity these past couple of years, after all, but you've done nothing. However despicable you are, I don't think you'd hurt Phoebe or your own brother just to spite me."

Their eyes met in a charged moment which seemed to last a lifetime. Rafe looked away first. Shoulders slumping, he turned his back on her to stare out of the window. Carla permitted herself a satisfied smile before slipping from the room and down the attic stairs. Served him right. Had he really thought he could go on manipulating her forever? If she'd only had the courage to call his bluff all those years ago, it would have saved her so much heartache.

***

Lottie lay in Adam's arms, her body heavy with a delicious languor. Slivers of sky showed through the cracks in the hayloft's roof, and she drank him in by their feeble light: his thighs, taut and muscular as a jockey, the fine golden hairs covering his chest, his eyes half-closed in drowsy contentment. How was it possible that this gorgeous, self-assured boy had fallen for her, Lottie, so shy she had always been more at home with her horse than her contemporaries?

Yet, even as she revelled in her good fortune, reality nudged at her happiness. With every minute that passed, her precious time with Adam was slipping away. Before long they had to join the rest of the family to see in the New Year, when they would have scant chance of snatching a private moment. The following morning he'd be gone, and who knew when they would see each other again? Just thinking of the imminent separation, of having to say goodbye for the foreseeable future, made Lottie's heart feel as though it were cracking in two.

"I wish you didn't have to go," she said against his neck. "I wish we could stay here like this forever."

"Me, too." Drawing her closer, Adam kissed her. They clung to one another, their limbs so tightly entwined that Lottie wondered whether even an earthquake could tear them apart.

"You know," Adam said some time later, "there are some advantages to us being cousins."

"Such as?"

"Well, for one thing, we can invite each other over to stay whenever we like without our parents thinking anything of it."

"I suppose. But are you sure I wouldn't get in the way of your friends and stuff?"

"Idiot. You know I'd rather be with you than anyone else. Let's sort something out for half term. Dad'll be at work all day, and Mum and Emma are hardly ever in, so we'll have loads of time to ourselves."

"Can't wait." Lottie's spirits lifted as she imagined hour after hour spent alone with Adam, with no one to interrupt them. "And once we've both left home to start uni, we'll be able to see each other whenever we like."

Adam grinned. "And as soon as we've finished our degrees and got jobs, we'll tell our families and move in together, and there'll be nothing they can do to stop us."

Lottie bit her lip, wondering how her parents would react to the news. Mum took most things in stride and would probably be okay with it once she got over the initial shock, but Dad was another matter. Much as he was generally easygoing, Lottie had the feeling he would be furious when he learned what his little girl had been up to.

"It's as good as incest!" She heard the words as clearly as if the confrontation had already taken place, though she suspected her dad's anger would have less to do with her and Adam being cousins, and a whole lot more to do with the rift between him and her uncle.

"How do you think your parents will take it?" Lottie asked.

Adam grimaced. "Badly. Oh, I think Dad will try to understand and maybe he'll even get used to the idea, but Mum'll go ballistic. You know what she's like. She'll have me down to marry the daughter of some millionaire business tycoon, perhaps the owner of another bank so the two firms can form one big moneymaking superpower. You're not what she would have chosen for me, at all."

A coldness stole over Lottie. She grew very still. This was Aunt Carla he was talking about, the Aunt Carla who always made such a fuss of her. Okay, so she had never made any secret of the fact that she and Uncle Tim were so much better off than Lottie's own parents, but surely that didn't mean she considered them beneath her?

Adam looked stricken. "God, I'm sorry. That was a stupid thing to say."

"It's okay," Lottie said, though the joy had seeped out of her.

"No, it isn't." Adam cupped her face in his hands, forcing her to look at him. "You mustn't think I share Mum's prejudices. I love her to bits, don't get me wrong, but even I can see she's obsessed with upholding her status in society. Unless you drive the right car and your kids go to the right school, don't expect an invite to her dinner parties. But none of that's important to me. I couldn't care less how much your parents earn or whether they own a villa in the south of France. It's who you are that matters, nothing else."

"I know, Adam, I know."

"So what is it?"

Lottie shook her head. "It's just, well, what if you'd be better off with the sort of girl your mum wants for you, the sort of girl who'll fit into your world?"

"Don't say that. This isn't about your world and mine. It's about us." Adam gazed deep into her eyes. "I love you, Lottie, and nothing Mum or anyone else says will change that."

***

The moment he heard the crunch of footsteps in the snow behind him, Joel knew he'd made a mistake leaving the house. Without needing to look round, he knew it would be Tim. Damn! He had only wanted some fresh air, to escape the oppressive atmosphere for a while. Still, he should have stuck it out in the drawing room with the others. True, he would have been forced to endure the combined condemnation of Olivia's hurt and Violet's accusing glares, but at least there was relative safety in numbers. Damn and blast it!

"Wait up," Tim said. "We need to talk."

Joel didn't slacken his pace. "I already said everything I had to say yesterday."

"Well, I think there's more to be said. For a start, I owe you an explanation."

"Don't tell me. Your memory's miraculously returned and you've seen the light."

"Something like that. Give me a minute, that's all I ask."

Joel snorted and put on a spurt, widening the distance between them. Why did Tim persist in deluding himself he gave a shit about his so-called explanations? Something heavy thudded into Joel's back, knocking the air from his lungs, and before he knew what was happening, he hit the snow as his twin rugby-tackled him.

"Right," Tim said, knees planted on Joel's chest. "Now will you listen?"

"Get off me," Joel snarled. Icy rivulets oozed down the back of his neck and into his ears, and he tried to shift his brother's weight.

Tim pushed down harder. "Not until you agree to hear me out. Just a few minutes of your time, Joel. That's all I need."

"All right," Joel spat. It wasn't like he had a choice.

Tim removed the pressure from Joel's chest and stood, reaching down to help him up. Joel glowered at the outstretched hand but otherwise ignored it. Shivering with cold, he clambered to his feet and stomped away without another glance. Tim fell into step beside him and they continued in silence for a time. The crisp brightness of the morning had faded to gloom and the snow was a grayish slush beneath their boots.

"Firstly," Tim said, "I had no idea until yesterday why things went wrong between us."

Joel didn't respond.

"No, really," Tim said. "In fact, it was Carla who figured it out."

"Carla?" Joel threw him a sharp look. "Yeah, I might have known the two of you would have a cozy little chat about me."

"She's my wife, Joel. Of course I discuss things with her, just as I know you do with Liv."

Hidden in his coat pockets, Joel's hands clenched into fists. Tim couldn't know how those words taunted him, but resentment seared his insides just the same.

"Still," Tim went on, "whatever my loyalties to Carla, I would never betray your trust. I would never have discussed with her anything you told me in confidence, and I swear to you I haven't so much as breathed a word to Carla or anyone else about the Langdon business."

Joel released his anger in a snort. "Right, silly me. You and Carla have learned to communicate telepathically."

"No." Tim's voice remained calm. "Just give me a minute to explain."

Joel shrugged but did as Tim asked. First with skepticism, then with dawning comprehension, he listened to his brother's story of how, twelve years ago, Carla had come in search of them as they sat by the pool and overheard Joel confessing the lengths to which he had gone to secure Langdon's custom. With each word, Tim stripped the hurt and bitterness from Joel's heart, only to replace these with another emotion he found almost as hard to take.

Once Tim finished, Joel was unable to meet his eye. "So you never did tell Carla."

"Course I didn't." Tim looked at him, his expression sad. "I'd cut out my tongue rather than betray your trust. I thought you knew that."

Neither of them spoke for some time. Only the squelch of their boots in the melting snow infringed on the stillness. Guilt ate away at Joel's stomach like an ulcer. What an idiot he'd been. He should have trusted what he knew of his twin's character, trusted that he would never willingly break his confidence. Instead, he'd allowed his prejudice against Carla to blind him to the truth, and, in so doing, wasted twelve years nursing a grievance that had no grounds.

"I know it isn't enough," Joel said, stopping to face his brother, "but I'm sorry. I should have believed in you. I just put two and two together and made a hundred."

Tim smiled. "Anyone else would have thought the same. I only wish you'd had it out with me years ago."

"Yeah, it was stupid." Joel hesitated, riddled with awkwardness, then held out his hand. "Look, can we start again?"

"There's nothing I'd like more." Tim's seized his hand, his smile broadening. "How about we seal it with a drink? Looks like you could use something to warm you up."

"Thanks to you," Joel said, but he grinned. Spirits lighter than he would have believed possible only moments before, he led the way back to the house.

"Just one more thing," Tim said. "Please don't blame Carla for what happened. When she mentioned the Langdon business to you, she swears she had no idea you'd told me about it in confidence. She never imagined that was the reason behind all the bad feeling, or she would have told me about it years ago. Don't hold it against her. She feels terrible."

Joel considered. Carla had taken a huge risk in revealing so much to Tim, and he could no longer ignore what that meant. Whatever he thought of her, however much he might loathe her guts, her love for Tim was greater than he had ever given her credit for.

"It doesn't matter," Joel said, though the words left a foul taste in his mouth.

* * *

Rafe couldn't stop shaking. He paced the tiny attic room as though the movement might drive that last image of Carla's face, glacial with loathing and contempt, from his mind. Memories leapt out at him from every corner: Carla's eyes greedy with desire, the thrill of her touch on his skin, her laughter warm and teasing against his neck …

He shook his head, trying to clear it. Could he really have been so deluded over her feelings for him? Okay, so he'd pulled a mean trick to get her into bed, something he certainly wasn't proud of, but he only did it because he was so sure Carla's attraction to him equalled his own. Now, his conviction leaked away. Had she truly continued the affair all these years solely to protect her marriage and closest friend? Had she merely been humoring him, pretending to return his passion when really he aroused in her nothing but revulsion? Has she, in fact, never loved him at all? Bile rose in Rafe's throat.

"Uncle Rafe, what're you doing in here?"

He started at the familiar voice, but, with Carla's dire warnings still throbbing in his ears, didn't glance round. Why did his niece have to seek him out now of all times? Her appearance felt like a temptation from the devil, a test to discover whether he could keep his word.

"Uncle Rafe?" Emma repeated, sounding uncertain.

"Leave me alone, Em, would you?" He stopped pacing, but didn't look at her. "I'm not good to be around just now."

"I know the feeling. When I heard someone moving about up here, I thought it might be Lottie and Adam. You haven't seen them, have you?"

"'Fraid not." Rafe went to stand by the window with his back to her, a deliberate dismissal. Every muscle tensed, he waited for the sound of Emma's feet retreating down the attic stairs. The door clicked shut and he relaxed. Yet, instead of fading, her footsteps drew nearer, and, a moment later, she was beside him. Rafe edged away as far as the confined space allowed. His hands balled into fists. For Christ's sake, couldn't she take a hint? If Carla caught them up here alone together, however innocent the circumstances …

"Don't be like that," Emma wheedled. "Everyone else is too busy to talk to me and I'm literally dying of boredom. Even Lottie and Adam keep going off by themselves, like they don't want me around. They're always laughing about something but never let me in on the joke. I hate being left out."

Staring out of the window, Rafe barely heard her. Tim and Joel had gone inside and the grounds were deserted, an expanse of dirty gray snow beneath a darkening sky. In his mind's eye, he pictured the scene in a different time, a different season: sunshine painting the lawn a vivid green and sparkling on the surface of the pool; the smell of charcoal singeing the air; a scream splitting the afternoon stillness, shooting an arrow of fear straight to his heart.

"I don't even have a boyfriend anymore," Emma went on. "So you were wrong about him, Uncle Rafe."

Grateful for the distraction, he turned to look at her. "How so?"

"You said there was no way Jerry would finish with me, but he has. When I finally got hold of him just now, he told me he'd hooked up with some tart at the party on Friday. Well, he didn't exactly call her a tart, but she has to be one, pinching someone else's boyfriend. Anyway, clearly I'm not as irresistible as you think."

"Oh, you don't need to worry on that score. If you remember, I actually said this Jerry would need his head tested to throw away a stunning girl like you. It's his loss."

Emma flashed him her tantalizing smile. "I know. Jerry's an idiot and I can do so much better. I certainly won't lose any sleep over him." She moved closer, putting a hand on his arm. "So, why are you hiding away up here?"

"Oh, you know." Rafe's gaze reverted to the window. Her touch burned through his jumper like a branding iron. "Just thinking about your Uncle Scott."

"Poor Uncle Rafe. It must be hard for you, being back here."

Taking him off guard, she leaned close and pecked him on the cheek. Her long hair tickled his neck and he breathed in her perfume, as addictive and intoxicating as opium. In that moment, as he stared into the eyes dancing like sapphires mere inches from his own, reality drifted away. It was no longer his niece in the room with him. It was Carla, young and beautiful, her expression dazed with desire.

Emma made to step back, but Rafe was too quick. Seizing her by the wrist, he forced her against him and crushed his lips down on hers, prying them apart with his tongue. She struggled, shoving at his chest with desperate strength, but he scarcely noticed. He kissed her on and on, revelling in his power, the delicious softness of her mouth, until the need to breathe compelled him to release her and he pushed her away. She stumbled, but Rafe made no move to help her. He merely watched as she steadied herself against the wall and stared at him, eyes wide with horror.

"Don't look at me like that," he snapped. "You've been driving me to this all weekend and you know it."

"How could you?" Emma said, and her voice shook. "Just you wait till I tell Mum."

Rafe took a step towards her. "You really don't want to do that. I know things about your mother that would make your lovely hair curl. So, unless you want to be responsible for destroying your parents' marriage, I should keep your mouth shut."

"You're bluffing, just trying to keep me quiet."

"Am I? Well, if you're so sure, go ahead and run to Mummy, but don't blame me if your safe little world comes crashing down around your pretty ears."

Emma hesitated, fear battling defiance in her expression, then turned.

"Just one piece of advice," Rafe said. "In future, don't promise what you're not prepared to put out, or, one of these days, you'll get yourself into trouble."

With a strangled sob, Emma flung open the bedroom door and fled. Rafe listened to her clatter away down the stairs. Spite dissipating, overcome with weariness and disgust, he turned to rest his hot forehead against the windowpane. *Christ, Carla, how am I expected to get through the rest of my life without you?*

Eighteen

"That smells delicious," Tim said, as Olivia set a large dish of chilli con carne on the dining-room table.

She smiled, and Joel noticed how much it cost her. "I expect you're used to something a bit grander for a New Year's Eve feast, but it's Lottie's favorite. Can I leave you men to help yourselves? Joel will see to your drinks."

"Aren't you eating anything?" Joel asked. He wanted to say how pale and thin she looked but knew she would resent his concern.

"I'll have something in a bit," she said, avoiding his eye, and made a hasty exit.

Once she had gone, Joel helped himself to a jacket potato and began piling it with chilli, though more to keep up appearances than because he was hungry. Guilt roiled in his stomach and he felt sure he would be unable to keep down a single mouthful. Glancing across the table at Rafe, Joel noticed that he, too, appeared to have lost his usually voracious appetite and was merely toying with his food between huge slugs of whiskey.

Before he could comment on it, Tim touched him on the arm. "Is everything okay between you and Liv?"

A lie sprang to Joel's lips, but, in deference to their recently repaired friendship, he bit it back. "Not really, but I'd rather not talk about it."

"Sure." Tim nodded, though disappointment flickered in his expression.

Joel placed a hand on his shoulder. "I'm not fobbing you off. I will tell you. Just not now. Need to get my head straight."

Tim's smile was warm. "As long as you know I'm here if you need me."

"I know." Conscious again of what a fool he'd been, Joel looked away and found Rafe staring morosely into his empty glass. "And what's up with you, big bro?"

Rafe lifted his head with a grimace. "Nothing getting back to London won't cure. In the meantime, though, I'll have to make do with another drink."

"What a bunch of merry-makers we are." Tim grinned, slapping Joel on the back. "Come on, you two, it's New Year's Eve. We should be celebrating, looking forward to what the next year has in store. Something tells me it's going to be a good one for all of us."

"I wish I shared your optimism," Joel said, and went to refill Rafe's glass.

***

"How're you feeling, Aunt Phoebs?" Lottie asked, curled on one of the drawing room sofas between her paternal aunts. *Merry Christmas, Everyone* played in the background and the fairy lights edging the ceiling cast beads of red, blue, and gold over their faces. "Can I get you anything else to eat?"

"This is all delicious, but if I eat any more I'll burst." Though still pale, Aunt Phoebe smiled with her usual sweetness. "I'm so sorry I haven't seen as much of you as I would have liked." She turned to include Adam in her words.

Lounging on the floor at their feet, he glanced up from his enormous plate of food. "That's okay. Lottie's staying with us over half-term so we'll come and see you then."

Aunt Phoebe's face lit up, but Lottie glanced anxiously at her other aunt. "That is all right, isn't it, Aunt Carla?"

"Darling, you're welcome any time, you know that," she said, at the same time shooting her son an exasperated look. "Although it would have been nice to be asked."

Adam grinned. "I knew you'd want me to be polite and return the invitation."

"Why is it, whenever you put on your best manners, I get the feeling you're up to something?"

"Mum, I'm hurt."

The four of them laughed. Under cover of their mirth, Lottie caught Adam's eye and he flashed her a private smile.

"Last Christmas, I gave you my heart," sang George Michael, "but the very next day, you gave it away."

"Seriously, though," Aunt Carla said, still smiling, "Adam's right. Now that your dad and uncle have patched things up, Lottie, you'll all have to come and stay with us."

"That'd be great." Lottie bent her head over her food. Having her whole family in the London apartment, however spacious it was, would certainly make it harder for herself and Adam to be alone together. As though sensing her disappointment, Adam nudged her knee with his shoulder. Lottie's insides turned to liquid at his touch and her appetite fled.

"Is your mum all right, Lottie?" Aunt Phoebe asked.

Lottie followed her concerned gaze to where her mother knelt before the fire, talking quietly with Aunt Violet. She couldn't help remembering previous New Year's Eves, when, egged on by several glasses of Dad's infamous punch, Mum would be the life and soul of the party, the first to get up and dance or propose a game of Twister.

"I think she's found this weekend tough," Lottie admitted. "Nearly as tough as Aunt Vi. Too many memories, I suppose."

All at once, Aunt Phoebe's expression grew wary.

"You know then?" Aunt Carla said. "And I thought your parents were so set on keeping it from you."

Lottie shrugged, wishing she hadn't brought it up.

Aunt Carla must have taken her silence as a confession, for she flashed Adam a suspicious glance. "I do hope this isn't your doing."

"No," Lottie assured her. "I guessed something was going on when Aunt Phoebs got upset at dinner the first evening, and I asked Mum about it."

Aunt Carla nodded. "You had to find out sooner or later. What exactly did your mum say?"

Lottie shared a fleeting look with Adam. Not wanting to get him and Emma into trouble, she hadn't repeated what they'd told her about Uncle Scott committing suicide. Probably best to keep that to herself for the time being, at least until she had a chance to discuss it with her parents.

After a pause, she said, "Just that Uncle Scott got really drunk and drowned in the pool."

Her aunts exchanged a look, plainly relieved. It seemed all the adults were in agreement that the precise nature of Uncle Scott's death should remain a secret.

"Where's Emma?" Aunt Carla asked, and Lottie had the impression she was deliberately changing the subject. "I haven't seen her since I came downstairs."

"Probably getting something to eat." Adam seemed unconcerned.

Lottie, however, set her plate on the floor and stood, guilt like a stitch in her side. How could she have failed to notice her cousin was missing?

"I'll go and find her," she said.

***

Kneeling to stoke the fire, Olivia found she couldn't get up again. She stayed on the hearthrug staring into the flames, while her family chatted and laughed around her and *I Wish It Could Be Christmas Every Day* drifted through the speakers. The lights had been dimmed, giving the room over to the magic of the fire and the strings of colored bulbs draping the Christmas tree. Olivia couldn't have dreamed up a more perfect setting in which to welcome the New Year. Nor could she remember a time when she had felt less like celebrating.

"You look as though you could use one of these." Kneeling beside Olivia, Violet thrust a tall glass into her hand.

"Thanks." She took a gulp, then choked. "Gosh, Vi, did you put any tonic in this gin?"

Violet shrugged. "Think of it as medicinal, a pick-me-up."

"Is it really so obvious I need picking up?"

"Liv, you look like you're attending your own funeral. Now, drink up."

"Yes, Doc." Olivia took another slug. A comforting fuzziness spread through her and when Lottie wandered over a while later, she was able to smile without too much effort. "Everything okay, sweetheart?"

"Great. I'm just going to find Emma. She's probably still fussing over her make-up." Lottie's worried gaze settled on her face. "But are you all right, Mum?"

"I'm fine," Olivia said, irritated with herself for letting her unhappiness show. "Once everyone's finished eating, we'll have a game of Twister."

Lottie's face brightened and she hurried from the room, graceful and long-legged as a colt. Olivia smiled after her, though her heart ached for what the New Year would bring. Joel's actions had hurt her beyond imagining, but Lottie was just as much a victim. She would lose everything that was familiar to her: the only home she could remember, the wild countryside she adored, her beloved Gypsy and, worst of all, the security of her parents' marriage.

"You see?" Violet's voice broke into her thoughts. "Even Lottie knows there's something wrong and she never notices anything."

Olivia sighed. "I know, but it's so hard sometimes putting a brave face on things. How about you, though? I think you hoped this reunion would bring you some kind of closure."

"I did hope that," her sister confessed, "but if it's one thing this weekend has shown me, it's that I'll probably never know for sure what happened to Scott. It's high time I accepted that and looked to the future."

"I'll drink to that." Refusing to think what her own future held, Olivia drained her glass and stood. "Right, then, let's get this party started."

***

Poking her head around her bedroom door, Lottie found Emma curled on the camp bed still in her casual clothes, her eyes red from crying.

"Em?" Lottie hurried to sit beside her. "What's wrong?"

Emma sniffed and gave her a weak smile. "Nothing. Just being silly."

"Doesn't look like nothing to me. Is it Jerry?"

"Kind of. I know he's a jerk and everything, but, well, it's never nice being dumped, is it?"

160

Lottie only shook her head. Since Adam was her first serious boyfriend, she didn't feel qualified to comment.

"Then," Emma went on, "you and Adam have been getting on so well, and it's obvious you don't need me around."

"That's not true," Lottie protested, but remorse pinched her conscience. She and Adam had been so wrapped up in each other that they hadn't noticed, or even cared, whether Emma might be feeling left out.

"Of course we want you around," she said. "It's just, well, you're so grown up. We didn't think you'd want to fool about with us."

Emma's expression lightened. "You mean that?"

"Cross my heart." Lottie flinched, half expecting a lightning bolt to strike her down for the lie. She smiled at Emma and took her hands. "Come on, come and have something to eat before our dads scoff the lot."

***

"There." Olivia finished spreading the plastic sheet dotted with colored circles on the drawing room carpet, then stood. "For anyone who hasn't played Twister before, Lottie will explain the rules."

"Aren't you playing?" Tim asked. There was such concern in his eyes that Olivia wondered whether he'd guessed all was not well between her and Joel.

"No." She dredged up a smile. "I'll keep Phoebe company and watch you lot making fools of yourselves."

"You'll play, though, won't you, Aunt Vi?" Lottie said.

Violet grinned. "Why not? Reckon I can show you young people a thing or two."

"How about you, Carla?" Tim's eyes twinkled. "Gonna show us what you're made of?"

"No point. I'd only put you all to shame." Tossing her hair over her shoulders in a gesture identical to her daughter's, Carla knelt on the floor at one end of the plastic sheet. "I'm in charge of the spinner. Right, who's playing?"

As the cousins gathered around the board with Joel, Tim and Violet, Olivia went to sit beside Phoebe on the sofa. "How're you doing? You still look pale."

"I'm fine. It's lovely to see the young people enjoying themselves." Phoebe smiled over at them, and Olivia thought for the thousandth time what a tragedy it was that a woman with so much love to give had never had children of her own.

"Okay," Carla called, "we'll play in order of age, starting with the eldest." She spun the pointer with a deft flick of her wrist. "Tim, right foot, blue."

"Think I can manage that one," Tim said, and stepped onto the nearest blue circle.

From the safety of the sofa, Olivia and Phoebe watched as the game grew in hilarity, the players becoming increasingly entangled, their bodies contorting into ever less likely positions. Frequently Phoebe's gaze rested on Rafe slumped in an armchair by the fire, working his way through a bottle of Scotch.

"Anything up with Rafe?" Olivia asked. "He doesn't seem his usual, er, exuberant self."

"He'll be okay," Phoebe said. "I know he acts as though nothing fazes him but, deep down, he's found it just as hard being back here as I have."

Olivia laid a hand on her arm. "I'm so sorry. This reunion seemed like a good idea, a chance to put the past to rest, but it was too much to expect of any of us, me included."

"Oh, Liv, please don't think I was criticizing. It's only me who's behaved like a mad woman. I've been a terrible nuisance, I know."

"I bet you've never been a nuisance in your life. It's little wonder it's been so hard for you. I shouldn't have put you through it. Can you forgive me?"

"There's nothing to forgive," Phoebe assured her, though she didn't meet Olivia's eyes.

Across the room, Carla announced, "Adam, left hand, green."

"You're kidding. I'm not a contortionist."

"Just reading what it says on my spinner. But if you're not up to the challenge, I'm afraid I'll have to disqualify you."

"Okay, okay."

Olivia exchanged an amused glance with Phoebe, and then they both turned to watch as Adam twisted his body in an attempt to reach the only green circle still free. Almost there, he lost his footing and fell on top of Emma. She in turn knocked into Violet and the entire group collapsed in a confusion of limbs, while Olivia, Phoebe and Carla cried with laughter.

***

"What're you doing?" Lottie giggled as Adam pulled her from the drawing room. "Someone might see."

"No, they won't. They're all far too busy having fun to notice us. Come on, we might not get another chance."

Craning her neck to make sure no one was watching, Lottie let him draw her across the hall to the sitting room. With the door kicked shut behind them, they felt their way through the blackness to the sofa and tumbled onto it, limbs entangled, hands seeking bare skin beneath clothes, lips exploring one another's faces. In a distant corner of Lottie's mind, caution warned her that this was dangerous, that someone might walk in at any moment and catch them. Above the thud of her heart and the desire sweeping in a hot tide through her body, she barely heard it.

"I'll miss you," Adam murmured, his breath warm and ragged against her throat.

"Really? You won't just go back to London and forget all about me?"

"Never. Even if my parents locked me up for the rest of my life to stop us being together, I'd still—"

"Lottie!" Her mum's voice sounded as loud as though she stood right beside them. They sprung apart so quickly that Adam fell off the sofa. Lottie fumbled to pull down her top.

"Lottie, Adam, you'd better get yourselves back here. It's almost time to see in the New Year."

"Coming," Lottie called, and, shaking with nervous laughter, groped for Adam's hand to help him up.

He crushed her against him for a final lip-bruising kiss. "I love you," he said, his tone fierce against her mouth.

"Love you, too. More than anything."

They held each other a moment longer, and then left their secret world to join the rest of the family in the drawing room.

It happened in an instant. As she and Adam paused on the threshold, Lottie took in the scene at a glance: Mum and Aunt Vi trying to tune the ancient TV to the live footage from Trafalgar Square, Aunt Carla shooting Uncle Rafe a look of pure hatred as she accepted a glass of champagne from him, Dad and Emma helping a laughing Uncle Tim to his feet while Aunt Phoebe watched, her expression torn between anxiety and amusement. Lottie saw it all with crystal clarity. Then, everything was obscured as a picture blazed across her mind: a summer sky visible through a canopy of leaves, sunshine sparkling on turquoise water, a figure leaning over it, full of malice …

In a blinding flash of realization, she knew. Her world, the safe, familiar world in which she had grown up, tilted on its axis and was changed forever. Horror washed over her, dark and unstoppable. She couldn't breathe; she was going to drown. She opened her mouth, gulping for air, and screamed.

"Oh, my God. Lottie? Lottie, what is it?"

"What's wrong with her?"

"Looks like she's having a fit."

"Lottie?" Hands grasped hers, firm and reassuring. "Sweetheart, it's okay. Everything's okay. I'm here now. You're going to be all right."

Soothed by her mother's voice, Lottie came back to herself. She blinked. The room she had known since childhood swam into focus, but

163

all was different. Nothing would ever be the same again.

Her mum pulled her into a hug. "There, you're all right now. What happened?"

Lottie clung to her, while the tremors racked her body. "Uncle Scott." Her voice sounded distant, as though coming from outer space. "It wasn't an accident. He didn't just drown." She moved her gaze over the concerned faces of her family, settling on the one that was white with alarm. "You killed him."

A hush fell over the room. From the television, horribly loud in the silence, Big Ben tolled the hour. It was midnight.

Nineteen

Dread seeps into Scott's consciousness even before he's fully awake. He screws his eyes tight, just as he had as a child in the hope that their nanny would be loath to disturb him and so let him miss school. Blocking out everything but Violet's warm body nestled against his, he tries to sink back into oblivion. As in his childhood, however, reality won't be ignored.

Giving it up as a bad job, he surrenders to the inevitable and opens his eyes.

Dawn mist shimmers beyond the window, promising yet another glorious day. What a joke. If this were a film, the director would have organized a backdrop of roiling clouds to symbolize the emotional storm to come. Then, just as he drops his bombshell, thunder would crash overhead and lightning rip the sky in two, illuminating for an instant the shocked faces of his family. Scott smiles, though there is no amusement left in him. This is not a film. There is no manipulating the weather to suit his mood, and no assurance that all will come right in the end.

Unable to lie still any longer, he eases himself from beneath Violet's arm and slips from the bed. He stands there for some time, simply gazing down at her sleeping face. How lovely she is, hair falling across her flushed cheek, expression peaceful and trusting. Guilt punches Scott in the gut. Damn his weakness, his blatant selfishness in putting his own feelings before what's right for Vi. Now she'll get caught up in the mess he's created whether he likes it or not. If only he hadn't been such an arrogant fool as to think himself infallible. If only he and Violet could run away, leave it all behind them and start afresh. If only...

Scott shakes his head, dislodging the pointless questions. What's done is done. Nothing he might do can change anything, no matter how hard he wishes it were otherwise. No, all that remains is to confront his folly head on, confess the whole sordid business, and deal with the consequences.

***

Olivia is back in the nightclub where she and Joel met. He holds her close as they sway on the dance floor, the music so loud it's impossible to distinguish the drumbeat from the pounding of her heart. Alive with the exhilaration pulsing through her bloodstream, she looks up at Joel, laughing with wonderful abandon. The mirth dies in her throat. The fair-haired man gazing down at her, his eyes dark with lust, is certainly not her husband.

"I have to go," she says, pulling away. "I must get home. My husband … he'll be wondering where I am."

Her companion leers at her. "Should've thought about that before you took your clothes off."

Olivia gasps, looking down at her naked body. What is she doing? If Joel catches her here like this with another man, it will be the end of her marriage, her dreams … everything. She has to escape. Must get home before he realizes what she's done. Heedless of her nakedness, she wrenches herself from the young man's arms and pushes her way through the crowded nightclub until she emerges onto the darkened street. Once outside, she begins to run. She runs until her chest aches and the concrete has cut her bare feet to ribbons. She trips on a crack in the pavement, arms moving in an instinctive gesture to shield her unborn son, but he isn't there. Her stomach is flatter than it has been since her pre-puppy fat days. Where's her baby? What has she done with him? Her mouth opens in a silent wail of anguish and then she crashes to the ground, the shouts and laughter from the club ringing in her ears.

Olivia opens her eyes but the racket goes on. Heart still thudding as though she has indeed been fleeing the shame of her dream, it takes a few panicked moments before she realizes where she is. Her taut muscles relax. She's safe in the bedroom of her new home, with Joel lying warm and familiar beside her, and the noise is, in fact, issuing from the next room.

"Oh, no." She groans and struggles to sit up. "Why is it that children are incapable of understanding the concept of a lie-in?"

"I'll sort them out." Yawning, Joel pushes back the covers. "You try and get some more sleep."

"Are you sure? A few more minutes would be heaven." The dream fresh in her mind, Olivia blinks back tears of gratitude.

Joel leans across to kiss her. "Leave the horrors to me. Don't want you tiring yourself out again."

"You're an angel," she says. "I don't know what I'd do without you."

"Then it's a good job I'm not going anywhere, isn't it?" Joel smiles at her, then pulls on his dressing gown and pads from the room.

With a sigh of contentment, Olivia burrows deeper under the duvet and wraps her arms protectively around the reassuring swell of her belly. In this moment, with the memory of Joel's touch on her skin and their baby snug inside her, she feels truly blessed.

***

"For crying out loud," Carla snarls, yanking the duvet up over her head. "Anyone would think World War III had broken out next door."

"Bad night?" Tim's arm slides about her waist from behind, but she shakes him off.

"Oh, just fabulous. You know what time I finally got to sleep? Five o'clock, that's when, and the last thing I need is a load of shrieking kids waking me up at the crack of dawn."

"Poor you. I'll go and tell them to keep it down."

"Stop being so bloody nice to me," Carla wants to scream at him. "Don't you know I shagged your brother last night?"

Instead, she waits until Tim closes the bedroom door behind him and then buries her head in the pillow. The images that kept sleep at bay return in force, confronting her with the bitter reality of what she's done. She sees it all again in her mind: herself stealing up the attic stairs to Rafe's room, the glint of triumph in his eyes as he bends to kiss her, the two of them falling naked to the floor, all her resistance gone.

She lets out a soft moan, swallowing the bile that burns her throat. God, she's disgusting, depraved, not worthy of a man like Tim. His consideration, his unfailing patience, only make her feel worse. If only he would snap back at her, bawl her out for being a moody, ungrateful bitch, it might ease her guilt just a fraction. Oh, God, how could she? How could she betray the person who means more to her than anyone else in the whole world, and with a man not fit to lick his boots? In answer, Phoebe's face swims across her vision, eyes anguished and flooded with tears. She had no choice. If she let Phoebe harm herself, knowing it was within her power to prevent it, she could never live with herself.

The bedroom door opens and Tim pokes his head into the room. "Joel's taken the kids downstairs and is going to put the kettle on. Want a cup of tea, or are you going to try and get some more sleep?"

"I would, if people didn't keep disturbing me."

Hurt flickers in Tim's eyes and Carla turns her face away, hating herself. A moment later, the bedroom door closes softly behind him. Insides knotted with shame, Carla attempts to lose herself in oblivion, but to no avail. Tossing the covers onto the floor, she puts on her dressing gown and drags her weary body along to the bathroom to splash water on her face, before deciding to check on Phoebe. She has her hand on the door of her friend's room, when a creak on the attic stairs makes her glance up.

"Good morning." A smirk plays about Rafe's lips. "Sleep well?"

"What do you think?" Remembering how those same lips moved over her skin, Carla grows hot. "If you don't mind, I'm going to see how Phoebe is after the damage you caused."

Rafe's fingers close around her wrist. "Allow me. Seeing as you're blaming me for this whole situation, I'm sure you'll agree I'm the one who should put it right."

"Don't touch me." Carla snatches her arm away and glares at him with more loathing than she has ever directed at anyone before. "What do you mean, put it right? What're you going to do?"

"Let's just say I have a little surprise for Phoebe when she wakes up. I promise she'll like it."

"Rafe, your promises are worth even less than Cameron's shares."

He chuckles. "You really should learn to trust me, Carla. As long as you stick to our bargain, you have no reason to worry. Still, just to put your mind at rest, why not meet me in the hayloft later? That should ensure I watch my step."

"Are you mad? It was risky enough last night, but during the day, anyone could catch us. I won't take that chance."

"Oh, I think you will." Rafe runs a lazy finger down her cheek. "At least, you will if your friend's happiness means as much to you as you claim. Wait for me in the stables after breakfast. If you don't show, you know what to expect."

***

Phoebe opens her eyes to find Rafe perched on Violet's bed, watching her. Hastily she screws them shut again. *For pity's sake, pull yourself together. He doesn't want you anymore, remember? You're too wet, too inexperienced, too ugly. It's just your mind playing tricks, taunting you with the one thing you long for above any other.* The pain, deadened during her long, dreamless sleep, returns with a vengeance, twisting her heart until it feels as though it will tear in half. She clenches her fingers around the edge of the duvet, fighting back the sobs.

"Angel?"

That voice, so achingly precious and familiar, nudges its way into her thoughts. She almost opens her eyes, but stops herself. He isn't really there. None of this is real; it's only a figment of her imagination. There's no use hoping.

"Phoebe, I know you're awake. Listen, I realize I don't deserve it after yesterday, but won't you at least look at me? Please."

If this is a daydream, it's a remarkably vivid one. Rafe's voice is so solid, so clear. Perhaps she's going mad. Before Phoebe can prevent them, her eyelids flutter open and she peers through the curtained dimness. Rafe is still there, hunched forward on the edge of the bed, chin in hands, expression full of concern. She blinks, but the image remains.

"Rafe?" Still she dares not believe it. "Is that really you?"

"You *are* awake." He's at her side at once, kneeling by the bed to take her hands in his. "Angel, I'm so sorry. I said such terrible things to you. I haven't been able to sleep for thinking about them. Can you ever forgive me?"

"There's nothing to forgive." Aware she must look a fright, Phoebe tilts her face away from him. "I *am* wet, you were right. There's nothing about me a man would want, least of all a man like you."

Rafe's grip tightens on her hands. "You mustn't say that. You're beautiful and sweet and I love you. Don't ever think otherwise."

Phoebe's heart stutters, then careers out of control. She must be dreaming. He can't possibly mean what he said; he merely feels sorry for her. She turns her head to search his face, questioning him with her eyes.

"I can see you don't believe me, and who could blame you when I was so hateful? I owe you an explanation." Rafe drops his gaze, reminding Phoebe of the boy he must once have been. "When you asked me yesterday about the business and I told you there was nothing to worry about, I wasn't being entirely honest. Oh, it's only a temporary blip, nothing I can't handle, but the fact is, Phoebs, I couldn't have chosen a worse time to fall in love. How can I even be thinking about getting deeply involved with someone when I have no stability to offer, no security for the future? It wouldn't be fair."

A heady joy, comforting as mulled wine on a winter's night, warms her heart and spreads to every inch of her body. It must have required a great deal of courage for Rafe to bare himself to her like this, revealing the vulnerability beneath the self-assurance. How wonderful that he should put such trust in her. With new confidence, Phoebe reaches out a hand to stroke his hair, luxuriating in its course thickness.

"Rafe, listen to me. None of that is important. Of course I care about the business, but for your sake, not mine. I know how much it means to you. As for money and stability, they're irrelevant. It wouldn't matter if you were a pauper with nothing to offer me but a rundown shed. It's you I want, only you."

Rafe lifts his gaze to hers and Phoebe blushes, unused to speaking out with such passion.

"You mean that? You'd marry me, even though I might end up penniless?"

"Of course I would," Phoebe assures him, then gasps as the full significance of his words sink in. Did he really just ask her to marry him? She attempts to subdue her racing pulse. He was speaking hypothetically, nothing more. Don't get carried away.

Rafe smiles at her confusion, pressing her hands to his face. "In that case, there's nothing to hold me back. Phoebs, will you marry me?"

She blinks, sure even now that she must have misheard, misunderstood. "What did you say?"

"I said." Rafe looks straight into her eyes. "will you marry me?"

For an instant, she can only stare at him. Then, half-laughing, half-sobbing, she flings her arms around his neck. "Yes! Yes, please."

***

"Na-na-ne-na-na, you can't catch me," Lottie taunts, then dives under the kitchen table with a shriek as Adam and Emma lunge at her.

Round and round the table they run, scraping chairs aside as they crawl on the floor from one side to the other, hollering at the tops of their voices. At the cooker, trying to bully her brain into conjuring up breakfast for eleven people, Olivia is on the verge of screaming herself.

"Can you three keep it down?" she says. "I can't hear myself think."

The children pay her no heed, too wrapped up in their game. Olivia closes her eyes. Roll on this afternoon when the house will finally be her own again. After luxuriating in a hot, bubble-filled bath, she'll send Joel out for fish and chips from the village and collapse on the sofa in front of *Birds of a Feather*. Bliss!

"Okay, you lot," Joel bellows, coming through the back door from the patio, "away from the hot food, please."

"But we're having fun." Lottie pokes her head out from under the table.

"You can have fun outside. In fact, if you're not out of here by the time I count to three, there'll be no going in the pool today. One … two…."

Smiling, Olivia watches the children vanish into the garden as though wearing Perseus' winged sandals. "Thanks for that, although I'm not sure threats would be approved of in the handbook of perfect parenting."

"Worked, didn't it?" Joel grins. "Now, what can I do to help?"

"You could see if anyone wants a top up. It is a celebration, after all."

"It certainly is. I was starting to think it would never happen, but it seems my big brother has finally found a woman who lives up to his high standards. I'm chuffed for him. For both of them."

Joel retrieves another bottle of champagne from the fridge and returns to the patio. Olivia watches through the window with a smile as he refills Phoebe's glass, saying something to her that makes her blush. Phoebe has clearly recovered from last night's touch of sunstroke and now looks positively radiant. Rafe, too, appears even more complacent than usual as he accepts another drink and a clap on the back from Joel. Even Tim has put aside the previous days' quarrel to join in the congratulations. For all their differences, the Cameron boys are always ready to celebrate each other's good fortunes, or to help one another up when they fall. Much like herself and Vi.

As if on cue, her sister wanders into the kitchen with her hair tied back in a ponytail and a pair of denim shorts showing off her long, suntanned legs. She looks barely older than sixteen, and more animated than Olivia has ever seen her.

"Something smells good," Violet says, perching on the edge of the table. "I'm starving."

"And I thought people in love were supposed to lose their appetite. Breakfast won't be long. Has Scott risen from the dead yet?"

Her sister frowns. "Isn't he down here?"

"Haven't seen him. I assumed he was upstairs with you."

"He must have got up early and gone for a walk. Not like him at all. He'll normally sleep half the day, given the chance."

"Definitely sickening for something." Olivia flips the bacon over in its pan. "Root him out and tell him breakfast's nearly ready, would you? Oh, and you might want to congratulate Rafe and Phoebe. They just got engaged."

"So Rafe's finally found someone fool enough to marry him. Poor girl."

"Vi, keep your voice down. I know you don't think much of Rafe—"

"He's an arsehole."

"Yes, well, if you could just pretend to be pleased for them. Phoebe's over the moon, and you never know, she might turn out to be the best thing that ever happened to Rafe."

"And I might decide to take up pole dancing. Okay, okay, don't look at me like that. I'll be on my best behavior. I might even congratulate them." Grinning, Violet leaps lightly down from the table and lopes onto the patio.

***

She finds Scott slumped on the lawn at the pool's edge, drawing deeply on a cigarette and staring into the water. Violet sits beside him, but the teasing remark dies on her lips when she catches sight of his face. There is something in his expression she has never seen before, a tense desperation that frightens her.

"How long have you been out here?"

Scott doesn't look at her. "Dunno. A couple of hours, maybe."

"Not like you to be such an early riser. Coming back to the house for breakfast? There's not much nutritional value in nicotine, you know."

"Don't think I can face it, Vi. Too much going on in my head."

Dread slides into Violet's stomach, cold and heavy as lead. Only last night he said he loved her, his eyes full of tender promises. Now he seems as unreachable as the stars that twinkled down on them as they made love in this very spot.

"You're having second thoughts," she says, keeping her tone devoid of the emotion raging inside her, "about us."

Scott's eyes snap to her face. "No! Christ, Vi, how can you think that?"

She sags against the hedge, weak with relief. "Really? No regrets?"

"Oh, plenty of those." Scott returns his gaze to the pool, squinting against the cigarette smoke. "I regret being a gullible fool with not enough sense to see a ditch from a goldmine, and too much pride to ask for advice. I regret letting my brothers down, when all they've ever done is support and take care of me. Most of all, though, I regret allowing myself to get involved with you, not because I don't love you like mad, but because it means you're going to get caught up in this whole shitty mess." His voice crackles with self-loathing.

Taken aback, Violet lays a hand on his shoulder. "What mess? How have you let your family down? I wish you'd tell me."

"I will. What choice do I have? This isn't exactly something I'm going to be able to keep quiet. We can't talk now, though. The others will be wondering where you've got to."

As if to support his words, Olivia's voice floats across the grounds. "Hurry up, you two, breakfast is getting cold."

"Go on," Scott says, "before they suspect something's up. Just tell them I'm feeling a bit queasy. I can't face food, let alone my brothers."

"If you're sure." Scrambling to her feet, Violet looks down at him. "Just try not to worry. Whatever's happened, we can sort it out."

"Thanks, Vi, but you might not be so keen to be with me once you hear what I've done."

"Don't be a clot. As long as you love me, that's all that matters. Anything else I can deal with."

Scott's mouth twists in a smile. "I only hope that's true."

Twenty

"Wonder what's got into your wife this morning," Rafe muses, watching Carla's rigid figure retreat into the house. He and Tim are alone on the patio, Joel and Phoebe having left to supervise the kids in the pool, Olivia to clear away the breakfast things, and Scott and Violet to indulge in a bit of hanky-panky in the attic room.

Tim rests his arms on the table, looking weary. "She had a bad night, poor love. You know how she sometimes has trouble sleeping. She'll be fine once she's had a lie down."

Rafe suppresses a smirk. Even as an unsuspecting Tim imagines Carla climbing the stairs to their bedroom, she is doubtless slipping out of the side door and doubling back to the stables. Guilt pricks Rafe's conscience, but he brushes it aside. Serves Tim right for being so trusting, so complacent as to believe a woman like Carla would ever be content with one man. Besides, he can't help himself. He's wanted Carla from the moment he set eyes on her, and she's remained out of reach, the one prize neither his charm nor good looks have succeeded in winning. Until now. Perhaps he should take this opportunity to dispel any lingering resentment between himself and Tim. He can afford to be generous, after all, and he hates falling out with any of his brothers.

"Look," he says, laying a hand on Tim's shoulder, "sorry if I spoke out of turn yesterday. You know Carla better than any of us. If you trust her, that should be good enough for me."

"Forget it. I know you're only looking out for me." Tim rewards him with his easy smile. "And I'm so happy for you and Phoebe. I wish you both all the luck in the world."

"Cheers, but I'd save your luck for Scott and Violet, if I were you. They're going to need it a damn sight more than us."

"Why do you say that? You don't think Scott's serious about her?"

"Only as serious as Scott's ever been about anything. Besides, it'll never work. Vi's as straight as they come, while our little brother lives for breaking the rules." Rafe shrugs. "If you ask me, Scott's already having second thoughts. Why else do you think he's been avoiding everyone all morning?"

Tim hesitates. "I did wonder whether it has something to do with this fantastic business deal he's supposed to have pulled off. What if it wasn't as fantastic as he made out? What if he's messed up and is too ashamed to tell us?"

"What does he think we'd do? Fire him?" Rafe snorts. "We all know how it is in this business. You win some, you lose some. We're not going to give him a hard time just because his judgment let him down. It's not like it happens very often. No, you take it from me, whatever's bothering Scott is personal, not business."

"I hope for Violet's sake you're wrong. It'll break her heart." Tim stands up, mopping his brow. "I'm going to cool off in the pool. Coming?"

"Think I'll pass." With Tim otherwise engaged, it will be easy to slip away to the stables unnoticed, and he has kept Carla waiting long enough.

***

It's dim and cool in the hayloft after the heat outside. Carla can't stop shivering. Huddled on the bed of hay, she gulps down air to try and quell the nausea, arms hugging her knees to still her trembling. She must be insane. If they're caught, it will be the end of her marriage, of everything that matters to her. And what about Phoebe? How could she ever recover from what she would see as the worst possible betrayal by her closest—no, her only friend? Carla buries her face in her skirt, unable to bear the possible consequences of her actions.

Is this worth it? She asks herself for the hundredth time. Is she actually doing Phoebe any favors by allowing her to become increasingly involved with Rafe? After all, he can't love Phoebe if he's desperate to cheat on her before they're even married. Might it not be better that Phoebe suffer now, however painful the fallout, so she has a chance of finding a man who'll care for her as she deserves? But would Phoebe ever heal from the trauma of losing Rafe, the only man she believes has ever wanted her? Even if she were prevented from taking her own life, would her heart mend sufficiently for her to be able to love again? Could she, Carla, play Goddess with another person's life like that? She almost laughs out loud. *A bit late to worry about that.*

The creak of the stable door drifts up from below. Carla tenses. Perhaps it's Tim, having found their room deserted and come to look for her. She'll simply tell him that she needed to be somewhere quiet, somewhere she wouldn't be disturbed. Oh, please let it be Tim. Carla watches the top of the ladder, willing with all her might. Rafe wouldn't dare try anything if Tim knew she was here. An instant later, Rafe's face appears in the opening and her stomach drops.

"You didn't chicken out, then," she mocks, going on the attack. "I wasn't sure you had the bottle."

Rafe chuckles. "Really, Carla, I think you know me better than that. In fact, after last night, I'd say we know each other extremely well."

He swings his stocky frame into the loft with surprising agility and drops the hatch into place, sealing them in.

Carla sucks in a breath, fighting claustrophobia. "Rafe, this is too risky, you must see that. If we're caught, if Tim or Phoebe—"

"Oh, don't you trouble yourself about them. They're far too busy entertaining the kiddiewinks in the pool to spare a thought for what we might be up to. Besides," he adds, inching towards her, "I demand your full attention."

Pressed into a corner, Carla flinches from his touch as he reaches for her.

Rafe sighs. "Must we go through this whole charade every time? It was a turn-on at first, I admit, but it's getting a bit tiresome. After all, it's no use pretending you don't want me when you were so obviously gagging for it last night."

As he leans in to kiss her, his smug expression visible even through the gloom, something inside Carla snaps. Who does this man think he is? How dare he presume he can manipulate her. No one gets away with treating her like a victim. No one! Catching Rafe unawares, she seizes him by the shoulders and shoves him unresisting into the hay. Then, using her knees to pin his arms to his sides, she straddles him and meets his gaze with defiance.

Rafe only smiles, expression hungry. "Christ, I love a dominant woman, but if you wanted to go on top, you only had to say."

"No talking," Carla snarls. Still pinioning his arms, she bends over him to crush her mouth on his, hands sliding beneath his T-shirt. Rafe's eyes, centimeters from hers, glaze over with lust, and Carla experiences a thrill at her power. He might have forced her into a situation she can't get out of, but if he believes he's going to hold all the cards in this sordid affair he has underestimated her.

***

"Goal!" Emma shrieks, sending the ball flying over Phoebe's head to land in the water with a splash. "Bad luck, Aunt Phoebs."

"I'm not very good at this, am I?" Laughing, Phoebe retrieves the ball and tosses it to Tim. "Here, you're the expert."

"No, you do it," Lottie says. "Come on, Aunt Phoebs."

"Yes, go on." Grinning, Tim passes the ball back to her. "Think of it as a family initiation."

"Well, if you insist." Phoebe takes it with a grimace. Turning to face her opponents, her expression contorts into one of intense concentration before she hurls the ball over the rope.

"Yes!" Adam catches it easily. Lottie and Emma cheer and hug each other in triumph.

Phoebe shakes her head. "I did warn you I'm not very good."

Lounging on the grass, Joel smiles as he watches the haphazard game of water polo, Tim and Phoebe on one team engaged in an exaggerated pretence at missing the ball, the children on the other, fighting to be the one to catch it and throw it back to the adults. How different Phoebe looks from the shy, awkward girl who arrived two days ago. With her face animated and dark curls escaping their ponytail to cling to her damp cheeks, she is quite lovely. And it's all Rafe's doing.

"Daddy," Lottie calls, waving an arm adorned with a pink water-wing, "come in and play."

"Excellent idea." Tim pulls himself to the side of the pool. "You can take over from me while I have a breather. This lot are beating us good and proper."

"You should be ashamed of yourself, losing to a bunch of kids," Joel says, then jumps back laughing as Tim clambers out of the water and shakes himself like a dog.

While Tim settles down to dry in a patch of sunshine, Joel perches on the edge of the pool and dips his feet into the water. "Blimey, it's freezing in there. You lot must have alligator skin."

"You wimp, Uncle Joel," Adam jeers. "Come on, get in."

"Wimp, wimp, wimp," Lottie and Emma join in.

"Okay, okay." Joel raises his voice over the hilarity. "You three practice for a minute while I get used to the water."

"Wimp, wimp, wimp," they taunt, then converge in a heap of giggling bodies.

As the children embark on a game that involves wrestling the ball from one another's grasp with much shrieking and laughter, Joel smiles at Phoebe treading water nearby. "I know I've said this already, but congratulations. It's taken my brother a long time to find the right girl, but he couldn't have chosen better."

Color floods Phoebe's cheeks. "Thank you."

"I mean it. Anyone can see you love him."

"Oh, I do. All I want is to take care of him, to make him happy."

"And you will. I only hope my brother knows how lucky he is."

"Not as lucky as I am. I must be the luckiest woman alive." Phoebe smiles fondly at Lottie and Emma's attempt to wrench the ball from Adam, all three helpless with laughter.

"You're great with the kids," Joel says. "I'd say they consider you their aunt already."

"And they may as well be my nieces and nephew. I've really loved spending time with them. They're wonderful children."

"Who knows, perhaps you'll have one of your own soon."

"I do hope so." Phoebe's expression grows dreamy. "Apart from Rafe, there's nothing more I want in the whole world."

Before Joel can respond, Lottie's insistent voice forestalls him. "Come on, Daddy, you have to come in now and play."

"If I must." Joel shares an amused glance with Phoebe. Then, taking a deep breath, he plunges into the water.

***

Worn out from another round of water polo, Tim wanders into the kitchen, his hair drenched from the pool. He casts an appreciative glance over the plates of sandwiches, cakes and scones Olivia is arranging on the table. "Wow, that looks amazing."

She turns from the fridge to smile at him, a jar of strawberry jam in her hand. "I wanted to give you all a treat, seeing as you're going home this afternoon."

"Upon which you'll breathe a sigh of relief at having the house to yourselves again."

"Well, perhaps just a small one." Olivia laughs. "No, really, it's been lovely having you all. Will Carla be up to eating, do you think?"

"I'm sure she will. She won't want to miss out on this feast." Tim moves towards the door. "I'll go up and see how she is."

"Thanks, Tim. Oh, and will you let Scott and Vi know lunch is ready? I think they're in one of the attic rooms."

"Will do." Leaving the delicious-smelling kitchen, Tim makes his way along the passage and up the stairs. With any luck, Carla has managed a couple of hours sleep and is feeling more herself. Pushing open the door to their bedroom, he stops short at the sight of Carla curled on the bed, knees drawn up to her chest like a child, shoulders shaking with silent anguish.

"Carla?" He's beside her in an instant, pulling her slender body into his arms. "Sweetheart, what's wrong? Tell me. Is it one of your migraines?"

He half expects her to shove him away as she had earlier. Instead, she clings to him, burying her face in his T-shirt.

"Oh, God, I'm sorry," she sobs, the words barely distinguishable. "I'm so sorry."

"Hey." Taken aback, he strokes her silky hair. "What's all this? You've got nothing to be sorry for."

"I have. I'm such a bitch and you're always so good to me, putting up with my moods. I don't deserve it."

"Carla, if this is about this morning, forget it. I know how you get after your bad nights. It doesn't matter."

"It matters to me." Carla pushes herself away to gaze into his face, tears pouring down her cheeks. "You shouldn't have to take shit like that

177

from me. Sometimes I wonder why you put up with it. You should be with someone nice, not a selfish cow like me."

"Now you're being silly," Tim says, and takes her face between his hands so she can't look away. "I don't want anyone else. I wouldn't be with you if I did. I loved you the moment we bumped into each other in the library, and I still do."

Carla gives him a weak smile. "And I love you. No matter what Rafe or anyone else says, or how badly I behave, I want you to know that."

"I do." Tim draws her close and kisses her, holding her until the last sobs subside.

"Tim," she says softly, head on his shoulder, "can we go home? I've had my fill of family for one weekend."

"Course we can." He tucks a strand of hair behind her ear. "We'd better have some lunch, seeing as Olivia's gone to so much trouble, but then we'll go."

***

She can't take it in. Scott's words echo in the silence, but her brain refuses to absorb their meaning. Sitting beside Scott on the very bed they'd shared only a few hours earlier, she has listened to his story, listened as he tore her happiness into shreds like so much waste paper and tossed it on the fire. This can't be happening. None of it makes sense. She wants to shake her head, to deny the evidence of her ears, but shock clamps her muscles in place.

"When did this happen?" Her tone is expressionless, as though the answer holds little importance.

Scott keeps his head bowed, as he has throughout his narrative. "Friday morning."

"Well, at least that explains why you turned up so late and reeking of booze. When faced with a problem too big to handle, lose yourself in alcohol, that's your motto. Actually, I'm amazed you showed up at all."

"Give me some credit, Vi. I may have made one God-awful cock-up, but I'm no coward. I knew I had to come clean. I just needed a bit of Dutch courage to get me down here, to face you again."

Violet raises her eyebrows. "I don't follow. Why would you be more worried about facing me than your own brothers? It's their business, not mine."

"But don't you see?" He jerks his head up to look at her, eyes flashing. "I'd already been trying to distance myself from you, trying to save you from getting mixed up with someone as unsuitable as me. Then this happened. How could I see you again knowing how you felt about me, how I felt about you? I was terrified I wouldn't be strong enough to resist you, that I'd give into my feelings and you'd be caught up in it all."

"What I don't understand," Violet says, "is why you didn't tell me all this from the start. If you were so anxious to protect me as you claim, surely it would have been kinder to be up front rather than letting me believe everything was fine."

"You're right. I'm sorry." Scott once more drops his gaze.

His weakness stokes Violet's fury into life. She leaps off the bed to pace the floorboards, mindless of cracking her head on the sloping ceiling.

"How could you be so stupid?" she flings at him, her shattered dreams mutating into spite. "We all know you're a sucker for a soft story, but this was just plain foolhardy. I never thought you could be so selfish!"

"Oh, I see." Scott stood to confront her, anger combining with the hurt in his expression. "Well, if I'm selfish, you're fickle. What happened to all your big promises, Violet? You'd love me no matter what, you said. It didn't matter what I'd done, just as long as we had each other. So much for your love."

"That's not fair and you know it. This has nothing to do with you and me. This is about you ruining your family's lives with your irresponsibility."

"And what would you know about irresponsibility, Little Miss Never-Put-A-Foot-Wrong-In-Her-Life? The way you're talking, anyone would think I did this on purpose, that I actually take pleasure in causing trouble. I thought you knew me better than that. I only did what seemed right at the time. Right for the company and my family. Fact is, it turned out to be the worst decision I ever made and I'm more sorry than I can say." Scott's voice breaks and he turns away.

Violet storms on regardless. "Oh, I'm so glad you're sorry. I'm sure that'll be a huge comfort to Liv and Joel when they have to sell the home they love. Have you any idea how much work they've put into restoring this place? Of course you have, but none of that's important to you, is it? And what about the rest of your family? What about Tim and Carla, the kids?"

"What about them?"

Violet freezes, mouth half open. Slowly, she turns to find Tim standing in the doorway. She glances at Scott, but he still has his back to her, unmoving.

Tim breaks the silence. "Sorry. I came to tell you lunch is ready. I couldn't help overhearing." He looks from one to the other, clearly taking in the atmosphere. "Would one of you like to tell me what's going on?"

Twenty-One

"Let's watch *Pinocchio*," Adam says, grabbing the video from the bookcase.

Emma shoves him aside. "I hate *Pinocchio*. We always have to watch it. I want to watch *The Jungle Book*."

"Come on, this is getting us nowhere." Olivia tries to stay calm, to hide her growing dread. All the while, she is conscious of her family waiting for her in the kitchen and that something must be horribly wrong. "If you can't decide between yourselves, I'll have to choose for you. What would you like to watch, Lottie?"

"I want to go swimming."

"Yes, well, I'm afraid that isn't an option. You've been in the pool all morning. Now it's time to have lunch. So, what will it be? And I'm warning you, I won't ask again."

"*Pinocchio*."

"*Jungle Book*."

"Swimming!"

"Right, you had your chance," Olivia says, stepping over them to reach the shelving unit. "Whatever I pick out you're watching, and I don't want any arguments."

Selecting a video at random, careful to shield the cover from view, she drops to her knees before the telly. Her hands tremble as she pops the tape into the player. She can't shake from her mind the image of Violet's face, set and white as marble. Awful possibilities tumble through her brain. Scott's been seeing someone else. He has a child by another woman. He's already married. Surely none of these scenarios would call for a family conference. Though his brothers would undoubtedly have something to say about it, it would be a matter for Scott and Violet to work out between them.

A still more dreadful possibility occurs to her. Scott's very ill, perhaps dying, and has only just plucked up the courage to tell his family. No, anything but that. Olivia's heart squeezes painfully at the thought. Well, one thing's for sure, the suspense isn't doing her any good. She needs to know, however hard the truth might be to accept. Fast-forwarding the trailers, she presses play and struggles to her feet, one hand to her swollen stomach. All of a sudden, this baby feels like a dead weight inside her, dragging her down.

"Oh, no, not *Sleeping Beauty*." Emma groans as the opening credits appear on the screen. "I hate *Sleeping Beauty*."

"Yuck, this is a girl's film. There's no way I'm watching it."

"Not *Sleeping Beauty*, Mummy. I want to go swimming."

"For heaven's sake, I'm not in the mood," Olivia snaps. "I don't want to hear another peep out of any of you. Just sit down, shut up, and eat your lunch."

Shocked into silence, they plonk themselves in front of the telly and begin picking at the sandwiches and crisps she's set out on the coffee table. Lottie looks close to tears and Olivia hesitates, longing to hug her and say she's sorry. There will be time for apologies later, once she's dealt with whatever bombshell Scott means to drop. Contenting herself with planting a kiss on the top of her daughter's head, she closes the sitting room door and makes her way along the passage.

No one is talking much when she enters the kitchen. Pretending to be enjoying the spread she took so much trouble over, they exchange stilted small talk and avoid one another's eyes. Tim has one arm around a pale-faced Carla, while Phoebe watches Rafe with a mixture of concern and compassion normally reserved for the terminally ill. Olivia's gaze darts to Violet, who is staring down at her hands as they lock and unlock on the tablecloth. She looks at no one, least of all Scott seated next to her at the head of the table. Trepidation lies heavy in the atmosphere, tangible as the humidity before a storm.

As Olivia closes the door behind her, Rafe looks up with obvious relief. "You're here. Come on and take a seat. We're all dying to find out what Scott has to say for himself."

Too anxious to mind being invited to sit in her own house, Olivia moves around the table to take the place between Joel and Phoebe. Seeking reassurance, she slides her hand into Joel's and he grips it hard.

"Okay," Rafe says, fixing Scott with a level stare along the length of the table, "now we're all here, perhaps you'd like to explain what this is all about. I'm assuming it has something to do with this fantastic new business venture of yours?"

"Yes." Scott glances around at the faces turned towards him, before once more dropping his gaze. "Only, as you've probably guessed, it didn't turn out to be as fantastic as I'd hoped."

After a pause, Tim leans forward in the chair across from Olivia. "Scott, you can't expect to get it right every time in this business, not even with your luck. God knows, we've all made mistakes over the years."

"Not like this, you haven't. None of you would be so stupid." Scott draws in an audible breath. "It started just over two weeks ago. I didn't have anything on that night, so I stopped off in the pub for a couple of pints after work."

Nothing new there, Olivia reflects.

"I got chatting to this bloke at the bar. Turns out he's a racehorse trainer, just beginning to make his name in the business. He built up his yard from scratch with the money he inherited from his grandparents, buying up horses he predicted would do well and training them up. He even rides them himself, and has been placed in several races. Still, there's only so far you can go without a large injection of capital. What he needed, he told me, was a backer, someone who believed in him enough to stake up the cash for a cup-winning horse to put him and his yard on the map."

"I have a horrible feeling I know where this is going," Rafe says. "Please tell me I'm wrong. Please tell me you didn't gamble the company's money on a race horse."

Scott looks up at him, defiance in his eyes. "Why not? It isn't as if stocks and shares are very reliable at the moment. I reckoned Cameron's needed to put its money into something completely different, something not so entirely at the mercy of the economic crisis, and Rick seemed to be the answer. He had his eye on a horse, he said, a fine black stallion with several prizes under his girth already. With a horse like that, his yard couldn't fail to get the recognition it deserved. He would be flooded with owners fighting to pay him to train their horses, and he'd be made. You should have heard him. It was impossible not to be caught up in his enthusiasm."

"I'm sure," Rafe drawls, "but before we get carried away, how much of an investment was he asking for this superhorse?"

Head bowed, Scott mumbles a figure so exorbitant that Olivia sucks in a breath. Joel's hand tightens on hers. The faces of the others mirror her shock. Only Violet doesn't react, still staring down at the tablecloth as though her mind is elsewhere, and Olivia guesses she must already have heard the worst of it.

"How much?" Rafe splutters. "You mean to say you committed almost half the company's value to buy what could have turned out to be some old carthorse, and on the say-so of some bloke you met in a pub? For all you knew, he might not have been a trainer at all, or at least he could have exaggerated his ability."

Scott's face hardens. "Give me some credit. I may take more risks than the rest of you but they're calculated risks. Rick gave me a couple of weeks to think over his proposal and I used the time to do my research, asking around in the business to check Rick's reputation, going to see for myself this horse he set so much store by. It all confirmed what he'd told me, and so I saw no reason not to go ahead. I met Rick in the same pub on Wednesday evening and we closed the deal."

"You don't think you should have consulted the rest of us?" Joel asks. "Seeing as you were committing so much of the company's money?"

"I should have, I know, but I didn't think you'd go along with it. I was so sure this was just the boost Cameron's needed, and it would have been, if not for—" Scott breaks off, shaking his head.

"What happened?" Carla stares at Scott with fear in her expression. "What went wrong?"

"Just about everything that could go wrong. Rick had already agreed to the sale in principle, so all he had to do on Thursday was transfer the money and pick up the horse. He called me that evening to let me know it all went through okay and the new addition to his yard was happily installed in his stable. I went to bed keyed up with the thought of seeing you all the following day and announcing my coup. Then I woke up and heard the news." A shadow passes over Scott's face. "I turned on the radio and there it was, one of the top stories, champion horse dies in suspicious fire."

"Oh, my God." Olivia puts a hand to her mouth. "I read about it in the paper. The owner called the fire brigade, but they were too late to save the horses."

Scott nods. "The moment I heard what had happened, I got straight on the phone to Rick. He was beside himself, everything he'd worked for up in smoke, and he confirmed my worst fears. The horse that was to make his name and secure Cameron's' future was dead."

"How did it happen?" Joel's tone is flat. "Was it an accident?"

"Too early to say for sure, but the police are treating it as suspicious. Rick reckons someone might have been jealous of his success and wanted to sabotage his business."

"Which is all very tragic," Rafe says, "but surely not the end of the world. You wouldn't have been so stupid as to throw away so much capital without some sort of guarantee. I mean, this horse was insured, right?"

Scott doesn't answer, but the expression in his eyes reveals the truth.

***

"Be quiet, you two." Lottie turns from the telly to scowl at her cousins. "I can't hear *Sleeping Beauty*."

"You didn't even want to watch it," Emma points out, "and Adam ate my bit of cake."

"I did not."

"Did so, you big fat pig. There was one piece each and I never had one. You ate it. Lottie, go and ask your mum for some more cake for me."

"Why should I?"

"Because you're the youngest and you have to do what I say."

Sighing, Lottie pauses the film and scrambles to her feet. Mummy will probably be cross if she interrupts the grown-up stuff going on in the kitchen, but if she doesn't her cousins will tease her for being a scaredy cat. She can't wait until it's time for Emma and Adam to go home. Then she'll have the house and her parents to herself again.

Opening the sitting-room door, Lottie pads along the hall and down the passage. At the end, she pauses, biting her lip. The kitchen door is closed. They must be talking about something very important, something they don't want little people to hear. Even as she stands there, unsure what to do, raised voices reach her through the solid wood.

"How could you be so bloody careless?" That's Uncle Rafe shouting. "Have you any idea what you've done? Well, have you?"

"I don't believe this," Aunt Carla storms. "I always knew you were irresponsible, Scott, but I never imagined you were so selfish."

Lottie begins to tremble. Why are they all shouting at Uncle Scott? She can't make sense of the words, only the anger. But Uncle Scott is fun and kind and makes everyone laugh. He wouldn't do anything bad. At least, not on purpose. Perhaps this is like the time when she was playing in her parents' room and broke her mother's favorite ornament, a china bowl that had belonged to Nanna Brown, who died when Mummy was a baby. Mummy was very cross, but she understood it was an accident and forgave Lottie when she said sorry. She can hear Uncle Scott saying sorry now in the kitchen, but it makes no difference. If anything, the voices grow even louder and crosser.

Lottie turns away; she doesn't want to hear any more. But she doesn't want to go back to the sitting room, either, and have to tell Emma and Adam what's going on. What should she do? Blinking against the hot tears, she creeps back along the passage. Instead of returning to her cousins, she slips into the drawing room where she hurries to the open patio doors and out into the garden. Hoping the adults are too busy to look through the window, she breaks into a run and doesn't stop until she is safely up in the tree house. There, huddled on the wooden boards in the shady quiet, she hugs her knees and waits for the storm to blow over.

***

Silence follows Scott's wordless admission. Joel struggles to absorb the implications, head reeling. Half of the company's value wiped out, just like that, as though it never existed. In better times they might have survived such a blow, but in the current crisis … This can't be real; it must be some appalling nightmare.

Echoing Joel's thoughts, Rafe says, "Please tell me this isn't happening. Tell me this is some kind of sick joke."

Scott only shakes his head, plainly unable to meet their eyes.

"I don't understand," Tim says. "You're no idiot. Surely you checked the horse was insured?"

"I thought it was all in hand, even had Rick show me the paperwork."

"So what went wrong?"

Scott sinks his head into his hands. "Turns out the policy didn't start until nine o'clock Friday morning, six hours after the police reckon the fire broke out. If it had happened the following night, we would have been covered. As it was," he falters, looking wretched. "I swear, it never occurred to me for a second Rick would've been so stupid. Still, I should have checked it out myself."

"Too damn right you should." Rafe explodes to his feet and glares down the table. Phoebe puts out a hand to him but he knocks it aside. "How could you be so bloody careless? Have you any idea what you've done? Well, have you?"

"I don't believe this," Carla snarls. "I always knew you were irresponsible, Scott, but I never imagined you were so selfish."

She rises from her chair to stand beside Rafe, hands gripping the edge of the table, face ghostly pale. Tim gets up to put an arm around her trembling body and the three of them stand shoulder-to-shoulder, united in their anger. Phoebe shields her face with her hands, but not before Joel glimpses her expression, distorted with fury and anguish.

"I'm sorry," Scott says, chin still in his hands. "I'm so sorry."

Joel barely hears him, is scarcely even aware of Olivia's hand in his. Fear has seized him in an icy grip, draining the strength from his limbs. He signed a contract with Langdon, guaranteeing a return on his investment, a guarantee Scott has just blown to smithereens. If they can't survive such a loss and Cameron's goes into administration ... if the authorities want to see the company's paperwork and uncover the agreement with Langdon ... Worse still, if his client sues him for breach of contract ...

Rafe lets out a bitter laugh. "Sorry? You calmly throw away the company our great-grandfather built up over a hundred years ago, the company we've helped to make a success and which we would have passed down to our own children, and all you can say is sorry?"

"What else can I say?" Scott shoves back his chair to confront them, eyes blazing. "Do you honestly think I wanted any of this to happen? How was I supposed to know Rick had upset someone so much they wanted to destroy his business, or that he was negligent enough to allow a horse like that to spend a single second in his yard without insurance? I didn't plan any of this but, the way you're talking, it's like you think I started the fire myself."

Rafe's own eyes are flint-like. "You may as well have. Either way, the result's the same. You've still lost half the company's money, and almost certainly forfeited our livelihood in the process. You couldn't have wrecked our lives so thoroughly if you'd planned it. And what about Dad? You know how he dotes on you, how you've always been his favorite. This will destroy him."

"Scott doesn't care about that," Carla says. "He never cared about anyone but himself. He's always treated Cameron's as an easy ride, knowing he can get away with being a sloth because he's one of its directors. Why should it matter to him if the company goes under, if we lose everything we've worked so hard for over the years?"

"How could you?" Olivia looks at Scott with tears in her eyes. "You know how much Joel and I love this place, and Lottie, too."

Tugged from his own preoccupation, Joel puts his arm around her and glares at Scott. "See what you've done? See where your meddling has led? Didn't you even stop to think how it would affect the rest of us if your bit of fun blew up in your face?"

"Of course he didn't." Carla tosses her head like an enraged mare. "He doesn't give a damn if you lose your dream home, or if Emma and Adam have to be uprooted from their school and their friends because we can no longer afford the fees. None of that matters a jot to him."

"I was trying to help!" Scott slams his fists onto the table; the china rattles in protest. "Why can't you understand that? I thought this deal was going to get Cameron's out of trouble, and it would have done if Rick hadn't trodden on too many toes on his way up the ladder. Christ, I can't believe you're saying all this. How can you even think I'd want this to happen?"

"And how can you still defend yourself? I don't know how you had the nerve to show up here after what you've done."

"Look, Carla, I've said I'm sorry and I am. I'm more sorry than you can possibly imagine. What more do you want me to do?"

Rafe regards Scott as though he's a stranger. "You can drown yourself for all I care. Just as long as I don't have to look at you a moment longer."

Scott doesn't move; the room holds its breath.

"Go on," Rafe says, "get out of my sight."

"Okay." Scott's voice grows deadly calm. "If that's what you want. Vi?"

He appeals to her, though whether asking her to come with him or simply hoping she'll beg him to stay, Joel can't tell. For the first time since they sat down, Violet raises her head to look at him. They gaze at each other for a long moment, a silent exchange indecipherable to all but themselves, and then Violet looks away.

"You should go," she says without emotion.

Scott's expression twists and he turns from the table. He leaves without another word, banging the door behind him. Then there is silence, broken only by Phoebe's quiet sobs and the ticking of the kitchen clock.

Twenty-Two

Scott chokes as the vodka burns his throat. Welcoming its rawness, he swallows and lifts the bottle once more. The second mouthful goes down more easily. Fire soothes his battered heart and spreads throughout his body, numbing the ache of loss, of betrayal.

Slumped on the grass, the sharp twigs of the hedge digging into his back like accusing fingers, Scott stares into the pool. Again and again he raises the bottle to his lips, until the rectangle of water blurs before his eyes, a mist of shimmering turquoise obscuring his vision. But nothing can stop the images from mocking him. Even with his eyes screwed tight, they remain branded on his retinas: the faces of the people he loves most in the world, the family who have adored him all his life, looking at him with anger and disgust. Vi's face is clearest, her expression devoid of emotion as she meets his gaze before turning her back on him. A pain unlike anything Scott has ever known knifes him in the chest and he doubles up, hugging the almost empty bottle as he'd once clung to his favorite teddy.

"Uncle Scott?"

Starting at the tap on his shoulder, he opens his eyes and attempts to focus on the small figure. "Where did you spring from, little one? Are you a fairy, able to appear out of thin air?"

Lottie giggles. "Can you keep a secret?"

Scott smiles without humor. As if his family would give a damn about anything he had to say. "My lips are sealed."

She leans in close, hand resting on his shoulder, to whisper in his ear. Her breath tickles his cheek and Scott inhales the wholesome smell of her, the smell of sun and chlorine and chocolate cake, the smell of innocence. It brings a lump to his throat.

"A tree house, huh?" He pulls her into his side, finding comfort in her warm presence. "So that's where you were hiding. I thought you were watching a film with the terrible two."

"I came to ask Mummy for some more cake for Emma because greedy pig Adam ate it, and I heard everyone shouting at you. Why were they shouting, Uncle Scott?"

"Nothing for you to worry about. Your silly old uncle's been a bad boy, that's all. Sorry if you were frightened. Is that why you came out here? To hide from all the shouting?"

Lottie nods, nestling against him. Her eyes alight on the bottle cradled to his chest. "What's that?"

"This? Oh, it's just some medicine to make me feel better."

"Like Calpol? Mummy always gives me Calpol when I'm under the weather."

"Yeah, just like that," Scott says. Heat pricks his eyelids and he turns his face away so Lottie won't see. How innocent she is, so untouched by this sordid, unforgiving world.

Lottie slides her arm about his neck to pat him on the shoulder. "Don't be sad. They'll forgive you. I know they will."

"You know, huh? I wish I could be so sure. They were really mad at me, especially your Aunt Vi. I don't think she'll ever forgive me."

"She loves you, silly. She said so yesterday, and you said you were going to get married. You haven't gone off her, have you?"

Fresh pain shoots through Scott's heart. He takes another slug of vodka. "No, but I think she might have gone off me."

"I bet she hasn't," Lottie says. "Bet you ten Mars bars. Come on, let's shake on it."

Scott opens his mouth to protest, then shrugs. What the hell?

"Okay, ten Mars bars it is." He allows Lottie to slide her small hand into his and pump it up and down.

"Be back soon." Beaming, Lottie scampers towards the gate in the hedge. "Wait there."

Don't worry, Scott thinks bitterly, I'm not going anywhere. The summer afternoon spins past as though he's on a roundabout, the colors running together like wet paint, blue sky merging with sun-yellowed grass and the sparkling water of the pool. Sunshine gilds everything in a harsh brilliance that hurts his eyes. He doubts his legs would support him even if he wanted them to. Turning his back on the retreating figure, he angles the bottle to his lips. It's empty.

Scott flings it to the grass and grabs a second. He'd pinched it from the drinks cabinet without glancing at the label, and he doesn't look at it now as he unscrews the cap. The distinctive tang of gin hits his nose. He hesitates. He's already had a skinful. His body can't take much more. Scott shrugs. What does it matter? His family won't care. He could drink himself into a coma, choke to death on his own vomit, and none of them would give a damn, least of all Vi.

Her face drifts once more into his mind, features stone-like, eyes regarding him as though he were a stranger. Despair crashes over him and he grits his teeth against a howl of misery. Thrusting the bottle to his lips, he gulps. Without Violet, life has no meaning. She's the only woman he has ever loved, the only woman he would have given up his wild days to settle down with. Now he's lost her and nothing matters anymore.

***

"Mummy," Lottie calls, hurtling through the deserted kitchen and along the passage. The house is unusually quiet. "Aunt Vi, where are you?"

"I'm right here." Her mother holds out her arms to hug Lottie as she rushes into the hall. "There you are. I just looked in to tell you your aunt and I are going for a walk, but you weren't there. Emma said you went to find me and never came back. Did the shouting frighten you?"

"A bit."

"My poor love. Have you been hiding all this time?"

"I went outside to play in the garden, then Uncle Scott came out. He says he's been a bad boy and everyone's cross with him. He said Aunt Vi doesn't love him anymore." Lottie peeps around her mother's belly to where her aunt is staring out of the window by the front door. "That's not true, is it, Aunt Vi? I told him you still love him. You do, don't you?"

Her aunt turns from the window with a shrug. "Right at this moment, Lottie, I honestly don't know."

"But you must." Tears sting Lottie's eyes. The vision of having ten Mars bars all to herself fades like a dream. "You must still love him. You held hands yesterday when we were playing ball, and Uncle Scott said you were going to get married and I would be the prettiest bridesmaid ever. You must still love him."

"For heaven's sake." Aunt Violet sighs, but her face softens. "Don't get upset. I didn't mean to snap."

Lottie blinks away the tears, suddenly hopeful. "So you do still love Uncle Scott?"

"Oh." Her aunt shakes her head as if to dislodge something caught in her hair. "All right. If that's what you want to hear, then, yes. Yes, I do still love Uncle Scott."

Lottie beams in triumph, and, disentangling herself from her mother's arms, races back along the passage.

"Where do you think you're going?" her mum asks. "I want you in the sitting room with Emma and Adam."

Lottie replies without slowing. "I need to go and tell Uncle Scott he owes me ten Mars bars. I'll come back in straight away, promise."

"Well, make sure you do."

Lottie barely hears her. Already at the back door, she crosses the patio and runs flat-out across the lawn towards the pool.

"Uncle Scott." She bursts through the gate in the hedge, breathless with excitement. "Uncle Scott, you owe me ten—"

She stops short. Her uncle has fallen asleep stretched out on the grass, the empty bottle of medicine beside him. Lottie pouts. Now what should she do? She promised Mummy she'd go straight back inside, but wants to see Uncle Scott's face when she tells him Aunt Vi still loves him and that he has to buy her ten whole Mars bars. She shifts from one foot to the other, dithering. Mummy said she and Aunt Violet were going for a walk. She won't know if Lottie doesn't go in straight away. Perhaps she should wait a while, just until Uncle Scott wakes up.

Deciding to hide in case her dad looks out of the window, Lottie creeps back through the gate and climbs the rope ladder to the tree house. It's dim and cool up here, and very still. Lottie yawns, suddenly worn out. Curled up on the wooden boards, she rests her head on her folded arms. She must stay awake, must watch for Uncle Scott. Despite her good intentions, her eyes grow heavy, until she can't keep them open any longer, and she sleeps.

***

Alone in Olivia's study, Joel hunches forward in the swivel chair, arms resting on the notebook-strewn desk, and stares out of the window. To him, the grounds look particularly lovely at that moment, an acre of trees and sloping lawn bathed in sunshine: the perfect rural idyll. An ache starts deep in his gut. He and Olivia have such plans for this place, plans which will now never be realized.

Joel closes his eyes, blocking out the view. What a wrench to lose this house after they've lavished so much time and money, not to mention love, on making it their dream home. Even if by some miracle they can save Cameron's from going under, there's little hope for him. The chance of him delivering on his contract with Mr. Langdon is non-existent, and when his client brings it to the attention of the authorities, he'll be lucky to escape a jail sentence. At best, he'll be banned from working in the financial sector for life. Either way, he's ruined. He has lost everything. Damn you, Scott. Damn you to hell.

The door opens and Joel glances round as Tim slips in. "Kids okay?"

"Fine." Tim comes to perch on the desk. "They know something's up, but I've told them it's nothing to worry about. They're watching *Pinocchio* now, so that should keep them quiet."

"And Carla?"

"Gone to lie down. This has hit her pretty hard."

"Join the club." Joel rubs his pounding forehead. "I can keep an eye on the kids for a while if you want to be with her."

Tim shakes his head. "Thanks, but I think Carla's best left alone for the time being. Besides, what can I say? What can any of us say?"

Joel doesn't answer. Nothing anyone might say will alter the bleakness of their situation. He drops his chin on his folded arms, fingers digging into his temples as though to will the reality away.

Tim grips his shoulder. "We'll get through this, Joel. Somehow or other."

"Not me," Joel says. "I'm finished."

"Snap out of it." His twin gives him a shake. "You'll make yourself ill, thinking like that. Look, why not come and sit with me and the kids? It's no good you sitting here brooding."

"Thanks, but I don't think I can cope with *Pinocchio* just now."

"All right, but try not to worry, okay? We'll find a way to beat this, you'll see. We Camerons always do."

***

Carla paces her bedroom floor, unable to keep still, though every movement is an effort. Her limbs are heavy and sluggish as if she's trapped in a nightmare, struggling through quicksand while the nameless terror draws ever closer. This time, however, there is no escape, no opening her eyes to find herself safe in bed. And it's all Scott's doing. Passing the window, she spies him hunched by the pool beyond the hedge. Fury leaps up to scald her throat. This is all his fault.

Carla turns her back to him and collapses on the bed, face buried in the pillow, teeth clenched against the scream welling like molten lava inside her. Staring into darkness, she tries to shut out the truth. It's no use. Not even her immense willpower can make her forget. Her worst fear has been realized, the business ruined, all her hopes for the future in tatters. They'll lose the beautiful penthouse with its balcony overlooking Holland Park. The children will have to be taken from private education and dumped in an ordinary school to mix with children from ordinary families, while she and Tim are cast out from society, forsaken by those who have been proud to call them friends. She, Carla Louise Cameron, will be a nothing, a nobody.

Oh, God! She moans into the pillow, nails clawing the bedspread. Oh, God, this isn't happening. It can't be real. It's all a dream, a horrific nightmare. Oh, let it be a dream. Please, God, let it be a dream.

***

Rafe stalks across the lawn, his strides eating up the grass as though only speed will drive the horror from his mind. He scarcely knows where he's going. It doesn't matter. Nothing matters anymore except getting as far away from the house as possible, far away from the memories, the betrayal. Phoebe calls his name but he walks on, deaf to all but his own ragged breathing.

"Rafe, please." Breathless from running, Phoebe clutches his arm. "Talk to me. You don't have to go through this alone. I'm here for you."

Rafe slows to look at her, at the eyes soft with anxiety and tenderness in her pale face. His throat closes. How easy it would be to rest his head on Phoebe's slender shoulder, to pour out his frustration and bitterness and let her soothe him with gentle words. He averts his gaze. No one must see his weakness, not even Phoebe.

"Leave me be, Phoebs, there's a good girl. This is something I have to do on my own."

At once, she drops her hand and falls back. Rafe continues through the grounds, oblivious to his surroundings, until his feet bring him to a stop outside the stables. He feels no surprise. Perhaps this is where he's been headed all along. Stumbling into the shady interior, he sinks onto the dusty floor and covers his face with his hands. Safe from scrutiny, he lets himself cry. He has lost everything: his respect for Scott, the younger brother he adores; the business that is his whole world; all his ambitions for Cameron's future. He has lost his very reason for living. *Christ, Scott, I could kill you for this. I could fucking kill you.*

***

"Feeling better?" Olivia asks as they wander along the winding country lane, shaded on either side by English oaks.

Inhaling the meadow-sweet air, Violet feels her muscles relax. "Much. It makes such a change to be able to hear myself think without the constant noise of London."

They continue in easy silence, the afternoon stillness broken only by birdsong and the stirring of leaves overhead.

After a while, Violet says, "How about you? This was as much a shock to you as to me."

"It was a shock," Olivia admits, "but out here, away from it all, I can believe we'll come through this, somehow or other."

"What about the house? Will you lose it?"

"Not if I can help it. It took Joel and me a long time to find our dream home, and I'm not giving it up without a fight. The advance my agent's hoping for should tide us over for a while, and, if Cameron's does go under, Joel will just have to buy a greenhouse and start growing vegetables. He's always fancied doing that."

Violet shoots her an amused look. "I never knew that."

"Nor does Rafe, so don't go shouting it about. Can you imagine how he'd react if he found out his own brother has dreams of being a lowly gardener?"

Violet laughs, filled with a sudden sense of well-being. Perhaps, after all, everything is not lost. Scott might have sunk the company, but, in spite of her harsh words earlier, she knows he acted with the best intentions. He can find another job, if not now, when the recession is over and, in the meantime, she earns more than enough to keep them both. They can still have a life together, a good life.

Olivia seems to read her thoughts. "You and Scott will be okay, won't you? You do still care for him?"

"I care," Violet says. "Nothing he does will ever change that."

"I'm glad." Olivia squeezes her arm. "Whatever anyone else says, I know you're made for each other. Ready to go back now?"

Violet hesitates, then shakes her head. "Not just yet. This might be the last quiet moment we get for a while. Let's make the most of it."

***

After watching Rafe out of sight, Phoebe walks on more slowly, blind to all but the anger pulsing behind her eyes like a migraine. How dare Scott hurt Rafe like this. How dare he. She has thought his devil-may-care attitude charming. Now, it just seems foolhardy, irresponsible. Phoebe recalls Rafe's face, eyes dull with horror, features strained and scored with new lines of disappointment. Her heart aches for him. If only there was something she could do, some way to ease his pain and wipe the desperation from his expression. She would do anything, anything in her power to make him happy, and yet she can do nothing. She balls her hands into fists, despising her utter uselessness, her inability to help the man she loves.

As she draws near the hedge around the pool, Phoebe notices the gate swinging open. Surely she shut it behind her when they came in for lunch. At least the children are safely installed in front of the telly. Phoebe shudders to think what might have happened if they'd come out here unsupervised. Hurrying forward to close the gate, her breath catches at the sight of the supine figure on the grass.

"Scott?" She falls to her knees beside him. "Scott, can you hear me?"

Receiving no response, she shakes him gently by the shoulder. His head lolls on his neck but he doesn't stir. Phoebe freezes, like an image paused on a television screen. Only her eyes move, flicking to the empty bottles of spirits lying in the grass a short way away and then back to Scott, limbs thrown out at careless angles, eyes half closed, face as peaceful and vulnerable as a sleeping child's …

Twenty-Three

After an age, the shock releases Phoebe from its grasp and she scrambles to her feet, away from Scott's unconscious body. Heart pounding, she tears through the gate in the hedge and across the lawn towards the house. Scott's face, slack-jawed and unresponsive, remains imprinted on her mind, spurring her on. Must find someone. Get help before it's too late. In her fear, it's as though the grounds have trebled in size, becoming an endless patchwork of trees and grass. Never have they seemed so sprawling, nor so utterly deserted.

Though she strains her eyes for any sign of movement, Phoebe sees no one on her mad dash to the house, and when she hurtles onto the patio the umbrella-shaded table is empty. Clutching the stitch in her side, too short of breath to shout for help, she staggers into the kitchen. Please let there be someone here. But the kitchen, like everywhere else, is unoccupied. *Oh, God, where is everyone?* Coming to a skidding halt, she rests her trembling hands on the table to steady herself and gasps for air. What to do now? *Think, Phoebs, think. A man's life is in your hands.*

***

Blind to her surroundings, Carla crosses the lawn and slips through the gate in the hedge. If she doesn't have it out with Scott soon, vent her anger and frustration, she'll go mad. She finds him sprawled by the water's edge, mouth hanging open, dead to the world. Well, isn't that just typical? Here's the rest of the family, agonizing over how to piece their shattered lives back together, while Scott, the wreaker of all the damage, falls asleep with the untroubled conscience of a baby. Bloody typical! Her gaze alights on the empty bottles lying nearby. He's not asleep, then, but has drunk himself into blissful oblivion. They'll soon see about that.

"Wake up," Carla orders, jabbing Scott in the side with the toe of her sandal. He doesn't move, so she squats and shakes him roughly by the shoulder. "Damn you, Scott, wake up."

His head flops from side to side, heedless as a rag doll's. Carla's heart rate speeds up. She presses her fingertips to his neck. *Come on, Scott. Don't do this to me.* As if in answer, a pulse flutters against her fingers, fainter than a butterfly's wings. He's still alive, but barely. If he'd been in the pool when he passed out, he wouldn't have stood a chance. Unbidden, Rafe's words creep into her mind. "You can drown yourself for all I care."

Carla looks from the pool to Scott's peaceful expression and back again. An idea spawns inside her, the one sure means to put everything right. She shrinks away from it; she mustn't think like that. Yet, it won't be ignored, oozing through her veins like poison, setting her entire body alight with the dreadful simplicity of it. Sickened and trembling, she shoves the notion back into the darkest recesses of her soul. *Get a grip, girl. Fetch help before it's too late.*

An image of Tim's gentle face, white with shock, blazes across her vision. He's such a good man, so honest and hard working. He doesn't deserve this. None of them do. Once again, she has a stark glimpse of the future: she and Tim living in a poky terrace with neighbors who hold raucous parties late into the night; Emma and Adam attending a state school with rough children from broken homes; the whole family shunned and in disgrace.

Carla's chest tightens. None of this is her fault. Why should she have to suffer because of another's recklessness? She's going to lose everything important to her, everything that makes her life worthwhile, and there's nothing she can do about it.

"Oh, but there is something you can do," whispers a voice in her head. "You have the power to stop Scott's actions from destroying your life. It won't hurt him. He won't feel a thing. It will be as gentle as falling asleep, and all will be well again. No one will suspect the truth. Not when it looks like such a tragic accident. The insurance company will pay out, Cameron's will be saved, and your lives can go on as normal. It's as simple as that."

Still on her knees in the grass, Carla gazes down at the man responsible for turning her world upside down. She recalls all the years she has known him, laughing and shaking her head in equal measure at his exploits, helpless to resist his easy charm. The notion that the blue eyes will never again sparkle with mischief, infecting them all with his enthusiasm for life, that he will never light up a room just by entering it and break a dozen hearts with a smile, is too awful to contemplate. Tears scald her eyes, tears of grief and resentment. How can life go on without this vital spark? Yet how can it go on while his actions cast a shadow over them all?

And what of Violet, the determined young woman who truly believes they have a future together? What will it matter to her that Cameron's survives if the man she loves is gone? Carla shakes her head. Violet's hopes and expectations are nothing more than dreams. Scott is a free spirit; he'll never be tied down to one woman, not even one as clever and strong as Violet. He'll break her heart as surely as he's broken so many hearts over the years, as surely as he has destroyed the lives of the family who adore him. Better that Violet should lose him now while certain of his love, rather than travel the long and painful road to disillusionment. Better, too, that she squash her own affection for him and act while the situation can still be salvaged.

***

Call an ambulance. The answer shines through Phoebe's confusion, a torch lighting the way along a dark tunnel. Yes, telephone for help, that's what she has to do. Her heart bounces off the walls of her ribcage. Now, where do Joel and Olivia keep the phone? She scrambles around in her brain, trying to remember if she has seen the phone during her stay. Her mind remains blank, refusing to cooperate. For heaven's sake, Phoebs, how hard can it be? Think. Where do most people keep their phones?

With renewed energy, Phoebe careers along the passage and across the hall to the telephone table by the front door. Thank goodness! The phone is there, nestled amid a profusion of pens and discarded envelopes, and she pounces on the receiver as though it is the first food she has seen after days of starvation. Phoebe is about to dial 999 when the awful truth locks her in place. She doesn't know Olivia and Joel's address. Even if she gets through to the emergency services, she won't be able to tell them where to come. A sob catches in her throat. This can't be happening. Scott is desperately ill, maybe dying, and there is nothing she can do, no one to ask for help.

"Phoebe?" Joel emerges into the hall. "I was in the study. Saw you running like a mad thing. What's happened?"

"Oh, thank God." Sobbing with relief now as well as fear, Phoebe runs to him and seizes the front of his T-shirt. "It's Scott. He's unconscious. Drunk, I think, out by the pool. I came straight away to get help but everyone's disappeared. I was going to call an ambulance, then realized I don't know your address."

Joel detaches her hands and grips them. Phoebe can feel him shaking. "Scott's unconscious, you say? Christ." Pulling himself together with a visible effort, he snatches an envelope from the telephone table and thrusts it at her. "Right, our address is on here. You call an ambulance and I'll go and see what state he's in."

***

The tears flow unchecked down Carla's cheeks. She can't do this; she hasn't got the strength. Resolve sets like concrete around her heart. *You have no choice. This is the only way.* Trembling all over, she takes a steadying breath and slides her arms under Scott's shoulders. Though slighter than his brothers, he's as heavy and awkward as a sagging mattress. Carla pants with the effort, sweat pouring off her, muscles screaming in protest. Yet she doesn't rest. At any moment someone might come through the gate in the hedge and catch her.

Gradually, by shifting first his shoulders and then his feet, she hauls him to the water's edge. That done, she pauses for a second to gulp in air. *Come on, girl, you're almost there.* She readies herself for the final push. With Scott's body already hanging over the side of the pool, it's surprisingly simple to roll him over and let him fall facedown into the water. He breaks the surface with a decisive splash and sinks several feet, before floating up again. Carla watches, frozen. At the sight of Scott's defenseless body, reality crashes around her. She can still change her mind. There's still time to go back.

A sob forces its way from her aching chest. Once she starts crying, she can't stop. There is no alternative, no option open to her. This is the only way to save both Cameron's and their lives as they know them. She can't falter now. Placing her shaking hands on Scott's neck, trying not to imagine the water rushing down his throat to flood his lungs, Carla holds his head under the surface. She holds it there until she loses track of time. How long does it take a person to drown? How long before their body is starved of oxygen and they slip away into eternal oblivion?

"Oh, my God!" A voice, sharp with shock, jolts Carla from her morbid reverie. "Oh, my God, what have you done?"

***

Joel sprints over the lawn, anxiety warring with exasperation inside him. Trust Scott to pull a stunt like this. Even as they are trying to sift through the wreckage of his bombshell, he has to recapture the limelight by drinking himself into a stupor. Perhaps he hopes the worry will soften their hearts, that this demonstration of his remorse will win their forgiveness. This really is so like him!

Pounding through the gate in the hedge, Joel skids to a halt. Disbelief knocks the air from his body and he almost stumbles. It's like a scene from a television drama: the figure on her knees by the pool, hair draped in a golden curtain about her shoulders, forearms submerged in the water as she holds the dark head under the surface. This can't be happening. Joel closes his eyes, then opens them again. Nothing has changed.

"Oh, my God." The words burst from him in a harsh cry. "Oh, my God, what have you done?"

Starting, Carla turns a tear-stained face to him but doesn't reply. The feeling rushes back into Joel's legs. He closes the distance between them in three strides and drops to his knees beside her.

"Get away from him." With an animal snarl, he shoves Carla hard in the shoulder so that she falls back onto her heels and has to remove her hands from Scott's neck to save herself. Joel ignores her, reaching into the water to grasp his brother's T-shirt. "Christ, we have to get him out of here."

"It's too late," Carla says without inflection. "You're too late, Joel. He's—"

Joel rounds on her. "Don't say it. Just help me get him out."

He takes a firm grip on Scott's shoulders, bracing himself to bear the strain, and tries to haul him towards the side. The water resists his efforts, sucking at Scott's sodden clothing, dragging him down.

"Help me, damn you," Joel roars.

Without speaking, face very pale, Carla seizes Scott's legs. Grunting with the effort, they heave him out of the pool and onto the grass.

"Now, get away." Warning Carla back with a glare, Joel bends over Scott. He puts his mouth close to his brother's blue-tinged lips and breathes out, hands working the chest in rhythm, all the while alert for a response. Nothing. Fear creeps into his mind but he forces it aside. Must stay focused. Forget everything but the task in hand. *Come on, Scott, don't do this to me. To all of us. You can't fail me now. I won't let you. Oh, Christ.*

A metallic clang breaks through Joel's concentration. Hands stilling on Scott's chest, he glances up as Phoebe hurtles through the gate.

"I've called the ambulance," she says, clutching her side. "It's on its way. How's…" Her eyes widen as they take in Scott, his clothes dripping, hair plastered to his pale forehead. "What happened?"

Releasing his brother's lifeless body, Joel gets unsteadily to his feet. "He's dead." Though he understands the words, it's as though he, too, is dead inside. "She drowned him."

"W-what?" Phoebe stares between them, her expression blank.

A bitter edge steals into Joel's voice. "You heard me right. Your precious Carla drowned Scott in the pool. I caught her holding his head under the water. She must have held it there until his lungs filled up and he choked to death."

"Stop it! I don't … no, I won't believe it." Phoebe turns beseeching eyes to Carla. "This can't be true. Please, tell me it isn't true."

"Yes, tell her," Joel says. "Go on, tell her what you did."

Carla appears scarcely to hear them. She stands as still as the dead man at her feet and her face is that of a stranger, features inscrutable, eyes hard and glittering as sapphires. Joel hardly recognizes her as his sister-in-law of the past eight years. Phoebe must have seen it, too, for the plea in her eyes darkens to incredulous horror. Her face drains of its remaining color and she looks about to faint.

"No," she whispers, as though to herself. "It isn't true. I won't believe it."

At last, their combined revulsion penetrates Carla's trance. She whirls to glare at them. "Don't look at me like that. I didn't do it for me, you know. I did it for all of us. For the company."

White-hot rage crashes over Joel, vaporizing his numbness. He takes a step towards her. "Don't you dare try and say this is what I wanted, what anyone of us would have wanted. Do you honestly think the business means more to me than my own brother? God, Carla, there's something seriously wrong with you."

"No, Joel, I'm just honest." She meets his anger with defiance. "Oh, I know you would never admit as much, but if anyone else had found Scott lying there they would have been tempted to do the same. I know the huge premiums Cameron's pays out, the sum you're set to get from the insurance if anything happens to any of you. Now it's time to put it to good use. Anyone could see this is the answer to our problems. The only difference is that I actually had the courage to go through with it."

"You're sick." Joel begins to shake. "This is my own brother we're talking about. Not some minor inconvenience. My own brother. And what about Violet? Spared a thought for what this would do to her, did you?"

"Come off it, Joel. We both know that was never going to last. Scott was toying with her, just like with all the women before. He'd only have broken her heart. This way is best for all of us. You must see that."

"It's murder. I see that much."

"Hardly murder. He was half dead already, and I very much doubt he ever would've recovered from that coma. All I did was make absolutely sure he didn't."

Joel raises his fist. He visualizes smashing it into Carla's perfect face, wiping the smugness from her expression. A quiet sob stays him. He turns, arm still raised. Phoebe has sunk to the grass, hands over her face, rocking back and forth in anguish.

"No," she moans into her palms, as though willing the truth away. "No, no, no."

Joel's fury solidifies into icy hatred. He squares his shoulders and turns back to Carla. He must stay calm, must keep his head.

"You won't get away with this," he says. "Not now. You can't expect us to keep quiet."

Carla shrugs and moves to stand with her back to the gate, barring their exit. "Oh, believe me, I can. Neither of you will be saying anything about this to anyone."

"Why's that? Going to drown us like you did Scott? What will you say, Carla? That we were all so distraught about the company going under we formed a suicide pact?"

"Don't be silly, Joel. You won't be saying anything because it's not in your interests, either of you." She reaches down to lay a hand on her friend's shoulder. Phoebe flinches but doesn't pull away.

"See?" Carla smiles as though she has proved a point. "Phoebe's my best friend in all the world. She would never betray me."

Phoebe looks up at her, eyes huge with fear. "Don't, Carla, please. I can't do this for you. Please don't make me."

"Phoebs, you know I would never force you to do anything, although I did hope our friendship meant more to you than that. I would have thought everything I've done for you over the years, all the times I've comforted you and protected you, the way I've always been there for you, would count for something. Maybe I'm wrong. Maybe you never cared about me at all and you've just been using me."

Phoebe lets out a cry, half denial, half despair. Burying her face in her drawn-up knees, she sobs as though her heart will break. Straightening, Carla gives Joel a look that says clearly, "You see? She'll never betray me."

Joel stares back, unmoved. "Very touching, I'm sure. The trouble is, Carla, while you may have some hold over Phoebe, there's nothing you can do to stop me going to the police."

"No?" Carla raises her eyebrows. "How about the little matter of an agreement between you and a certain Mr. Langdon?"

Shock slams into Joel's chest. He staggers, knocked off balance, as if the ground has shifted beneath his feet. Only one person knows about the deal with Langdon and he would die rather than break his confidence. Wouldn't he?

"How did you find out?" he asks, throat hoarse.

Carla tosses her lovely hair over her shoulders. "That doesn't matter. Nothing matters other than that if you breathe a word of this to anyone, anyone at all, I'll tell the police what I know. Fancy spending the next ten years behind bars? Think what it would do to Olivia. And what about little Lottie? How will she feel when she learns her precious daddy's in prison?"

Joel says nothing. Betrayal, more painful than anything he has ever experienced, forms a fist-sized lump in his throat. It oozes like snake venom into his heart, poisoning forever his perception of the twin who has been both brother and soul mate to him. Through his hurt and confusion, he is dimly aware of a siren wailing in the distance.

"There's the ambulance." Carla becomes brisk, rubbing her hands together as though concluding a highly successful business meeting. She fixes each of them with an intense gaze. "Now, pay attention, both of you. Here's what we tell them."

***

At the sight of the ambulance parked in the driveway, Olivia shares one terrified look with Violet and then they are running flat out towards the house. Horrific images flaunt themselves before Olivia's eyes: Lottie lying in a pool of blood, fragile limbs bent like snapped twigs, face white with pain and shock. Her hands are shaking so much that she fumbles with her key as she tries to unlock the front door. The moment she and Violet tumble into the hallway, Tim emerges from the sitting room and closes the door behind him.

"There's been an accident," he says in a low voice. "Out by the pool. It's—"

"Is it Lottie?" Olivia cuts across him. God, why hadn't she made her daughter come back inside, rather than letting her go running off on her own?

Tim shakes his head, eyes haunted, face gray and haggard. "No, it's Scott. He's—"

But Violet doesn't wait to hear the rest. With a strangled gasp, she darts through the drawing room door and Olivia hurries after her. The momentary relief at learning Lottie is safe flees in the face of this new crisis. As they sprint onto the patio and over the sloping lawn, her bruised mind tries to figure out what can have happened. An accident by the pool, Tim said, but what sort of accident? Rafe's words, spoken with such venom earlier that afternoon, slither into her thoughts. "You can drown yourself for all I care." Fear pushes her to run even faster. Please, no. Not Scott, not like that.

They burst through the gate in the hedge just as two paramedics are lifting Scott onto a stretcher. Olivia's heart turns over. Huddled on the grass by the hedge, Carla has her arms around a sobbing Phoebe, her own cheeks glazed with tears. Olivia spies Joel, standing with Rafe by the water's edge. Both so confident in the world of finance, they now look as helpless and desolate as Wendy's lost boys.

With a soft moan, Violet falls to her knees beside the stretcher. "Scott, I'm so sorry. I didn't mean to leave you like that, but I'm here now. Everything's going to be okay. Speak to me, Scott, tell me you're okay."

One of the paramedics, a middle-aged man with a fatherly expression, lays a hand on Violet's shoulder. "I'm so sorry. We arrived too la—"

"Don't say it." Violet knocks his hand away, eyes blazing. "It isn't too late. He's unconscious, that's all. Just unconscious." Hunching over the stretcher, she shakes Scott by the shoulder. "Wake up, Scott. It's me, Vi. I know you can hear me. Don't do this to me. I love you. Please, wake up. For pity's sake, wake up."

"Oh, God," Olivia mouths, head spinning. She should go to her sister, comfort her, but disbelief glues her to the spot. She can't take her gaze from Scott's face, so alien in its indifference. No compassion softens the handsome features, and the half-closed eyes that so often sparkled with vitality and mischief stare blankly at nothing.

Once again, the paramedic reaches out to Violet. "I really am sorry. There was nothing we could do. He's gone."

"No!" Her wail is pure anguish. "No, no, no."

Violet seems to crumple in on herself. Collapsing onto Scott's limp body, she buries her face against his sodden T-shirt and convulses with grief. She sobs as though her soul is being ripped apart piece by piece, an animal sound that goes straight to Olivia's heart. Emerging from her shock, she falls to her knees beside her sister. She doesn't speak; nothing she says will cushion the blow. She simply wraps her arms around Violet and holds her tight, as though only this will keep her from breaking apart. Violet appears not to notice. She merely clings to Scott as though she'll never let him go, weeping into his chest.

Helpless to comfort her, Olivia lets her gaze roam. The paramedics, looking awkward, have moved a short distance away to give them some space. Everyone else is exactly as she first saw them, like actors in a play awaiting further stage directions. Olivia catches Joel's eye, bleak with a sorrow too deep for tears. His pain calls out to her and she aches to go to him. She glances from Violet to Joel and back again, torn between two of the people she loves most in the world.

"Mummy?"

Though faint, the whimper drowns all other sound as though issuing from a megaphone. Olivia is on her feet in an instant. Her daughter mustn't see this.

"Lottie?" she says, looking around wildly. "Sweetheart, where are you?"

"Up here." Lottie's face, small and white, appears from between the branches of the nearby oak and seems to hover fifteen feet off the ground. Fear shoots through Olivia's heart. How many times have she and Joel warned Lottie not to go in the tree house? Oh, God, how much has she seen?

"Lottie, don't move." Joel's voice is calm as he comes up beside Olivia, but she hears the strain behind it. "I'm coming to get you."

He hurries towards the gate in the hedge, Olivia barely a pace behind him. Passing Phoebe and Carla still huddled on the grass, she sees her own shock frozen in their expressions.

"Want to get down," Lottie says, close to tears. "I don't like it."

"It's okay, sweetheart." Olivia tries to reassure her. "We're here now. Just sit tight."

She isn't sure what happens next, whether Lottie misjudges the distance between herself and her parents and expects one of them to catch her, or whether she simply misses her footing on the rope ladder. All she's aware of is the frightened cry splitting the air, and then her own scream as Lottie tumbles towards the ground. Joel lunges forward, arms outstretched to break her fall, but he's too far away. Olivia knows the sickening crunch as her daughter's head smacks an exposed root at the base of the trunk will haunt her forever.

"Oh, my God!" She drops to the grass beside Lottie, gripping the hand which suddenly seems so fragile. Already blood is trickling from beneath her daughter's hair. "It's okay, sweetheart, Mummy's here. You're going to be all right. Oh, God, Joel." She looks up to find her terror mirrored in his face. "She isn't moving."

"No need to panic." The fatherly paramedic rushes over to them, his colleague close behind. "If you could both stand back, we'll take a look at her."

"No." Olivia tightens her hold on Lottie's hand. "I won't leave her."

The paramedic squeezes her shoulder. "It'll only be for a moment. I promise your daughter's in safe hands."

"Come on," Joel says, "we have to let them do their job."

He holds out his hand and Olivia takes it, allowing him to pull her to her feet. As she stands and steps away, a warm wetness slides down her legs. Puzzled, she glances down.

"Oh, Joel." Her voice is little more than a whisper.

His gaze snaps to her. He looks as though another shock will finish him off. "Liv, what is it?"

Olivia doesn't speak. She simply directs his attention down to her skirt and the dark, reddish-brown stain spreading across it.

Part 4
Monday

Twenty-Four

"You killed him."

Lottie's words dangled in the silent drawing room, horribly out of synch with the champagne glasses waiting in readiness on the coffee tables, the game of Twister abandoned in one corner. No one appeared to breathe. She had the conflicting sense of being unable to believe what she'd just said, while knowing with a horrified certainty that she spoke the truth. Lottie stared at Carla, the aunt who had always been so generous to her despite the rift between their families. Had her kindness in fact been nothing more than guilt? Disgust bubbled in her stomach; she felt sick. Aunt Carla returned her stare, the initial alarm that had betrayed her now hidden away. Her face revealed nothing but innocent concern.

Lottie averted her gaze and found every eye upon her. Through a numbing haze, she noted their reactions by the muted glow of the fairy lights: her parents tense and anxious, Uncle Tim uncomprehending, Aunt Phoebe pale with fright, Uncle Rafe blinking in bleary-eyed confusion. Only Aunt Violet appeared unperturbed. Standing in a shadowy corner, she observed the gathering with keen concentration as though watching a particularly complex play. This is what she's been waiting for, Lottie realized.

Incongruous in the aghast hush, the revelers in Trafalgar Square began to sing *Auld Lang Syne*. Aunt Violet bent to switch off the television, breaking the spell.

"Sweetheart," her mum said, gripping Lottie's hands, "come and sit yourself down. You've had a nasty scare."

"Wait." Adam, visibly shaken, grabbed Lottie by the arm. "What the hell are you playing at? Why would you say something like that?"

The hurt and anger in his eyes tore at her heart. She opened her mouth to speak but no sound came out. She could only look at him, pleading silently for him to understand that she didn't mean to hurt him, that she had no choice.

"Well?" Adam shook her. "Why are you making up stuff about my mum? If this is your idea of a joke—"

"Stop it, Adam," her mum said, dragging him off. "Can't you see she's had a shock? She needs to sit down."

Adam glared. "Not until she explains. That's my mum she's accusing. I have a right to know why she's doing it."

"We both do." Emma came to stand beside him. She looked at Lottie. "Why are you saying this? I thought we were friends."

Lottie barely noticed Emma; she was aware of no one but Adam and the accusation in his eyes. Her insides twisted. How could he even think she'd make up something like this? How could Adam, of all people, believe that of her? From a distance, she felt her mum squeeze her hands and allowed herself to be led over to the sofa to join a shattered Aunt Phoebe. Her dad moved to her other side, sliding a protective arm about her.

"Leave her be," Uncle Tim said behind them, and Lottie glanced over her shoulder to see him pulling his children back by their jumpers.

"Why are you on her side?" Adam demanded. "Didn't you hear what she said about Mum?"

"Yes, Dad, you can't just let her get away with spreading lies like that. It's sick."

"That's enough, both of you. Lottie isn't well. She doesn't know what she's saying."

"That's not true." Lottie stopped in her tracks and tried to twist around.

Her mum restrained her. "It's all right. Don't upset yourself. Just come and sit down and you'll feel better."

"There's nothing wrong with me. Let me go." Wrenching herself free of her parents, she turned to confront her uncle and cousins. She flinched at Adam's expression; it was as though they were enemies, as though he despised her. She forced herself to continue. "I'm not a liar and I'm not ill. I'm just saying what I saw."

Emma and Adam burst out in noisy protests, but Uncle Tim raised a finger to hush them. "What did you see?" he asked Lottie, his tone gentle as though speaking to a psychiatric patient prone to extreme violence.

She bristled. "I saw Aunt Carla murder Uncle Scott, saw her drown him in the swimming pool when he was unconscious."

"You liar!" This time Adam ignored his father's warning and advanced, face contorted. "You take that back."

"Yes, take it back," Emma spat. "I can't believe you'd say something like that."

"I said that's enough." Uncle Tim's voice held an uncharacteristic edge of steel. Clearly seeking reassurance, he turned to Aunt Carla who remained composed. "Is Lottie making this up?"

"No," Lottie yelled, "I'm not making this up. Why won't anyone listen? Aunt Carla dragged Uncle Scott into the pool and held his head under the water until he drowned. I saw it happen."

"No." Aunt Carla spoke with slow consideration, as though pondering an elusive crossword solution. "No, Tim, Lottie isn't making it up. I believe she's telling the truth, or at least what she believes to be the truth." She fixed her intense gaze on Lottie. "You are mistaken, though."

Lottie shook her head. "I know what I saw."

"You know what you *think* you saw." Her aunt gave her a smile full of understanding; Lottie swallowed the bile that rose in her throat. "I would never have hurt your Uncle Scott. I thought the world of him. You were only little then. You didn't understand. You thought you saw me pushing Scott into the water, when what you actually saw was me pulling him out. He was already drowned by the time your Aunt Phoebe and I found him. I got him out as quickly as I could while Aunt Phoebe went for help, but we were too late. It was a terrible thing for you to have seen. It's no wonder you're confused."

Lottie gaped. Aunt Carla should have been an actress. She was so shameless, so utterly convincing in her compassion. A sliver of doubt pierced her certainty. Could she have been mistaken? Was Aunt Carla telling it as it really happened? *For heaven's sake, Lottie, can't you see? This is what she wants. She wants to muddle you, to make you doubt your own mind. How else do you think she's managed to hide the truth for so long if not by being a mistress of deceit? But you know what you saw. You can't let her get away with this.*

Uncle Rafe nodded, his drink-befuddled brain catching up with the conversation. "Yes, that's how it was. A real tragedy."

Uncle Tim's face lightened and Emma and Adam looked relieved. Taken in, the whole gullible lot of them.

"No!" Lottie almost screamed in her frustration. "She's lying, twisting everything. You have to listen. She murdered Uncle Scott. I saw her."

"Come now," Rafe slurred, looking put out. "There's no need for all this unpleasantness."

"Yeah," Adam said. "There's only one liar around here and it's you."

Lottie gasped at the quiet venom in his voice. Instinctively, she bound her arms about her chest as though his words had gouged an open wound there. From a long way off, her cousins' insults flew at her, jumbled, disjointed.

"Lying bitch!"

"Sick in the head ..."

"Can't believe I ever trusted ..."

"Enough."

Through the pain, Lottie felt a hand on her shoulder and looked up to see her dad standing beside her. His face was ashen, but his expression held a fierce determination she had never seen before.

"Enough," he said again. His hand gripped Lottie's shoulder and she could have sworn it trembled. "She's telling the truth. I know. I was there."

***

For the second time that night, Olivia's head reeled. Along with everyone else in the room, she turned to stare at Joel. It was as though she was seeing him properly for the first time.

"What do you mean, you were there?" A terrible coldness closed around her heart.

Joel met her gaze, expression tortured. "I caught her. Phoebe found Scott passed out on the grass. I told her to call an ambulance while I went to see what state he was in. By the time I got there, she … Carla had dragged him into the pool. She was holding his head under the water. I pulled him out straight away but … but it was too late."

His face twisted and he looked away. Olivia's brain whizzed into overdrive, trying to assimilate this revelation about her husband of eighteen years. To think he'd kept the secret for all this time, kept the horror of it locked away inside him, and she hadn't even guessed. Lottie, too, was studying Joel, her forehead creased in concentration as though struggling to remember something.

"What is this?" Rafe found his voice first. He seemed to be sobering up. "Joel, if this is your idea of a unique way to see in the New Year, I'm telling you now, it's not funny."

"No, it isn't." Tim's expression was wary as he surveyed his twin, as though confronting a beloved pet who had turned savage. "What's this about, Joel? Why are you saying this?"

Joel looked back at him without flinching. "Because it's the truth."

Tim shook his head, eyes sad.

"You're mental." Adam pushed past his father to glare at Joel. "I can't believe you're playing along with this. If you were there, like you claim, how come Lottie can't remember it, seeing as her memory's *miraculously* returned?"

"I can remember something," Lottie said, still frowning. "There was a lot of shouting and someone crying, but I didn't understand what was going on. It's all confused."

"That's convenient," Adam sneered. "Now I know what's meant by selective memory."

Olivia opened her mouth to jump to her daughter's defense, but Carla got there first.

"Take it easy, Adam. She's only saying what she thinks she saw." She smiled at Lottie. If she was rattled, she hid it well. "The shouting you remember was probably the row you overheard earlier that same afternoon. It really upset you. That's why you were hiding in the tree house. It's hardly surprising everything's mixed up."

"Very clever, Carla," Joel said. "Very convincing, but you're forgetting one thing. I saw what happened with my own eyes, and I assure you there's nothing whatsoever wrong with my memory."

"Ah, yes." Carla's eyes flashed. "But your view isn't exactly unbiased, is it, Joel? You've never liked me, have you? I bet you'd love the chance to turn Tim against me."

"Is that what this is about?" Tim asked. He seemed genuinely anxious to understand. "Are you trying to come between Carla and me? But I thought you and I had sorted things out."

Joel shook his head. "Rafe always used to say you were too trusting, but he was wrong. Thick as a bloody tree trunk would be closer to the mark."

Emma and Adam both began shouting at once, but again Tim silenced them.

"There's something I'm not following," Rafe said. "Just supposing this nonsense about Carla is true, how come you've kept quiet about it all these years?"

"That's a fair question, Joel." Olivia took care to keep her tone free of accusation. "Why not speak up at the time? It makes no sense."

Joel spoke directly to Tim. "She blackmailed me with the Langdon business."

Tim's face went rigid with shock, and, for the first time that night, Olivia thought she detected a flicker of doubt.

"The what?" Rafe demanded. "What's Langdon got to do with this?"

Joel sighed. He suddenly looked much older than his forty years. "I knew it would come out in the end. Basically, I signed a contract with Langdon, promising a return on his investment way beyond what we could afford. You know how tough things were back then. It was the only way I could hold on to his custom. Without the insurance money, we'd have been in deep shit."

Olivia sat heavily on the arm of the sofa. Her husband, upright, hardworking Joel, resorting to fraud? Vi had been right. She didn't know what he was capable of.

"I don't believe this." Rafe shook his head, looking stunned. "I can't believe you put Cameron's at risk like that and didn't even think to tell me."

"What has this got to do with Carla?" Olivia forced the words past her dry throat.

Joel's gaze returned to her. "She overheard me telling Tim what I'd done, and when I caught her drowning Scott, she threatened me with going to the police if I told anyone what I knew."

Rafe snorted. "Now you really are sounding like a raving lunatic. A Cameron crumble under a bit of blackmail? Give me a break. I know you loved Scott too much not to have wanted justice for him."

"You know nothing," Joel said fiercely. "You don't know what it was like, seeing your own brother murdered in front of your eyes, knowing you'd arrived too late to save him. You can't even begin to imagine how that felt, and I've had to live with that for twelve years. Okay, so I know I did the wrong thing. I should have turned Carla in and to hell with the consequences, but I wasn't thinking straight. My head was all over the place. By the time I realized what I'd done, what Carla had talked me into, it was too late."

"It's all lies," Carla croaked, tears glistening on her lashes. "I can't listen to this."

"You don't have to." Tim put his arm around her and glared at his twin with something akin to hatred. "You've gone too far this time."

"For Christ's sake, open your eyes," Joel roared. "Open your eyes and see what's right in front of you. Your wife, your precious Carla, is a murderer, a blackmailer, and a barefaced liar! Do you honestly think I'd make up something like this?"

"Yes, actually, I do," Tim shot back. "Carla's right. You've never liked her, never passed up the opportunity to tell me how she's not good enough for me. Well, whatever you say, Carla's always been there for me, which is a damn sight more than can be said for you."

"Yeah, that's it, throw that back in my face. God, you're so smug sometimes, Tim. You with your posh car and snooty friends. I hope it makes you proud, knowing it's all paid for with blood money."

"How dare you! You know what your problem is, Joel? You can't bear it that I've made a success of my life. You're eaten up with bitterness because my marriage is as strong as ever and yours is obviously falling apart."

Joel lunged at him. "You bastard! I'll—"

"Stop it! Oh, please, stop it."

Olivia had leapt forward to grab Joel's arm but it wasn't she who spoke. Diverted, everyone turned to stare at Phoebe. She had risen from the sofa, face chalk-white, swaying as though the slightest breath would knock her down. Looking around at all the eyes fixed on her, she burst into tears.

"Oh, God." She covered her face with her hands. "God forgive me. It's all true. Everything. Oh, God, what have I done?"

"What is this?" Rafe seized his wife by the shoulders. He looked as if he'd had as much as he could take. "What have you to do with this?"

"Hey, go easy on her." Joel moved to put an arm around Phoebe. "She's been going through hell these past few weeks. I've had her on the phone countless times, practically hysterical about coming back here."

He looked at Olivia when he said this, a look heavy with significance. She stared back at him, seeking his meaning, and then it hit her. She dropped once more onto the arm of the sofa, dizzy with the realization. She lost track of the argument for a moment, as a single fact reverberated inside her head. *Joel isn't having an affair. There has never been another woman. He isn't having an affair.*

"She's my wife, for Christ's sake! If she's been keeping things from me, I have a right to know." Rafe's voice penetrated Olivia's daze and she roused herself in time to see him shake Phoebe hard. "What's this about? Tell me, damn you."

Phoebe lowered her hands to peer up at him. "Carla ad-admitted it. Right after I'd gone to call the ambulance. Scott was lying on the grass, dripping water everywhere, and Joel was trying to ... to revive him. He said Carla did it, that she'd drowned him. I wouldn't believe it, didn't want to believe it, but ... but then she confessed, said she'd done it for all of us. For the business. Oh, God. I wanted to tell you, Rafe, I swear it. I wanted to tell you so many times, but—"

"But what? What possessed you to keep something like this from me?"

"I w-was scared. I didn't know what she was capable of anymore, what she might do."

There was a silence as Carla gazed at Phoebe, her closest friend of almost thirty years. Her eyes brimmed with hurt, but, for the first time that night, Olivia perceived a trace of fear.

"Why?" Carla whispered. "Why would you do this, after everything I've done for you?"

Phoebe covered her face again, muffling her sobs. "I've tried, Carla, I swear I have, but I can't do this anymore. I have to tell the truth. It will kill me otherwise."

"She's gone crazy," Carla said. "She doesn't know what she's saying." She turned to Tim. "Let's get out of this madhouse. We don't have to listen to another word of this."

But Tim was backing away from her, his eyes blank with horror.

"Tim?" Carla's voice faltered. Hands outstretched, she took a hesitant step towards him. "Tim, I—"

"Get away from me," he hissed. "I don't want you anywhere near me."

"Oh, God," Emma moaned. She slid down the wall to huddle on the floor, face buried in her knees. Adam sat beside her and put an arm around her shaking shoulders, his face gray.

"You monster!" Rafe advanced on Carla, expression contorted. "You evil, twisted, murdering ... I'll kill you for this, you hear me? I'll break your fucking neck."

"How could you do it?" Tim seemed to have trouble forming the words, as though his lips were numb with frostbite. He never took his gaze from Carla. "My own brother. How could you?"

Tears sparkled in Carla's eyes. "Don't look at me like that, Tim. I can't bear it. Everything I've done these past twenty years has been for your sake. I've only ever wanted the best for you. Whatever I've done, you have to believe me."

"Believe you?" The ice in Tim's tone chilled Olivia's blood. "As if I can believe a single word that comes out of your deceitful mouth. Honest to God, I wish I'd never set eyes on you." He began to shake. "It's all been a lie, hasn't it? Our marriage, your love for me … everything."

"How can you even think that? I love you, Tim. You're the most important thing in the world to me." Dissolving in a storm of weeping, Carla flung herself at Tim.

Rafe yanked her back by the bodice of her dress. "Don't you dare touch him. As for you." He rounded on Phoebe. "You're as bad as she is. You may as well have held Scott's head under the water yourself. To think you've known about her for all these years and never so much as breathed a word of it in your sleep. You disgust me, you know that? You're not fit to call yourself my wife."

Phoebe opened her mouth but no sound came out. She swayed on the spot and the blood drained from her face, leaving her as white as a corpse. Then she collapsed. Olivia rushed forward, but Joel had already caught her and lowered her to the sofa.

"Now see what you've done?" he shot at Rafe. "Don't you think she's had enough worry without you turning on her?"

Rafe's body slumped as the fight went out of him. "Oh, God. Oh, dear God."

"Let me get to her," Olivia urged, trying to squeeze past him.

Rafe stepped aside, confused and docile as a child. Olivia picked up Phoebe's wrist, checking for a pulse.

"This is your doing," Joel accused Rafe. "She's been going out of her mind these past couple of days, trying her hardest to hold it together, and why? Because you were too pigheaded to see that coming back here might be too much for her."

Rafe opened his mouth, but seemed unable to find the words. He looked shattered, his face tired and drawn. Moved by his distress, Olivia reached up to touch him on the arm. "Phoebs will be fine. She's only fainted. This has all been too much for her. We should get her into bed."

"No," Rafe said, and his tone held a hint of his usual decisiveness. "I'm taking her home. She shouldn't have to spend another moment here."

"What about your things?"

"Phoebs packed them yesterday. She's always so efficient. Oh, Christ, this is all my fault."

Joel gripped his arm. "Come on, I'll help you carry your stuff to the car."

He led him towards the door. Just as they reached it, Rafe turned back to Carla.

"Don't think you've got away with this," he spat. "One way or another, I'm going to make you pay for Scott."

She appeared not even to hear him. Rafe knifed her with one last hate-filled glare, then left with Joel. Still kneeling beside Phoebe, Olivia clutched at the sofa arm with trembling fingers and surveyed the wreckage of the party. Save for Emma's soft crying, the drawing room was silent. Tim had sunk to the carpet between his children and was holding onto them as though they were the only three survivors of a plane crash. Carla stood like a deserted island in the center of the floor, desolate and alone, tears coursing down her cheeks.

Phoebe gave a soft moan and began to stir. Dragged from her numb shock, Olivia clambered to her feet and moved through the deadly hush to the drinks cabinet. As she poured Phoebe a large brandy, Violet, who had remained quiet and watchful throughout, left her corner and walked straight up to Carla.

"So, how does it feel?" she asked.

Carla didn't question what she meant. She only looked at her through a Niagara of tears. "This is what this whole weekend's been about, isn't it? You getting your revenge."

"Oh, yes." Violet smiled. "And, boy, does it taste sweet."

Twenty-Five

"What will you do now?" Olivia asked her sister as they stood on the driveway, watching the taillights of Rafe's Mercedes vanish into the early morning gloom.

Violet shrugged. "Go home, have a hot shower, and get down to some serious work. I'm in court first thing tomorrow."

"My sister the workaholic." Olivia was half incredulous, half impressed. "But I meant what are you going to do about all this. Will you go to the police?"

"I thought I would. I vowed if I learned who killed Scott, I'd stand for the prosecution myself and see them sent down for life. Now, though." Violet shook her head. "I never imagined it would be so complicated. There are so many more people involved than Scott and Carla. If I turn Carla in, Lottie will have to relive the whole experience on the witness stand, as will Phoebe, and Joel will have to confess to the contract business. This family has suffered enough already. I won't be responsible for putting them through another round of hell."

Olivia's heart swelled with love for her sister, a love mixed with relief and gratitude. Much as she longed to see Carla publicly named as a murderer, she couldn't bear the damage it might do to her already fragile loved ones.

"Of course," Violet said, "that doesn't mean Rafe won't do my job for me, although I doubt he'll want to put Joel in that position."

"Or Phoebe," Olivia added. "You saw how worried he was."

Violet snorted. "Riddled with guilt, more like. It suddenly occurred to him that if he had paid more attention to his wife over the years, she may have been able to confide in him and wouldn't have fretted herself into a mental collapse. Rafe will play the doting husband for a while to soothe his conscience, but it won't last."

Olivia bit her lip. She hoped, for Phoebe's sake, it was merely Violet's prejudice talking and that her cynical prognosis would prove mistaken.

"You're sure you're all right with this, though?" she pressed. "No one would blame you for wanting to see Carla hang."

Violet sighed, stirring up gravel with the toe of her trainer. "It all happened so long ago. Let's say I were to go to the police, there's no guarantee of a conviction or even a hearing. We have no evidence to prove Scott didn't just get hammered and pass out in the water. It would be our word against Carla's. Besides," she stared into the distance, "Carla's got what she deserved. She's lost the person who means most to her in all the world, just as I did. No legal punishment could be more effective than that."

"No," Olivia conceded. An image of Tim's face, bleak with loss and horror, floated into her mind. She shivered as a sharp wind gusted across the driveway. "But Carla's not the only one who's going to suffer."

"There are always casualties in a case like this, friends and relatives who had no idea what their loved ones were capable of." Violet glanced at Olivia. "You look done in. Get yourself in the warm."

"I think I will," Olivia said, and held out her arms. "Drive safely."

"Always the worrier." Violet hugged her. "Look, I am sorry about all this, taking advantage of your hospitality and everything."

"You had to know, Vi. I understand that." She stepped back as Violet climbed into her car and started the engine. When her sister rolled down the window, Olivia asked, "Did you ever suspect it might have been Carla?"

"Actually, I hoped it was Rafe." Violet's smile was rueful. "I've always wanted to nail the arrogant bastard for something. Still, there's always another time." And with a final wave, she pulled out of the driveway and purred away towards London.

***

"Adam, wait," Lottie said, catching hold of his arm as he headed for the door. "We need to talk."

He shook her off as though she were an insect, and started down the attic stairs.

Lottie followed, heedless of appearing desperate. "Don't go. I'm sorry. I never meant for this to happen, any of it."

"No." Adam refused to look at her. "But it did, all the same. Nothing you say will change that."

Lottie gasped. His coldness cut her far deeper than his earlier anger. Fighting tears, she hurried after him along the landing. "Adam, please, you can't just go. Not like this."

"Leave it, Lottie," Emma said, emerging from the bedroom with her suitcase. She looked dreadful, her face pale and blotchy from crying. "No point talking to him when he's like this."

"How can I leave it?" Lottie slumped against the wall. She knew the despair must show in her eyes but was past caring. "How can I let him go without even saying goodbye?"

Emma considered her. "You love him, don't you? I mean, you're, like, in love with him."

Lottie nodded; there seemed no point pretending. "And he'll never forgive me for this, will he?"

"I don't know, Lottie, I really don't." Emma shook her head. She didn't appear shocked. Probably nothing could shock her anymore.

After a brief pause, she said, "Dad will be waiting. I have to go."

Lottie nodded again. Too shattered to move, she merely watched Emma descend the stairs and disappear from view. How could the most magical weekend of her life have gone so disastrously wrong?

***

"You all right?" Joel asked.

Tim only shrugged, his gaze fixed on a point outside the sitting-room window. Following its direction, Joel peered through the darkness at the figure huddled still as a statue in the passenger seat of Tim's Audi.

"We can always call a taxi. You don't have to do this."

"Yes, I do." Tim looked at him, expression set. "I need to see she's all right."

"You what?" Joel slammed a fist into the window. "She murdered our brother, and you want to see she's all right? What's wrong with you, man?"

Tim looked back out at the driveway. "I've loved Carla for twenty years, Joel. Loved her more than my own life. Feelings like that don't disappear overnight. I may hate her for what she's done, may never want to set eyes on her again, but I can't pretend my marriage doesn't exist. I have to at least know she'll be okay."

"So what will you do? Where do you expect Carla to live?"

"We don't have any clients staying in the executive flat at the moment. Carla can stay there, just until she finds somewhere else to live."

Or until Rafe decided to go to the authorities, thereby providing Carla with accommodation courtesy of the state. The unspoken words hung between them, but neither acknowledged their existence.

Joel shook his head. "I don't get it. If I were you, I'd throw her out without a thought and make damn sure she spent the rest of her life behind bars."

"Would you?" Tim said softly. "If it had been Liv, could you really behave as though she'd never meant anything to you?"

Joel had no answer. "What about the kids?" he demanded instead, watching from the window as Emma and Adam carried their luggage onto the drive. "Are you going to let them continue seeing Carla as though nothing's happened?"

"They're virtually adults now. Old enough to make their own decisions. Whatever Carla's done, she's still their mother. They have a right to stay in contact with her. Somehow, though, I doubt they'll want to."

Judging by their rigid backs as they waited by the car, clearly reluctant to get in without their father, Joel thought he was probably right.

"I'd better go," Tim said. "The kids and I need to get home and start putting ourselves back together, if that's at all possible."

Joel pulled his twin into a bear hug. "Just remember, if you need anything, a place to escape to, someone to rail at, call me."

"Thanks." Tim drew away, blinking rapidly. "And I hope you and Liv can sort out whatever's gone wrong between you."

***

Olivia pulled on her boots and went out into the chill dawn. A faint opalescence shimmered on the horizon, and the last droplets of snow gleamed like pearls in the grass. She tracked Lottie down in the stables, her face buried against Gypsy's neck, body convulsing with grief. In two strides, Olivia crossed the hay-strewn floor and took her daughter in her arms.

"There," she soothed, stroking her hair as she had when Lottie was a child. "Everything's going to be all right."

"It isn't." Lottie sobbed into her shoulder. "Nothing will ever be all right. I love him, Mum. I love him so much, and he'll never speak to me again."

Sluggish from a sleepless night, Olivia's brain scrabbled to make sense of the words. For a moment, she even wondered whether Lottie's distress was unconnected with the night's events. "Sweetheart, who won't speak to you?"

Lottie burrowed her face deeper into Olivia's jumper, muffling her reply. "Adam. I didn't tell you before because Dad never liked to talk about the family. We got together on the geography field trip. He swore he loved me, said we'd be together forever. Now he hates me. It's all my fault what's happened to his family and he'll never forgive me, I know he won't."

Olivia continued to hold her but her mind was in turmoil. Lottie and Adam, in love and conducting a secret relationship under her roof? What had they been thinking? More to the point, how could she have failed to see it? Questions and recriminations leapt to her tongue but she bit them back. None of that was important now. There would be time enough for explanations later. Nothing mattered at this moment other than that her daughter needed her, that she was hurting.

"I'm sorry." Olivia hugged her tight. "I really am. I know it doesn't make it any better, but heartbreak is something we all have to go through at some point in our lives."

"Not like this." Lottie drew away to look at her with tear-stained certainty. "No one has ever loved anyone the way I love Adam."

Olivia smiled. "It feels like the end of the world now, but it isn't. One day you'll meet someone who'll sweep you off your feet and you'll wonder what you ever saw in Adam."

They were quiet for a while, Olivia rubbing her daughter's back until the sobs subsided to the occasional hiccup.

"Mum," Lottie said, when she at last drew away, "you won't make me go to court, will you? I don't think I can do it."

"No one will make you do anything you don't want to," Olivia assured her, and hoped she spoke the truth. She pressed a kiss on Lottie's forehead. "Now, shall we go in? I'm freezing to death out here."

"Actually, I think I'll go for a ride, if that's okay."

"Of course it is." Olivia gave her a squeeze to show that she understood.

Lottie squeezed her back, then set about tacking up Gypsy. Telling her to take care, Olivia made to leave her to it.

"Mum," Lottie said, staying her, "you won't say anything to Dad, will you? About Adam, I mean."

"No, I think that would be best," Olivia agreed, and Lottie's face lightened a shade.

As she headed back to the house, Olivia wrestled with her conscience. She had never kept anything concerning Lottie from Joel before, but it was better this way. She couldn't entirely shake the sense that she was in some way responsible. If she hadn't been so wrapped up in her own problems, she might have realized what was going on. Besides, the relationship was over now. No good would come of creating a fuss. Lord knows, they had been through enough already.

***

"Why didn't you tell me?" Olivia asked a short while later, seated beside Joel on the sitting room sofa. A fire crackled in the grate, warding off the gloom outside, and she curled her hands around her mug of tea to warm them.

For the first time in weeks, Joel looked at her directly. "I should have. I know that now, but, like I said earlier, I wasn't thinking straight. I was in shock, I suppose. One minute I saw my brother murdered by someone I trusted, the next, the ambulance arrived and Carla talked us into going along with her lie. Although I wanted to tell you, came very close many times, I couldn't do it. I was so ashamed that I'd given in to Carla like that, and yes, I admit it, I was scared what she would do."

Olivia nodded, trying with her writer's mind to put herself in his position. "Why not tell me a couple of months back, though, when Violet first suggested getting the family together? Phoebe couldn't have been the only one going out of her mind. You must have been, too."

"My only excuse is that I'd got so used to living a lie, I couldn't break the habit. Of course, I was stupid to think you wouldn't notice something was up."

"And rather than tell me the truth, you let me believe you were having an affair!" All Olivia's pent up resentment gushed out in a torrent. "Have you any idea what I've been going through, Joel? I've been in bits, wondering how the hell I was going to get through the rest of my life without you, and all because you were too bloody pigheaded to admit the truth."

"I know." Joel bowed his head. "This whole thing is my own stupid fault, but, if it's any consolation, I've hurt myself as much as you. It almost killed me having to watch you suffer, knowing I was responsible. I suppose I hoped, even if I couldn't tell you the truth, you'd know I would never, could never cheat on you."

They were silent for some time. Olivia stared into the flames, mentally going over everything that had happened over the past weeks: Vi's determination to reunite the family; her own discovery of what she had believed to be Joel's infidelity; the return of Lottie's nightmare, which had sparked the fiercest row she'd had with her sister in years; and finally last night's horrific revelation concerning that long-ago summer. It was all, she decided, far more sensational than any of the plots in her novels.

At length, Joel held out his hand. "Liv, I know it's a lot to ask, perhaps too much. I've messed up big time, I realize that, but can you see your way to forgiving me?"

"That depends." Olivia hesitated. "On whether you can forgive me for getting it all so wrong. However it looked, I should have given you the benefit of the doubt."

Joel's smile lit up his tired face, smoothing away the lines of strain. "Done."

Smiling back, Olivia slid her hand in his and let him draw her against him. In unspoken agreement, they slipped into their familiar position, his arm around her waist, her head on his shoulder. At the moment of contact, warmth spread through Olivia's body and the crushing weight lifted from her heart. She felt whole again.

"Liv," Joel said, "you do realize we're not out of the woods yet. If Rafe goes to the police—"

"Which he won't. If it's one thing I know about Rafe, it's that he always looks out for his brothers. He'd never drop you in it like that."

"Maybe, but if he does and I have to go to court, admit to the Langdon business and everything—"

"If he does." Olivia sat up, meeting his gaze head on, "We're in this together. Whatever happens, no matter how tough things get, I'll be right there with you."

Epilogue

The cemetery was deserted. Coat buttoned against the January chill filling her lungs, Violet sat by Scott's grave and watched the sun rise over London. The dome of St. Paul's and the slender finger of Big Ben shimmered in the winter sunshine, and it was as though she was seeing it all for the first time. For twelve years she had lived like a shadow in this city, existing without being part of it. Now the wall of grief separating her from everything around her shattered and sensation rushed in. The world seemed suddenly brim full of promise, urging her to come and join in, to enjoy all life had to offer before it passed her by.

Reaching out a hand, Violet traced Scott's name etched into the gravestone. Frigid air nipped her fingers but she scarcely felt it. Despite the horror of what she'd learned that day, her heart was lighter than it had been since Scott's death. She knew the truth now, the whole truth and nothing but, and though she would never be free of the pain, she could see her way through it. She could move on with her life, satisfied in the knowledge that justice had been done at last. Violet smiled, tilting her face up to the ice-blue sky.

"I did it," she said softly. "It took me a while, I know, but I got there in the end. You can be at peace now, Scott." Her voice dropped to a sigh. "And perhaps I can, too."

About the Author

Jessica Chambers started inventing stories even before she was old enough to hold a pen. She has a passion for writing contemporary novels packed with emotion, complex relationships, and often a touch of mystery.

Visually impaired from birth, Jessica currently lives with her family and Staffordshire bull terrier in the English town of Windsor. In addition to devouring fiction of all genres, she loves watching TV quiz shows and admits to being extremely competitive when it comes to a game of Trivial Pursuit.

Made in the USA
Lexington, KY
10 January 2012